Starkadder

Starkadder

Bernard King

NEW ENGLISH LIBRARY

Copyright © 1985 by Bernard King

First published in Great Britain in 1985 by
New English Library, Mill Road, Dunton Green, Sevenoaks, Kent.
Editorial office: 47 Bedford Square, London WC1B 3DP

Typeset by:
Hewer Text Composition Services, Edinburgh.

Printed in Great Britain by:
Biddles Limited, Guildford and King's Lynn.

British Library Cataloguing in Publication Data
King, Bernard
  Starkadder.
  I. Title
  823'.914[F]   PR6061.I43/

ISBN: 0 450 06100 0

To My Parents

Þann hef ek manna menzkra fundit hring-hreytanda
hrammastan at afli.

Of all human warriors, this is the strongest that
I ever met.

Fragment from an old LAY OF STARKADDER

Contents

Author's Note

I have not attempted to date the action of this story. Wiser heads than mine have tried and failed to establish a date for the final years of the Yngling dynasty. Let it suffice for a chronology that it takes place in Sweden in the closing years of the Dark Ages.

In that time and place, long ago and far away, a fact might be lost for eternity in the depths of the forests or the vastness of the mountain ranges. Most of the facts of Starkadder's life are now vanished beyond recall into the depths of legend. Yet the ancient skalds and tellers of tales believed that some, at least, of this story was true.

Those skalds are now gone, and their bones have long since turned to dust. They have given whatever truth they possessed to the worms, and may tell their tales no more. We who live on have been freed by their demise. We may doubt or believe as we desire.

This is a part of the legend of Starkadder. It is the story of his dying.

B.J.H.K.

Beside the waterfall

ONCE A man has found a place, a personal sacred place, he is free to come and go as often as he chooses. The place is his alone, and its beauty, be it wild and barren or secure and lush, will grow upon him with each new visiting. If he is at peace when first he goes there then it will be a place of peace for ever after. If his soul is troubled, if the lake of his emotions bears ripples or waves, the place will harbour his longings and doubts.

The traveller came upon such a place. He was leading his horse, resting it from the furious riding of the past hour. He travelled slowly, not because his thoughts were tranquil, but of sheer necessity. There would be further places to go to, other things to see and masters to serve before he died, and he would need this horse, and the next, and the next, as many as his weird made him outlive. He would need them to journey from betrayal to betrayal.

Once over the crest the hill declined sharply, rough with scree and broken rocks. Here and there grass struggled to bind the scree together. Stunted trees with knotted boles sent out tough roots to find a precarious purchase. The crest wound round in a semi-circle to the waterfall opposite where, as if broken by some giant hand, it fell away, collapsing into the valley below in a thunder of spume and fury. The water, clear both above and below the falls, was streaked with white and muddy brown for the length of its fall. The summit was set with rocks like broken teeth, between which flashes of foaming white appeared and vanished with the flow.

This was a place of wonder and mystery to the old man, though he knew it well.

He shaded his eyes from the sun with an upraised hand. Yes, the hut was there, the little hut built of grey stone where the old woman, if such she was, had chosen to live. There it stood, half hidden by the spray, with the runestone standing beside it, on the very edge of the waterfall.

She watched him approach even before he had reached the crest of the hill. There were no eyes like hers for watching mortals, except perhaps for those of Odin's ravens. As the dark-clad warrior began his descent, still leading his weary mount, she scanned the sky, seeking those dark shapes which watched even as she watched, though both they and their master would have paid dearly for her knowledge. After all, Odin had already purchased a draught from the well of wisdom with one of his eyes. What would he not pay for just a glimpse of the parchment scroll she carried?

No, they were not there. Only the gulls from the distant, storm-swept ocean wheeled and mewed overhead. Odin wasn't spying on her. He knew what was his business, and what would only become known in the fullness of the future.

The aged warrior's eyes were old, but they still saw as well as they had first seen, more than two hundred years before. That was why she pulled down her veil as he drew near enough to make out the features, the lines of age and sorrow on her face. No man might see that face, not even an accursed creature like Starkadder.

He had drawn close enough for her to hear the sound of his horse's hoofs upon the scree above the thunder of the waterfall. She smiled at him, a sad understanding smile hidden beneath her veil. She was dressed in rags befitting her office. Once the rags had been the most exquisite finery, but now they were old and torn. She affected tatters that none might ask for a future of riches and preferment nor guess what she really knew. Only the veil was whole and untorn, and it concealed her face completely. It was of thick

2

wadmal, homespun cloth in contrast to the faded, shredded Byzantine silks which clothed her. It signified the uncertainty of what was to come, the possibility of death or defeat for the unwary or the foolish.

Now she heard the footfalls of the warrior as well as those of his horse. Now she saw the steely glint of his eyes beneath the helmet of bronze-banded leather. His face, grizzle-bearded, was gaunt and tired. He had seen too much and lived too long, for he was old beyond the understanding of ordinary men.

'So you've come to me again, Starkadder?' she asked. Her voice was as old as her appearance suggested, bent like her body with age.

Starkadder, for all his years, stood erect with the bearing of the warrior he was. She had known he would come, as he had known. It was but a little magic to move this place nearer to him, as a token of respect and compassion for his suffering, though he would never know it as such.

His grey eyes studied her, seeking for some hint of pity or mercy beneath the veil. Yet they saw only the wadmal, and it was the voice of an old man tired of killing and deceit which replied to her greeting.

'Of all your sisterhood, Mother Skuld, you interest me the most. Besides, where else should I go when the betrayals are over? I come to you, as you knew I would, to ask if I have done enough, to ask if the time has come when I may die.'

Such a tired voice, so defeated, she thought. It was like this when Vikar died. His was the first betrayal.

'Will you tether your horse and step into my hut, Starkadder?'

'Is there some comfort there, Skuld?'

'I have a fire to warm you, for this sun is nothing to bones such as yours and mine. I have a little mead also, and beakers to drink it from.'

He sighed, and the sound was enough to still the torrent of the waterfall. 'That is not what I meant, as well you know.'

'There is the comfort of confession.'

Starkadder threw back his head and laughed into the sky.

3

It was a forced, raucous, bitter mirth that bubbled from his throat, mocking both himself and the aged crone before him.

'Confession?' he smiled sourly. 'Of what use is confession? You already know everything that I do. Your sisters tell you. And you know what I will do in the future, for that is your own domain. What then is there for me to tell you? When I accepted your offer before, and told you about Vikar, you already knew. You even reminded me of details I had been fortunate enough to forget. No, I will not relive what we both know already. Neither for your satisfaction nor for my purgation will I do it. That is too cruel, Skuld. Too cruel.'

'So the weary traveller will not take warmth or mead with me? Well now, what else is there that I might offer? My body, perhaps? Would you comfort an old woman with your own ancient love? Whatever remains to you, that is.'

'And now you're mocking me. You know what I want. You know why I've come to you, why I always come to you. I've come for hope, not for mockery. Is there hope, Mother Skuld? Can you and your sister Norns give me that?'

'There is always hope, Starkadder.'

'That isn't what I mean,' he spat. 'You know of the curse on me. I'm asking you if there is a way to defeat it. Freya's tits, woman! All I'm asking for is the chance to do as others do. All I want is to die. That's all, nothing more. I don't even care if I go to Niflhel or Valhalla any more. I just want death. Can you understand that?'

It was Skuld's turn to laugh. She brayed like the old crone she appeared to be, shrieking at the aged viking who stood before her. There was something of both mirth and malice in the laughter, and Starkadder inwardly cowered, though his face and bearing showed simply an impatient longing for her to be done.

'You ask if I can understand your desire to die, Starkadder? Should I not? Can you understand how *I* might yearn for the final dissolution? You have but three spans to live. I have already lived thirty-three thousand times three spans. Your lot is hard? Your curse is hard to bear? Then think of me.

4

Think of the Norns. Think of the gods of Valhalla. How much longer have *we* lived? How old, how tired, how sickened by the puny whines of men are we? Your life is but the blink of Odin's eye, old man. Oh yes, there will come an ending for you, but you may not cheat the curse. You shall live out your three spans and commit your three betrayals. You have Thor and Odin to thank for that.'

Her voice softened, and a smile stole across her features beneath the veil. 'Have you your comfort now?' she asked him. 'I have told you all, Starkadder. A third betrayal, and it will be over. Yes, over. It may be ten, a hundred years from now, but it will come. Your victim, if such he shall truly be, may not yet be born, but he will be born, Starkadder, he will. And you will betray him. And then it shall end for you. Is that comfort enough for you? Grasp it, then. Keep it by you in the long, dark hours of your night. Nurture it with the blood of those you kill, for each fresh killing brings you nearer to the end of your weird.

'Yet hear me well,' the Norn continued. 'There shall be a dread come upon you as the end draws nigh. You shall know the victim and serve him, as you both knew and served Vikar and Frothi. You will fear his death, even as you deliver the blow, for you will know that it heralds the end for more than just the ancient Starkadder. You will not live to see the passing of the old, for that will take many years and many battles, far more than we have allotted to you, but you will fear it none the less for that.'

The old warrior scowled his disgust. 'Even what you grant with one word you cancel with another,' he grunted. 'Is this what I came to you for, Skuld? To be told that there will be more dying even when my weird is over? Have you no pity left for me?'

'Of what use is pity, Starkadder? It aids neither the giver nor the given. I have no pity for you, but I have fire. I shall use my words to set it in your veins, to give you strength and courage for the years ahead. You must be strong and resolute. You must commit your last betrayal because it has already been written in my book. Yet in your age there shall be youth to aid you, and to kill you. Your last betrayal shall be a dreadful act, as you already know, but the years may

5

dull my words within your memory, and that last betrayal may not be the one which you expect.'

She paused and studied his face once more. He simply stood and listened to her. One gloved hand played with the pommel of his sword, but his face beneath the beard was as drained as she had known it would be. He heard, he understood, but he was beyond emotion. Skuld knew all too well what he was feeling. It was a feeling that she knew herself.

And then Mother Skuld felt pity, for both of them.

'I should not have come here,' Starkadder muttered. 'It was wrong.'

'It was inevitable. If you had not come to me, then I would have come to find you. I need you, Starkadder. I need you in ways that you may never understand. I need you to give me peace.'

He shook his head and turned away, leading his mount back up the scree slope. Then he turned back and stared at her.

'I don't understand you, Mother Skuld,' he called.

She nodded beneath her veil. 'Perhaps that is just as well,' she replied.

Skuld stood in the doorway of her hut, watching him go back to the world of men. Even without the armour of the curse he would have been a mighty warrior. With it he was perhaps the most feared man in the north. On the day of his death it would be given to him to understand. Like most warriors he worshipped Odin the Allfather, but had never been sure – no mortal man would be – of the rôle the Norns played in the affairs of gods and men. Well, on that day, in the moment of his death, Starkadder would know.

When he had gone she raised her veil again, revealing the face of a wrinkled old woman to the wheeling gulls. There were no ravens in the sky, and they would not be coming now. Odin was playing the game according to the rules.

Here beside the runestone and the waterfall, Starkadder's grandfather, the eight-armed giant, had been slain by Thor Odinsson. Here, in this hut, Starkadder had been born. It was only right that he should come back here to talk to her.

The waterfall roared on. It would never know that it was not where it should have been, never know that old Skuld had moved it for her meeting with Starkadder. Even if it could see her tears it would not comprehend them, other than to believe that its own spray had wetted her cheeks.

There was a bitterness in being more than mortal which made dealings with mortals painful. They were so trusting, so eager for pleasure, so vulnerable in both the body and the spirit. It was so easy to hurt them. Yet it was with pride that Skuld reflected that they would never know the pain they gave the immortals. The gods hid it too well.

In a little while the illusion would fade. In a few more moments she would join her sisters, Urd and Verdandi. But for now Mother Skuld wanted to snatch a few moments of pleasure from eternity, to sit beside the waterfall and cry.

And that is what she did.

THE FIRST PART

Images of times gone by

CHAPTER ONE

A watcher near the plain at Roliung

FOR A moment the raven hung suspended on the air, black as moonless midnight, its eyes of death-bright jet searching the snows beneath. Then it wheeled and swept away, beating the unseen draughts with dark and tattered pinions. It had seen, and it would remember. It knew, and it would tell.

The one-eyed man stood, at first glance, alone. He was tall and, whilst there was little grace in the figure beneath the blue travelling cloak, there was a hidden strength that spoke of challenges long mastered, of challenges yet to try his power. The bulk of chain armour reinforced with metal plates pushed and prodded at the cloak from underneath, adding a bulk of its own to his substantial frame. Little of his body showed beneath the close-drawn shrouding. Only the fingers of his gloved right hand protruded into the winter cold, damp-mottled with melting snowflakes, grasping the massive spear which was both weapon and traveller's staff.

His single eye, set deep and burning in a face mostly masked by a battered, low-brimmed hat and a greying beard, watched the raven's flight. Yes, it had seen and it would remember. Its name was Munin, and Munin was more than a name. It was the word for memory.

The other raven, the one that perched upon One-Eye's left shoulder like a death-black shadow, watched its mate.

Its ebony eyes glittered with a hardness that showed no trace of understanding as the black pin-prick on the pink-grey sky of limpid dawn drew nearer, regaining form and familiarity.

'Do you see her, Hugin?' One-Eye asked. 'Do you see? She's coming back to me. She's coming to tell me what she sees. Do you know what she will tell me? She'll tell me that my son is wrong. She'll tell me that there's a brave, silly old man out there, waiting for a death that will not come.'

The raven's croak sounded hoarse and feeble in the winter dawn. Its breath steamed shapelessly like its master's, mingling with the twin breaths which floated briefly upwards from the prowling grey shapes which paced the hem of One-Eye's cloak.

Munin flew nearer, growing in black clarity against the pallid sky. Hugin watched with his master, their three eyes bright in the early morning. Closer to the ground, like amber set in granite, other eyes watched the bird's return, eyes that showed the hungry thoughts behind them, eyes devoid of mercy.

One-Eye reached out his left hand and rubbed at Freki's ears. For some moments the wolf acquiesced, content to take affection from its master. Then the sharp-toothed head moved upwards, and its breath steamed out once more as a long, grooved tongue licked at the brown-gloved fingers.

'You see, Freki? Geri? She's coming back.'

And she was. The two wolves slowed their pacing and stood panting, steaming, shaggy-pelted to watch the form-less black speck take on the shape of their night-plumed companion.

One-Eye shifted the spear into his left hand, the glove moist from Freki's licking. His right hand and arm stretched out, revealing the heavy mail beneath the cloak, for the bird to alight.

Above them, remembering, Munin saw the waiting group, blue, grey and black against the snow. She was a bird. She could not speak. But she could tell. One-Eye would understand. He always did.

And yet . . . this was freedom. The air was cold around her feathers, but this was freedom. She circled and watched.

12

Soon, she knew, there would be carrion. Soon the old man would be dead. Or, if he survived, there would be other dead men. She tried to hover, to think, but the air currents were wrong. She had tried before, she remembered, but the air currents had been wrong then as well. Somehow she always returned. Somehow she always went back to the tall figure with only one eye, to Odin.

Her claws dug at his arm as she alighted. One day he might not be wearing armour. One day her timeless talons might cause him pain. After all, the world was full of ravens. Why had he chosen her?

She edged up the arm to his shoulder, digging her claws between the links of mail. He knew that she was trying to hurt him. He always knew. That was why he smiled. And yet she loved him, even though he denied her freedom, even though she could not make him feel pain. He was Allfather. Perhaps he was not the creator, but he was the one who came after the creator, the one who ruled this world of ice and snow. He was the god they called Terrible, Death-blinder, Flame-eye, and War-glad. He was the Giver of Carrion, the Taker of the Slain, and for that alone her hungry heart held love for him, and pride that she was his.

Her beak reached beneath the leather and metal flap that edged his helmet. It sought the flesh of his ear-lobe and waited, poised to draw blood. The god simply smiled and waited, knowing that the peck would never come.

'Have you seen, my dark beauty?' he asked. 'Is Starkadder there? Is the old man waiting?'

And she told him. Not in words, for ravens speak words only when they are taught to mimic men, not because they know what they are saying. Neither did she caw and chatter, as Hugin had done but a few minutes before. Allfather knew everything. He might understand her, but that was not how they spoke together.

The small brain in the feathered skull poured out its memories. The dark beak, nestling like carved ebony against Odin's ear, did not move as she told what she had seen. Their wild and savage thoughts merged in the telling, the bird sensing a feast as yet unset, the god seeing warriors to fill Valhalla, warriors still unslain.

Munin spoke of those things that she remembered. Her voiceless words told of the old, scarred warrior who waited. They told of the freezing flakes that covered his cloak and armour, piling in a glistening cone upon the iron-banded helmet of thick leather, covering him in a shroud of clotted snow. They spoke of the only sign of life Munin had seen in him, those deep-set, glittering eyes, unreadable as her own, as hungry as the twin wolves, Geri and Freki, who prowled at the hem of Odin's cloak. They described to her waiting master how those eyes had pierced her, glaring up at a solitary raven in a sky fresh with winter's dawn, a raven whose very blackness set her apart from the chill, grey world in which he sought his death.

'And has he seen the others?' Odin asked.

Oh yes, she replied. He had seen those other shapes, those snow-spattered shapes that stumbled nearer. His death-hungry eyes had picked them out, counting their number, roving amongst them like the liquid amber gaze of the patrolling wolves. They had not seen him yet, though they knew that, if he was not there, he would come soon. That was why they went on. He would be there, sooner or later. His honour alone dictated that he should face them in battle, and honour was more than a word to such as he. It was a code to live by, or to die for. He would be there to stand against them, seeking the death that they intended he should meet at their hands.

'But tell me, my lovely,' Odin smiled, his right hand reaching up to smooth the feathers on her back in a gesture which was at once half threat and half affection, 'will he defeat them? Will he see to your feasting, and kill them all?'

She hesitated. Allfather had been up to his special seat. He had looked out over the world and seen what was to happen. That was why they called him Allfather. He was not the creator, but he knew about everything that had been created. Only a brave fool dared to try his wisdom against that of the god. Those few that had tried, giants and dwarfs, lay long dead, or stood to greet the sun, turned to immortal stone.

His smile persisted in the frozen morning. 'You're learning wisdom,' he whispered. 'You know what you may not do, and that is truly wisdom. Shall I tell you, little Munin? Shall

I tell you what the Norns have written for the fate of this accursed old man? Or shall we draw nearer to this field of conflict? Shall we wait and see what has been written for his weird?'

He looked from the coal-black eyes that twinkled near his own, down to the tiny figures on the plain. Even his brilliant, single eye could not make out the snow-shrouded figure of the waiting champion. All that he could see was the tiny figures struggling nearer through the whiteness of a cruel winter.

Munin released her threat upon his ear. She knew that the spear-jab of her beak could never be delivered, knew it as surely as she knew his names. She and Hugin were his slaves. They would never nest, though they were mates. They would never seek a high place in the trees and hatch their eggs. But there were advantages. There was no counting the times she had flown across the world and seen her kin, other ravens, lying dead, their feathers fouled and bedraggled in the mud. She would never end like that. Her master was a god and, whilst she served, she shared his immortality.

Odin shuffled through the snow to the plain beneath them. The hem of his cloak, heavy with melted snow, stretched heavily and lazily behind him, granting a greater compass to the prowling wolves. Geri and Freki widened the circle of their patrol, ravening with greedy hunger. They too had pride, the same pride that Hugin and Munin, carried on Allfather's shoulders, knew and felt.

His tracks lay spread out behind him in the broken whiteness that blanketed the ground. The tiny figures, so remote, struggled nearer to a foe they could not yet see. And Starkadder, the old man, glared upon them from beneath his canopy of snow, his hollowed gaze seeking for the blade that might end his tired and tiresome life, and finding it not.

Odin felt his thoughts, though he could not see him. He would only see the old man when he shrugged off his cloak of velvet white. Perhaps then he would grant the mercy of death. No, not yet. The curse was not yet run. Three times the span of mortal men was Odin's promise to the warrior. Three dreadful deeds, one for each span, was the curse

15

with which Thor had countered his father. Starkadder had only two betrayals on his conscience. There had to be a third. Only then could the looked-for blade be seen. Only then could mercy intervene and the killer be released by death.

And the others, the ones who came to kill a man they could not see, what of them? Angantyr and his berserks had no knowledge of the curse. Only Starkadder and Thor and Odin knew. Angantyr could not know, and he would pay with his death for his ignorance.

The old man had killed often, and he would kill again. Many times the assassin's dagger had sought his unprotected back in vengeance or in spite, but each time the blow had been delayed or turned. Each time he had walked away unscathed, leaving a gutted corpse to add another line to the legend of Starkadder.

And now he waited in the snow for others to come, for others to seek to end his accursed life, though he knew it to be beyond their power. One more betrayal, he told himself, echoing the thoughts of the watching god; one more betrayal and you can die. Just one more and it's over, Starkadder. But this isn't a betrayal, Starkadder, this is not the time. You won't die yet.

How many are there? Ten? A dozen? Perhaps a dozen. What other man could stand alone, hampered by snow about his ankles, and kill a dozen men? Was there ever one? They envy you, you know. It's more than just a grudge against King Oli, the lord you serve. He's a hard man to kill, but could he stand against a dozen? He knows you can. That's why you're here, freezing in the winter dawn. That's why he's in his hall, wrapped warm in furs against the winter, and you're here alone.

Allfather smiled again. The curse must wait, as must the longed-for death. And while it waited there was time for things to change, time for life to grow and strengthen with every eager sacrifice before old Odin's altars. Perhaps red-bearded Thor had sought to spite his father with the curse. Perhaps his words were harsh and badly-framed. Yet there had been a care in them that even his thwarted father could appreciate. Three spans, three betrayals, gave them time to thwart the Norns, gave them time to seek an answer, to prevent the third betrayal from bringing down the Yngling dynasty.

The royal house had ruled the north since time or, at least, the rule of Allfather and the lesser gods, began. The Yngling dynasty had supported the old gods. With its fall other gods would rise to power; and the White Christ would storm from his cross, out of the sun-dried south, with a faith that would win minds but wither honour. Was this solitary, deathless old man to be the only hope? Must this third betrayal change the lives of men and banish gods for ever from the north? Somehow, somewhere, there had to be another way. There had to be an escape from the immutable decree of the unyielding Norns. Could they not see that the Christ would banish them as well? Could they not understand that the end of the Yngling dynasty would consign them to the silence of eternity, together with Allfather and his family?

Odin's single eye blazed as he looked down upon the plain at Roliung. His knowledge told him that the third span was drawing to its close, that Starkadder would soon commit that last betrayal, that he and his, Hugin, Munin, Geri, Freki, all, would fade and vanish with the fatal stroke.

Thus he watched. He watched every battle as he now waited to watch this one. Soon, be it this year or in twenty, thirty years to come, that last betrayal would take place. His fate, his immortality, his mastery of the northern world, not yet contaminated by the written word, were bound up with the curse upon the snow-mantled viking. With Starkadder's death his own decline would begin. When Starkadder fell the very foundations of Valhalla would begin to crumble, and the White Christ would begin his conquest of the North.

Odin, Allfather, the Greybeard, Death-blinder, watched from the ridge above the plain at Roliung, unable to warn or help, bound by the very curse which plagued his servant Starkadder. He wanted to call out, to tell the waiting warrior of the horror of his curse, but his tongue was bound by the Norns, by a power even greater than his own. Yet what he could do, he did, though it could not be much.

'Let him hear you, my children,' Odin muttered. 'Let him know that, even in his loneliness, he is not alone.'

Hugin and Munin launched themselves from the god's shoulders, cawing and circling above the snow-swept plain. Geri and Freki threw back their shaggy heads and closed their amber eyes, howling their death-song across the field of conflict. Odin, suddenly cold in the white of winter, huddled himself in the depths of his traveller'ᴗ cloak as his creatures sang, knowing that his time was running out.

And so it was, on that winter morning in the days before recorded history in Scandinavia, whilst Offa's subjects laboured on his dyke and Charlemagne was rocked in his cradle, an old, old man stood in the snow and watched his approaching adversaries, knowing that even if they had been a hundred, they could not kill him.

CHAPTER TWO

Starkadder killing

ANGANTYR DID not look up to see the wheeling ravens, but he heard the howling of the wolves. Their cries, borne by the skin-whipping wind, bit into his helmeted ears, pledging their desire to feast on the fallen.

'Do you hear?' he demanded. 'They've hunted through the night and found nothing. It's up to us to give them food.'

'Or our blades,' grunted Hervard, shuddering beneath his leather cape. He was a seasoned warrior, the veteran of many battles, but the mournful crying of unseen wolves sent chills down his spine, for he knew how they feasted, and on what. He had seen reindeer, pulled down and ripped open, stark brown and blood upon the white of snow, lifeless yet moving still beneath the slavering, snapping jaws.

Angantyr laughed at Hervard's distaste. His laughter was full-blooded and cruel, too selfish to hold humour, too cold to be covering fear. Some of the others joined that laughter as they struggled through the snow, but they were not so brave. They knew of Starkadder's immortality, and feared it.

'I don't like it,' Hrani Arngrimsson shuddered. His thick woollen cloak was soaked with melted snow and his shoulders steamed as he struggled onwards into drift after drift. 'There never used to be wolves in these parts. It's not right.'

19

For an instant the sun emerged from its grey-pink shrouding, suddenly blinding them, throwing long, blue shadows on the broken white tracks which stretched out behind them. Then it drifted behind the clouds again, restoring their sight.

'Do you see him?' Hervard asked. 'This is the place, Angantyr. This is the plain of Roliung. You see the stream over there, with the wooden bridge above it? This is the place all right. But do you see him, Angantyr?'

'Hold your woman's noise,' their chieftain spat. If their adversary were not there already, he'd be coming. As killers went, Starkadder was the best. They all knew that. The story of the curse that kept him alive made no difference. If enough men came against him, then one only was required to strike off his head. No man, whether blessed or cursed by all the gods of Asgard, could survive that.

Angantyr laughed again, throwing back his helmed head as Odin's wolves had thrown back their heads to howl. Even King Oli, the man Starkadder served, feared his killer's blade and wanted him dead. Men such as this gaunt, dry old warrior were the stuff of legends, the substance of the songs of skalds. Their deeds, whether commonplace or glorious, kept them alive and gave them majesty, majesty that rightly was reserved for kings. If Angantyr and his men died, Oli would reward old Starkadder. If Starkadder died, then Oli would be rewarding them. Not openly, of course. He would have to show due respect for the death of a man who was, after all, a formidable champion.

'Keep together,' Angantyr ordered. 'Keep your eyes open, and be ready.' Still, he thought, at least this hell-spawned winter will keep us from ambush. Only a storm-mounted valkyrie could come on us unseen through this.

They were drawing closer. Twin grey fires burned in Starkadder's hollowed sockets, fires that flickered about the twelve growing shapes, searching their strengths, probing for their weaknesses. He knew that they had not seen him where he stood idol-still in his shroud of settled snow. Even the brief awakening of the sun had revealed no more than a whitened hump which perhaps disguised a tree-stump or a standing stone. But they would see him. They would see

20

the grim old warrior, and he would be the last thing that they saw.

Perhaps King Oli had sent him there, to this snow-swept plain, to find his death. The thought struck true, and the aged killer stilled a nod, lest it betray him before his time. Yes, Oli wanted him dead. It was Angantyr who was supposed to walk away from Roliung. He had not, of course, told Oli of the curse, but it was obvious to all who knew him that there was nothing natural in Starkadder's age, or in his fighting skills. Men feared and hated him, leaving him friendless and solitary. Another, ordered to stand against these berserks, would have found others to stand with him, men who wanted the glory they would gain from such a battle. But Starkadder waited alone, his grey-whiskered mouth twitching into a knowing smile.

In other times, without the curse, he might have killed King Oli. Certainly, if he died, Oli would reward Angantyr, then seek out others who would kill the berserk for him. That way he would be rid of the most feared of his retainers, and the most formidable of those who threatened him. Perhaps the death of King Oli on Starkadder's blade would end the curse. Perhaps then he could find his sought-for death and sit with Odin in Valhalla. Yet there was pain in such betrayals, a pain that chewed and gnawed at him, biting into his aged bones like a frost-giant penetrating a woman. Perhaps even this life-in-death was better than feeling that pain again.

His ears were tingling, singing beneath his banded helmet. They felt the cold in their fleshy lobes like no other part of his scarred and wrinkled frame. Even so, through that inward singing, he heard another song, a song that echoed about him each time he plied his deadly art. A song that growled from deep in wolfish throats, a song that echoed through the frozen winter waste. And then he knew that even in his solitude he was not alone. There was one above him, unseen though not unfelt, who watched and waited for the final blow, the severing stroke that brought an end to life.

'Is it time yet, Allfather?' His lips formed the words, but it was his heart which spoke them, knowing as it asked that the question was still in vain.

21

He heard Angantyr's distant laughter. Then, from nearer, from a larger, closer shape, a deeper mirth began to bubble. Starkadder allowed himself the movement of his thumb, slipping the thong which held his sword down in its scabbard. Outside his cloak the snow cracked, but the coating was thick and the shrouding held intact.

They drew nearer still. Now he could see the breath that steamed out from their nostrils, spreading in twin streams from beneath the metal nose-guards they had hinged down into place. He wanted to shout to them, to tell them that the curse had not yet run its length, to tell them that their futile onslaught could only end in bloody death. But they would not believe him. They would laugh, confident in their own strength. They would rush on, anyway, blades of steel aswing before their faces.

One thing was in his favour. The clotted snow about their boots bound their feet to the frozen earth. Those on the flank could not rush to the centre, and those behind would lose precious seconds pushing forward. They wanted him dead, and it was up to them to come to him. He was the defender. If they could draw a little closer, seeing him only at the last possible moment, he would have won an advantage that might yet keep him safe.

And yet, he mused, as they drew those few feet closer, perhaps it could end here. Perhaps they would be the ones who took his life, ending his miserable solitude. But to die like this, cut down by these berserk mercenaries, could never be his way.

He was Starkadder. And Starkadder had his pride.

Besides, had his ears not heard the howling of the wolves? And did he not know that in their song of death was the omen of his winning? So had it proved before and so would it prove now. His time, though he longed for it, was not yet come.

Once more the sun slid out from behind the covering clouds, low and bright before the advancing berserks. Once more it cast long, blue shadows behind Angantyr's men. Once more its brilliance bit their unready eyes, spattering their sight with snow-dazzle, bringing their hands up from weapon-hilts to guard against its pitiless brightness.

And, in that moment, his deep-set eyes in shadow, his back to the light, Starkadder threw off his shroud of snow. The flakes broke apart and flew outwards from his cloak, catching the light, spreading a sunlit, shimmering aura about him, tracing the glittering arc of his sword, the sword which swept out, curving through the frost-bright air, slicing deep into the stomach of the nearest warrior. Only as the man screamed did the snow begin to settle, only as he clutched his spilling entrails, spraying blood onto the whiteness of the world he left, did the sun begin to fade. And by then it was too late for the man who came after him. The same blade swept his head aside, shearing the neck beneath, leaving the headless fountain to pitch away.

Only in Starkadder's early days would he have noted two deaths, and calculated the ten still to come. That was long ago, probably nearly two hundred years. Since then his instinct had become more finely strung than that of any viking in the north. No man could face the sweeping of his blade and walk away. No man could see the shimmer of his steel and live to tell of it.

'Kill him!' Angantyr screamed, tearing his blade from its leather scabbard. 'Gut him!'

Even as he spoke another died. The point of Starkadder's weapon, honed to a razor-edge, imbued with the magic of its owner's legend, clove mail and breeches, vertically down from rib-cage to genitals. The old killer had learned long ago to avoid the thrust in favour of the swing. A swing could be turned to kill again. A thrust required withdrawal, leaving the thruster vulnerable in the act.

Nine left. But nobody was counting.

One thrust. Starkadder, smiling grimly, sidestepped and knocked the sword aside. Then he doubled the movement at the wrist and sheared the sword-gripping forearm from its elbow, leaving the stump to spurt on sword-proud fingers. No need to follow up. The man was beyond fighting now, and his life or death had ceased to matter.

Hervard stumbled through the snow, seeking to get behind the aged warrior for a decapitating stroke. Angantyr hung back, ranting curses at his berserks, urging them to the fury that had made them so formidable in the past. Yet

23

even as he swore another died, one eyeball slit, the other swept away on the guard-shattering point of Starkadder's weapon. The ruined nose beneath ran gore down cloak and corselet. The death was worth it though, Angantyr smiled. Hervard was nearly there. At least he was beyond Starkadder's vision.

Two more blades thrust. Both were clanged aside by the old man's sword. A third warrior howled up, his sword held high, aiming a vicious swing at the ancient's head. As he approached Hervard drew his arms back, bending them across his face, preparing the stroke that would sever Starkadder's head from his shoulders. Then, with a wordless and triumphant howl, the stroke began.

The man in front lashed out. With an angry snarl Starkadder threw himself sideways into the snow, sweeping up at the groin of one of the men whose blades he had just deflected. His assailant's sword shimmered harmlessly on and down, cleaving nothing more than the empty air. Hervard, unable to check his stroke, gasped despairingly as the edge of his weapon bit into his comrade's neck.

Wordless in his fury, Angantyr began to count. Five left.

Hervard tugged at his sword. The weapon had cut deep into the berserk's neck bones and stuck fast. Starkadder's blade swung again, seeking for itself targets that the sunken eyes had not yet registered. The owner of the other deflected blade lost a leg above the knee at the beginning of the same upward stroke that tore out Hervard's throat.

Three.

The snow about their feet had long since ceased to shimmer white. Now it was trampled brown and pink, steaming and melting beneath stamping feet and flowing, spraying blood. As Starkadder scrambled to his feet two dying men, one prone, one thrashing in the recent agony of amputation, moaned their way towards bloodless unconsciousness. Seven more dark shapes flecked with falling white lay scattered on the plain, close by the bridge of Roliung. Only three remained to face him, but one of them was Angantyr.

He watched them begin to circle, picking their way between the bodies of the dying and the slain. As yet no sword had touched Starkadder's meagre flesh. No blade or point had yet found the way to shed the thin but powerful blood that coursed within his veins.

'Can you kill me, Angantyr?' Starkadder demanded. 'Can you strike the blow that will save both of us?'

'What, not dead yet?' his foe replied. 'It comes to all men, friend Starkadder. It can even come to you.'

The old man nodded. He stood, tall and gaunt, apparently oblivious of the berserk who had crept close up beside him. Only when the sword flashed down did he move, with the speed of a striking viper, lurching sideways beneath the glittering arc, wrapping his free arm about the warrior's legs, lifting him across his back and hurling him into the man who waited on his other side. As both went down in a tangle of limbs and weapons he towered above them, knocking aside Angantyr's sudden thrust with bone-jarring force, buying himself the time to kill both fallen berserks.

Allfather, why does it always have to end thus?

The brightness of his blade was dulled with blood. Eleven men lay dead about his feet, stretched in the darkened circle on the whiteness of the plain.

'Now, my friend,' he smiled, 'we shall see which one will die.'

And Angantyr, finally alone with this man of legend, tasted fear. Its rankness stung his mouth and seeped, burning, down into his stomach. For a brief moment he allowed himself the luxury of wondering if Starkadder shared that taste.

The old man felt suddenly weary. 'Go,' he said, 'if you want to. There's none will hold it against you. All men know me, but few would stand alone against me, Angantyr. There's no disgrace in choosing life over death. Leave this place. I'll not seek to stop you.'

Angantyr shook his head. 'Men know that I came here to kill you,' he replied. 'There's no honour if I leave here without your head at my belt.'

Starkadder stared at his enemy for a while, then slowly nodded. 'We're both trapped, you and I. You must kill me for your honour. I must prevent you for my own. Do you have a family, Angantyr?'

The berserk smiled faintly. 'I had a wife,' he muttered.

'She gave me a daughter before she died. Apart from the girl there's no one. Except my brother, of course. His name was Hervard, but now he lies over there.' He gestured with his sword towards one of the corpses on the bloodied ground. 'That's another reason why I can't leave you alive.'

'Your pride will make your daughter an orphan,' Starkadder cautioned.

'Perhaps her vengeance will prove stronger than your curse,' came the reply.

'Then so be it.'

They stood facing one another, weapons drawn, less than six feet apart. Their eyes burned, each into the other's, searching for that weakness that would grant an advantage to the stronger. Above them twin ravens circled silently. In the distance, high up, a blue–cloaked god watched with his single eye, the thunder of passing years loud in his ears. At his feet the wolves, Geri and Freki, stared hungrily at the waiting feast.

'Tell me, Starkadder. Through the years, have you always held the same sword?'

'Better in my hands than another's. And you?'

'My sword is called Tyrfing,' Angantyr replied. 'I took it from the corpse of King Svafrlami on the battlefield.'

'I've heard of it. It was forged by the dwarfs. They say that dwarfish steel is better than most. The sword that the god Frey gave for Gerda's love was dwarf–forged.'

'They say more than that of Tyrfing, Starkadder . . .'

As he spoke Angantyr raised the sword and aimed a cut at the old warrior's head. Had it struck it would have split apart his banded leather helmet like a nutshell, and dug deep into the brains beneath. Starkadder's own blade moved in a speed–blurred arc. Twisting and flickering in the air it caught the guard of Angantyr's weapon and continued upwards, tearing Tyrfing from its owner's grasp, sending it straight up, into the sky, like a giant silver arrow.

The eyes of both men followed Tyrfing's unexpected flight as it glittered towards its zenith. Then the sword turned, still shimmering, still alive, singing in the air and began its fall.

Starkadder wanted to cry out, to warn the berserk, but

his tongue was stilled, this time by a curse not his own. The point of the descending blade caught Angantyr in the throat. It buried its length in his body, plunging down behind the rib-cage, parting the heart, piercing the lungs and entrails. The warrior stood quite still, the hilt of the sword keeping his head raised, holding his dead eyes towards the ice-grey sky as the gushing, pumping blood sprang from his throat. Then, stiffened by Tyrfing's deadly length, Angantyr rocked backwards on his heels and struck the ground, spattering blood-thawed snow into the air.

Starkadder wiped his blade on the cloak of a fallen warrior and returned it to its iron-bound scabbard. 'They do say more of Tyrfing Angantyr,' he whispered. 'They say that Svafrlami stole it from the dwarfs, and that they cursed Tyrfing. You took it from Svafrlami's corpse, Angantyr, for it had killed him as surely as it has now killed you. That is the curse they laid upon it, that the sword should kill all who possess it.'

He bent down and closed Angantyr's eyes with his gloved fingers. Perhaps, he thought, they might have been friends, but for the curses that haunted them both.

In the distance, from the rise above the plain, Odin still watched, taking pride in the old fighter's prowess. In many ways he regarded Starkadder as the greatest warrior who had ever lived, who would ever live. Yet each of the old man's victories was as much a cause for sadness as for rejoicing. Each fresh killing brought that third betrayal closer. He knew, as Starkadder did, that one day the old man would kill King Oli. He also knew that Oli's successors were destined to be feeble, useless creatures who would squander their patrimony and bring the Yngling dynasty to its end. There would be other dynasties, of course. Other ruling houses would rise to govern the north, but then they would fall under the governance of Rome, or those who took their orders from that southern city almost as old as Asgard, who lied their way into the hearts of fools and undermined the ancient, venerable faith of their forefathers.

He knew, because the Norns had written it. And from their fatal weird there could be no escape, neither for Odin nor for Starkadder.

27

CHAPTER THREE

The awakening of Angantyr

HERVARA'S FIGURE, where it showed through the travel-stained rags of her clothing, was full for her age. The nipples of young breasts stood firm and proud against the cloth as she breathed and her hair, once bound but now loose and matted, hung long and fair about a face that should have, and would have, been beautiful, save for the pain and hatred on its perfect features. Her eyes were blue, not the pale, ice-blue of her father's, now some months slain by Starkadder, but the deep, rich blue of sun-bright sea. Even now, as the world sank into a summer twilight, the blue shone out, strengthened and hardened by a lifetime of sunless winters.

This was her fourteenth year and, though she had never known a mother's love, the first without her father Angantyr. Soon she would be a bride, for men loved her and wanted her. There was something hungry in the way they looked at her, something to do with her firmly moulded body, something that bespoke a willingness to ignore the festering hatred in her. Already court was being paid by one of King Oli's favoured retainers and, whilst there was no love in Hervara, she was responding to his games and promises. Oh yes, he could have her body. He could satisfy and soften the hardness she aroused in him.

But he would never have her love. At least, not whilst Starkadder still lived.

She slipped down from the pony's back when she saw the old fisherman walking up from the beach. His figure was bent with the long years of hauling at his nets. Now it was bent with the weight of the brimming basket he carried. The spring shoals might have thinned, but there were still fish shimmering silver in the coastal waters to be caught.

Beyond him, on the darkening sands beneath the sunset, lay his boat, its shadow long and black beyond it. Further away, its dark bulk threatening the sinking sun, was the Isle of Samsey, its sun-red summit proud with the burial-mound of her slaughtered father. This was the object of her journey, the land in the water, the abode of the sleeping dead.

The fisherman smiled and moved to pass her, but she stood scowling in his path, the pony across it blocking it behind him. He tried to push past her but she thrust herself against him, the touch of her breasts unnerving him, bringing forgotten life to his age-bent body. Yes, Hervera was lovely. Except for her eyes.

'Will you take me to the island?' It was both a question and a demand, and those deep blue eyes held no promise of the payment her body seemed to offer.

For an instant the fisherman, still tingling from their brief contact, seemed to waver. Then he shook his head.

'Take me to the island in your boat.' This time it was a command.

Again the fisherman shook his grey locks. 'It's the glimpses of the moon, Lady,' he replied. 'This is the dark time, the time when the dead wake in their barrows. And there are mounds for the slain upon that island.'

'Then I shall take your boat.'

'No, I cannot let you do that.'

Hervara did not know a great deal about men, yet. She was still virgin, and her knowledge of men's bodies was confined to the odd occasions when, as a child, she had glimpsed her father. Yet she had seen the young men wrestling at the games, and she knew from their faces that there was a place where they could easily be hurt. Her hand slid down into the old man's breeches and grasped him. His length stiffened as best it could at the touch, then softened as she repeated her demand.

'Then take me across, old man. Or I shall hurt you.' Her fingers began to tighten on him.

'And . . . if I do?' he asked, his eyes beginning to feel moist, but not with pleasure.

'Then I won't hurt you. Perhaps I will even reward you.'

The catch, now lying about his feet, mostly spilled from the basket he had dropped, was adequate. It was about the best you could expect from this area at this time of year. Up to this point the day had been good, but now it had suddenly soured. He studied Hervara's eyes and felt the tightness of her grip. If he refused, those strong young fingers could crush his balls and leave him writhing amongst his suffocated fish. If he complied he would have to face the possibility of the waking, walking ghosts of the slain. It was not the easiest of choices for him to make.

At length he nodded. 'I'll take you,' he said.

She released her hold and withdrew her hand, moving carefully and slowly in case he attempted to dart away. Men driven by threats could often be treacherous. So she tore open her dress, baring her breasts to him, watched his rheumed old eyes widen at the sight.

'I've shown you pain.' Her hollow smile was half-hidden in the twilight. 'Keep faith and take me across to the island. Then I might show you pleasure.'

They both knew that her promises would come to nothing, but the fisherman remembered the dull ache in his scrotum. Somehow this girl, almost but not quite a woman, held more terror for him than the waiting ghosts.

'I'll take you,' he repeated.

He left the spilled fish and the basket where they were. Slightly ahead of Hervara, his eyes lancing back in the sunset in anxious, nervous watching of this child who was already half a valkyrie, he led her down to the beach and dragged his boat into the water once again. She seated herself in the bows, her back to the Isle of Samsey, and watched his aged back and arms strain at the oars in the rowlocks. Although the old man could not see her, he felt those cold, deep-blue eyes burning him through the gathering gloom.

Her hand dragged pale and thin in the water, her arm crooked over the gunwale. Her fingers ploughed the surface into little furrows which trailed into lazy ripples. It was not so long since news had come to her of her father's death and, naturally, it had strengthened and deepened in the telling. The fine distinction between Starkadder having killed Angantyr and the deed being that of the dwarf-forged sword, Tyrfing, had misted and vanished completely. It was Starkadder and Starkadder alone who was responsible for the deaths of all twelve berserks, including her father and her uncle.

To Hervara, on that crossing to Samsey Isle, it was unthinkable that there might be other forces at work, that the games of others should determine the deaths and lives of those she held so dear, those that were all the Norns had left her by way of blood-kin.

Her memory of that dark, storm-laden day when the news came to her was unclear, overcast by the misery thrown so carelessly into her young life. Images, fragments of memory, clung to the thoughts of the child-woman in the boat. Men in heavy plate and chain armour, speaking in gruff, subdued voices. Rain falling against the parchment windows of the longhouse, beating out a rhythm to accompany the falling of her own uncontrolled tears. Strange shadows closing about her, moving stealthily, pervasively, enfolding her in their secret, unknown, unknowable recesses.

And then the old woman came to her.

Somehow the shadows clung to her face as she spoke to Hervara, masking her wrinkled features, hiding them from the girl's tear-swollen eyes. Yet by some magic her words cut through the girl's deep grief with a power and a clarity beyond her ability to measure.

'Conceive a son,' the old crone said simply. 'Give him your father's sword. Give him Tyrfing, and he will use it to kill Starkadder for you.'

She shuddered in the boat and drew her hand from the

31

water, suddenly chilled. For the duration of some of her grief she had forgotten the old woman, though not the thoughts which she had put into her head. Now, as the boatman beached his craft on the shore of Samsey Isle and she stepped once more onto land, they came back to her strongly, as they had done many times before.

The chill persisted, creeping through her flesh and setting its icy fingers about the marrow of her bones. Get Tyrfing, the old woman had told her. Go to your father's grave-mound and ask him for the sword. He will give it up to you. This is one time when the dead will give up at least some of their secrets.

'But . . . how should I make him give me his sword?' she had asked, her voice unsteady, choked with too much crying.

'Go in the dark of the moon,' said the old woman. 'Go in the glimpses, when the dead are so much nearer to the living. He will give you Tyrfing if you go to him then.' Hervara wiped her eyes and looked up, trying to make out those shadowed features, seeking some sign that the words were offered in charity and not as some black entrapment. If there was a face beneath the wadmal shawl Hervara couldn't see it.

The path up to the burial mound was dark and indistinct, reminding her again of the old crone's veiled features. As she began to make her way up from the shore Hervara sensed a growing weight in the air, presences beyond her comprehension. Yet she continued her progress, feeling the heather and the brambles claw at her legs to either side of the narrow, slightly beaten path.

The terrified fisherman remained behind, sitting on the shore with his boat. Not for all the promises of love or gold or torture Hervara might have muttered would he have ventured another yard towards the death-haunted heart of the isle.

Before her, in the centre of the island, the glow of hidden fires rose mistily towards the sky.

The old fisherman could see the corpse-lights from where he sat, and was tempted to push away, to leave this mad girl to whatever fate awaited her. Drawing deeper within himself

32

he muttered a hurried prayer to Redbeard Thor and continued his vigil.

Slowly, trembling in the darkening night, Hervara, still bare-breasted, approached the mound which held her father.

'For Thor's sake hurry,' the old man called after her. 'Only a fool would linger on this place in the dark of the moon. I can feel it in my bones, child. The graves are opening!'

She nodded in the shrouding evening. Yes, she felt fear. About the barrow tiny fires, perhaps fireflies, perhaps the will-o'-the-wisp, sparkled in the darkness. There could be no doubting that this was a place of the dead.

'What if he leaves you?' an unseen voice demanded. 'What if he goes back to the mainland, leaving you here amongst the unquiet dead.'

Even that, she thought, if it must be, will be. I have come here for a purpose, and I will not leave before that purpose is accomplished, though all the ghosts of Hel rise one by one to seek my maidenhead. I shall go on. I shall speak with my father. I shall take the sword from him for the son I have not yet conceived.

She walked on, closer to that dead-holding summit of Samsey Isle. Perhaps her heart fluttered with the fright of a hunted butterfly, beneath those perfect child-woman breasts, but her eyes did not show her fear.

And then the death-mound rose before her, lit with the unholy fires whose source was hidden from her eyes, circled by the flickering flames, blue and cold as her eyes. Yet Hervara walked on in her proud beauty, defying the nameless dead who lay about her father, clinging to her purpose, fired by hatred greater than her fear. Then she stood still, facing the mound, her eyes bright once again in the unhallowed light of the corpse-fires, fires from which no smoke was seen to issue.

'Father,' she called. 'Father, awake. Angantyr, wake! It is your daughter who calls you.'

About her the silence echoed, but there came no answer.

'Angantyr, it is your daughter, Eyfura's daughter. I seek the sword, my father. I seek Tyrfing, the sword which Svafrlami stole from the dwarfs who forged it.'

33

And still there was nothing, save the silence. And the fires.

'Is this my father's resting-place? Is this where mighty Angantyr lies in the sleep of death? Surely only pale corpses lie here, their valour burned out. Surely only the craven dead lie in this mound. My father, Angantyr the Mighty, would make answer.'

Still only silence lingered, but the fires flickered with uncertain life.

'My father is not here. Only the worm-eaten corpses of dead cowards ward this tomb. There is no one here worthy of the respect of the living. Only the ant-chewed bodies of dead fools lie here!'

And then the answer came, shocking and thrilling her with its hollow might, ringing in the air like broken bells, banishing the silence from Samsey Isle, cursing at the ears that heard it, sending the distant fisherman to hide, shaking, in his rotting boat.

'Hervara!' howled the voice. 'Would you wake me from the sleep I've come to love? Daughter, will you abuse my deathly calm?'

For a moment she was helpless against the uncontrolled, fright-born tremor which possessed her limbs, shaking her as a dog might play with a dead ermine. Then the hidden face of the old woman rose to confront her, to give her strength and power, to steady her trembling and give her the will she needed to complete the enterprise.

'Get Tyrfing,' came the old crone's whisper. 'For your son.'

The terror which her dead father's voice had called forth began to subside beneath her efforts to master it. It had arisen because, despite her faith in the ancient woman's promptings, despite her burning, consuming desire for revenge upon Starkadder for Angantyr's murder, she had never really believed that such things could be possible. It had always seemed unthinkable, despite the tales in the legends and sagas recited by the skalds, that the dead might actually respond to the summons of the living.

Yet now, with her fear mastered and Angantyr's hollow, tomb-deep voice still echoing in her ears, her disbelief was

34

banished for whatever span of years remained to her. With its passing she entered a world which bore little semblance to the secure, warm, stable realms of vanished childhood.

The terrors of the night could be real. They might not be soothed away by the gentle stroking of a loving nurse ever again.

Would she waken him from his deathly calm, he had asked. Could she tear him from the slumbers of the grave-mound to demand he give her Tyrfing? With the realisation that her enterprise might not be in vain her resolve strengthened. For an instant the ancient crone, her face still wrapped in shadow, stood beside her once again, urging and prompting Hervara to make answer to her buried father.

'Ask for Tyrfing. Ask him for Tyrfing for your son.'

Will you disturb him further, Hervara? Abandon your fear. It has no place in what you have to do.

'You've left me little enough,' Hervara said, her voice becoming stronger as she conquered her fears. 'Give me the sword, Father. Give me Tyrfing. Now!'

'It . . . is . . . not . . . here.'

She had never thought to hear Angantyr answer. Somehow she had believed that the sword, Tyrfing, would be thrust up through the earth, into her waiting grasp, without this ghostly discourse with the dead.

'It is here. And you shall give it to me, that I may give it to my son. For I shall have a son, Father. I shall have a son, Angantyr, a son who will avenge your death, a son who will kill Starkadder. Will you give me the blade? For him?'

Angantyr sighed, and the earth about his burial-mound cracked and opened at the dreadful sound. 'I will not,' he answered, 'for there is a curse upon that sword. Let it lie here, daughter. Let its curse end here, in the depths of the earth, with me.'

'Curse or no, it is a symbol. I need it for my son. Let it be mine, Father, or I will curse your bones. Give me Tyrfing, Father, for my son, or I'll lay the spell my old nurse taught me. I'll bind your dead flesh to lie here, in the grave, eternally rotting, giving you no peace, in Hel or in Valhalla. Now, will you give me the sword?'

'It is not here, Hervara.'

She shook her head. 'Your lies will force the curse, unwilling, from my lips. None would take Tyrfing from you. It lies with you in the grave, beneath your back, ringed with the witch-fire of the dead. Deliver me the sword, Father. I do not fear to curse you where you lie, but it seems hard to me to damn you to avenge you. Give it up, Angantyr. Give me Tyrfing.'

The dead man sighed again, and again the earth widened above his tormented corpse. 'Can you hold such a blade?' he demanded. 'Can any living woman hold such a blade?'

'Give me the sword,' she repeated, her blue eyes blazing down at the splitting ground before her feet, burning with the reflected corpse-light that hemmed her in. 'I will hold it.'

'I will . . .' came the reply.

And then, slowly, the ornate hilt of Tyrfing, one side of the guard chipped by the bite of Starkadder's own blade, came rising through the earth. Hervara reached out to take it, showing no fear at the lambent blue fire which glittered about its surface.

'Here is the weapon,' Angantyr cried, his voice echoing about the mounds of Samsey Isle, making the fisherman's teeth chatter where he waited in his boat. 'You're a foolish daughter, but my love can deny you nothing. Neither can my fear of your cursing. Are you truly flesh of mine?'

He awaited the reply in darkness, but it did not come. His bones felt the tugging as she reached out and grasped the hilt of the sword called Tyrfing. He sought to reach out with his thoughts, to touch her into caution, to warn her once more of the curse that had cost him his life. But the sword was already gone from the grave-mound, and Hervara with it, so Angantyr slid quietly back to death.

'Don't touch the blade,' he hissed. 'There is a poison on the edges . . .'

Did she hear? Did his last warning reach her as she trod the downward path, away from Samsey's dreadful summit, away from the flickering of the corpse-lights? The fisherman heard her approach and pushed his boat into the water. He sat there, at his oars, watching as the girl-woman, Hervara, stood upon the shore, holding Tyrfing aloft, thrusting at the night sky with the accursed blade, bare-breasted like no valkyrie the world had ever seen. And then he shuddered again.

Whatever reward this strange, lovely girl might offer, he did not want it.

'Is it over?' he asked. 'Can we go now?'

She seemed not to hear him. She simply continued to stand, half-naked, unmoving, where earth and sky and sea all met. 'I have stood between the worlds,' she whispered to the darkness. 'I have Tyrfing. Now I must get my son.'

She splashed through the shallow water and sat down in the boat, holding the blade across her knees. Her eyes still burned, but their fire was far away, across the years that kept her from the future. For a moment the fisherman feared for his life when they reached the mainland once again, but then he thought again. She would not kill him, though she held the power to do so. She was somewhere else, for she had stood between the worlds, and wise men said that no one stood between the worlds, unless they left part of themselves behind.

He beached the boat on the mainland, glad to be free of the fear of ghosts and his unnatural passenger. Hervara walked to the waiting pony, then flung him a coin. She mounted and rode off, leaving the old man to gather up his fish into the basket. The coin lay where it had fallen, and no one has touched it to this day.

CHAPTER FOUR

Eyes that watch from afar

HE SAT upon the balcony, perched like a sparrow upon the narrow ledge which circled the grotesque tower, watching with eyes amber and unfathomable as those of Odin's wolves.

She's taken the sword, a shape reported, black and tattered where it wheeled against the deepening darkness of the evening sky. She's taken Tyrfing from her father's grave-mound. Tyrfing no longer transfixes the dead berserk Angantyr.

Very good, the watcher nodded in reply, the eyes burning with a grim satisfaction beneath the shadows of the hood.

She's crossed back from Samsey Isle and paid off the fisherman. He's left her gold to its fate on the path. He doesn't want her money. She's frightened him too much for that.

The hooded figure sighed and settled down inside its robes, gathering its small body together where it sat upon an ornate throne above the acid lake. The trouble with the shapes was that they never knew when their work was done. They lacked the intelligence to sort out fact from worthless detail, so they reported everything. Better so, Dvalin mused. That way at least he could be sure that they were telling him everything.

He grinned to himself where he sat, huddled against the

depth of the young night. When sunrise came he would scuttle back to the halls and corridors far beneath the tower, fleeing the powerful, transmuting light it brought with devastating and detrimental effect into his kingdom. Yet for now, with the last of the sunset less than an hour gone by, he could sit and watch, enjoying the darkness, letting the intelligence which the shapes brought to his eager ears wash about his mind.

There was nothing more significant, more vital, which they would tell him before the dawn. That Hervara had gone to her father's grave-mound on Samsey Isle was enough in itself. The additional intelligence, that she had wrested the sword Tyrfing from poor, vanquished Angantyr's tomb, merely served to confirm what he had known all along.

Play had begun again in the fearsome contest which raged between those who controlled the destinies of simple men. One of the greatest factors in that contest, a length of accursed, dwarf-forged metal that had been named Tyrfing, something that was both a prize and a bane to those who held possession of it, had been wrested from the rusting earth by a woman, little more than a girl, who might hold it in trust for the works and deeds of a future generation.

And Starkadder, the old killer, the tired, life-weary hero who was feared and dreaded throughout the north, would come to him before the closing moves of the game were played out. Starkadder would come and, at his heels, his young eyes bright with fear and the dwarf-blade in its scabbard at his waist, would come another whose name was not yet known, another who had yet to be born into a conflict he might never understand.

Hervara's unborn son.

Yes, they would come. As surely as Dvalin knew that the servants of the White Christ his shapes had told him of would travel north with the fire of their books and sermons into a world of ice and snow, a world so unlike the warm, sun-bright climes where the faith had already taken insidious root, he knew that Starkadder and the boy would come to him. They had to. They had as little choice about their coming as he would have in receiving them.

And then they would be near the end. Then it would no longer be a question of whether they would do what they had to do. It would simply be a question of when.

Dvalin sighed and the lambent fire in his eyes died a little as he thought on what was to come. It would be an end for all of them, yet for others it would also be a beginning, and the beginning of another end.

'The riddles don't matter,' he whispered to himself. 'They serve only to make me ponder the unavoidable, to listen to the shapes and seek to piece their mutterings together. Yet even that is useless . . .'

There was no one to listen to him as he sat and watched. None approached, neither the sentry who waited beside the little door which led back into the grotesquely ornamented stone tower, nor any who might have been approaching up the staircase within its heavy walls.

'They must come to me,' he said softly to the night. 'They need me more than I need them. That's why they'll come. They have no choice.'

He stared into the darkness, his eyes seeking one of the grim, ragged shapes which flapped above him on tattered pinions. They all looked so alike, but they remembered their names. The names might be all that remained to them of whatever lives they had lived before, perhaps together with memories enough to make their present servitude the more painful and uncomfortable. Mercy, forgiveness, had never been a strong point with either Dvalin or his forebears. That was why the shapes still served. That was why they circled and obeyed, waiting for a release which, though it would be final, might never come to them.

'Can you hear me, Svafrlami?' Dvalin called, more to himself than to the circling shape. 'Little Hervara has taken Tyrfing from her father's tomb. She has the sword now, Svafrlami. She has the sword you stole from me so many years ago.'

The wheeling, tormented, night-black Svafrlami didn't answer. His shape had no need to respond to Dvalin's information. It wasn't much, but the little spite his silence offered was all that he might muster by way of retaliation.

Dvalin grinned at the lack of response. He knew its

meaning only too well. Yet his grinning hid a deeper fear, a fear not of the coming of Starkadder and the boy, but of something greater, something which travelled with them, in their shadows.

Something which even now, fifteen years before, threatened to engulf them all.

A sacrifice unbidden

'HANG HIM.'

The order was calmly, almost carelessly spoken. Oli's black eyes neither widened in anticipation nor closed in suppressed pleasure as he spoke. They simply maintained their habitual, disturbing emptiness. He might as well have been throwing a bone to a dog or rewarding faithful service from a follower as ordering the death of a human being.

Vermund Bjarnisson, riding beside his lord, rubbed at his chin with a gloved hand and scowled behind the gauntlet. It was nothing more than another of Oli's whims, and made about as much sense as they usually did. So the man was one of the priests of the new god, the White Christ, who were starting to make their first appearance in the north. That was no reason to hang him. The vikings had centuries of experience of tolerating the worship of a variety of gods. Their own pantheon, whilst it concentrated for the most part on the major deities, Frey, Thor and Allfather Odin, embraced personifications of almost every desire and aspiration man had yet conceived. This new god, this Christ, was yet another. He would have his priests and his devotees as all the rest had. But Oli wanted this priest, this brown-robed monk, dead. And really, when you served a despotic lord such as Oli, that was all that need be said or reasoned.

'Bring him along,' Vermund grunted, resignedly.

Oli shot him a glance from those disturbing dark eyes, then nodded. The column was traversing one of the treeless plains of southern Sweden. It made sense to drag the Christian along behind them until they came to somewhere where he could be executed in the prescribed manner.

'So I must wait for my entertainment until we meet Starkadder on the fringes of the forest,' Oli muttered.

Vermund studied his lord carefully. Oli's impatience and changeability already bordered upon madness. Vermund, a seasoned warrior and still, despite Starkadder's presence, marshal of the royal forces, knew that it was only a matter of time until some unmarked borderline was crossed and the mighty Yngling King Oli was stark mad. Perhaps the moment had already come, but Oli still reigned, still appeared competent to command despite his increasing cruelties. He had not yet put either the safety of the realm or the succession at risk, and until he did so there was no reason to suppose the worst. The fact that when he finally crossed the thin line dividing sanity from madness and jeopardised either the realm or the Yngling line it would probably be too late for action was neither here nor there. He still reigned and was still competent to reign, and that was all that mattered to Vermund.

He feared Starkadder. All men feared Starkadder. His legend was well known, and, even without it, the way he had disposed of Angantyr and his berserks was enough to make mere mortals suspect that there was something super-natural about so dedicated and proficient a killer. Yes, Vermund Bjarnisson was afraid of Starkadder. It was only wise to fear such a man. Yet he had no envy of him. The legend, the story of a man doomed to live three lives and find only the self-recrimination of betrayal in each of them, was enough to kill envy before it came to birth in his breast. It was true that Starkadder was the greater warrior, but he was bound by constraints that Vermund could scarcely imagine. He dared not betray Oli, not even if Oli was mad beyond redemption. Such a betrayal would be his third, according to Vermund Bjarnisson's information, and the third betrayal would seal the old warrior's doom.

They bound the Christian monk and dragged him behind their column. He fell into the dust regularly, stumbling upon tired legs during his forced march to the edge of the

43

forest. His companion, younger and wiser, though some might have said more of a coward, had remained hidden, cowering in a gully whilst his companion rashly approached the king's column and declaimed the virtues of his god. Consequently he had escaped discovery and capture, remaining in his hiding-place whilst Oli delivered his sentence of death. He would wait there until the column passed and vanished into the dust-hidden distance, before he moved, before he reiterated the message he had been spreading to the local people, the common folk to whom Oli was nothing more than a name and a distant legend.

Later that day, before they reached the forest, the priest fell down, his tired legs giving way beneath him. Oli had deliberately, though subtly, increased the pace of his column so that the prisoner could no longer remain upon his feet and had to be dragged behind a horse. The man's knees and elbows were beyond simple rawness. The dirt of the summer road had worn away both flesh and bone by the time the royal progress reached the edge of the forest and joined Starkadder and his waiting troops. Both arms and legs were as useless as mercy to a man who had been dragged that far. All that might remain to the monk was a quick, clean death, and that would never come from merely being hanged. The tying of the right knot, let alone where it should be placed under the jaw, was unknown to Oli and his men. Hanging was not a quick death, unless it was followed by the merciful spear-thrust which might constitute a sacrifice to the Allfather, to Odin.

When they met Starkadder saluted Oli as his king and liege lord. Then he turned to Vermund Bjarnisson and looked along the line of the king's escort to the prisoner they dragged behind them.

'Who's that?' Starkadder asked the marshal.

'A priest of the White Christ,' Vermund replied. 'He made the mistake of attempting to impede our progress. King Oli has ordered his death by hanging.' Vermund took off his helmet, showing the strap which held the patch in place across his missing eye. His hair, once gold-white but now merely a tired, dirty yellow, streamed in ringlets behind him in the wind. The gloved hand rubbed at his beard again, as if attempting to displace some of the dust of their progress. He was scowling as he spoke.

Starkadder nodded, suddenly chilled despite the summer warmth, and drew his black cloak close about his gaunt figure. The execution of the priest made as much sense as anything Oli had ordered recently. After all, with so many dead already what was the point in protesting about one more? There might have been some point to it if this had been the first, or if Starkadder had been an ordinary mortal. But he had to be careful. He had to avoid doing anything that might be seen as a betrayal. Besides, the bloody remains at the end of the column were too far gone to thank him for rescinding the order, for granting life. All that remained to the priest was the hope of martyrdom.

'Then hang him we shall,' he replied. 'There are plenty of trees over there.' He gestured behind him to the fringe of the forest, where firs stood waiting with their branches thick and ready to take the strain of a rope, and a body.

'Make a noose and get him ready,' Vermund commanded, his single eye closed as he spoke.

They cut the priest free of the horse which had been dragging him and carried him, mangled and pain-wracked, to the nearest tree. He accepted the badly tied noose willingly, staring up defiantly into Oli's black eyes, fired by a spirit neither the king nor his retainers would ever understand. Soldiers had to hold him upright. His kneecaps were gone, worn and dislocated by the merciless terrain he had been dragged over.

'I forgive you,' he began, his voice little more than a croak. 'In the name of Jesus Christ Our Lord, Who forgave those who persecuted Him even as He hung upon the cross, I forgive you . . .'

Oli grinned to himself. He had heard, but the words meant nothing. He could not understand them. Instead he raised his hand, giving the signal for his men to draw upon the rope, raising the hapless monk out of the arms of those who supported him. Vermund grimaced with distaste and turned away. This wasn't how he thought things should be done. It wasn't like a warrior's clean death in the heat of battle. It was something unnatural, dishonourable.

45

Starkadder remained mounted, regarding the spectacle of the slowly strangling priest with blank, emotionless eyes. The gaunt viking made no move either to hasten or prevent the Christian's death. He simply sat his saddle in silence, impassive as an image of a forgotten god carved from seasoned timber. In his right hand he held both the reins of his mount and the haft of his spear. His thin lips, a livid slash across the sallow drawn parchment of his face, mouthed no words either of comfort or admonition.

'That's it,' Oli ordered, no longer grinning, no longer amused. There was nothing left to watch but the tiresome struggles of the dying man, and that bored him now. 'It's time we were riding again.'

He dragged on the reins, turning his mount away from the execution, his black eyes expressionless dead fires.

With a backward glance Vermund ordered his men to fall into line behind the monarch. With a dismissive movement of his left hand Starkadder waved his men to follow at the end of the column. Only when they were in position and moving, escorting King Oli along the dark, sunless trail into the forest, did the old warrior nudge his horse forward.

He followed them to the fringe of the firs, to the borderline between light and darkness, where the damp of the forest floor met the summer dryness of the plain. Then he drew on the harness and halted his short-legged northern war-horse. His eyes, still blank, looked back to where the monk fought for breath, his feet still struggling vainly to touch the ground a yard beneath his kicking heels. That they were no longer capable of supporting him wasn't important. All that mattered was the effort. The monk's breathing was little more than a harsh gurgle, a forcing of breath down his constricted windpipe to the starving lungs. His face was purple with the effort, and his eyes, not yet sightless, were starting to bulge.

Starkadder nodded curtly to the doomed man. Then he hefted the spear above his shoulder and hurled it at the dangling body. The head struck the monk's chest and buried itself in his heart. As blood erupted from the wound, forcing its way out along the shaft, staining the tattered brown robe a deeper, glistening hue, the priest surrendered to the mercy of death.

The old warrior left his spear where it was, projecting from the spinning corpse. He raised his tired eyes to the blue, cloud-flecked sky and whispered a single word, almost as much a question as a dedication.

'Odin?'

Then, his question unanswered, he pulled at the reins with his gloved hand, turning his mount to follow the rest of the column into the ragged path which they travelled through the forest. He didn't see the watching, fear-chilled figure, its clothing the same colour as that of the dead monk, approach the spear-pierced figure which dangled from the tree.

Brother Gerard had seen it all. His heart burned with shame at his former cowardice. He blushed with the disgrace of having stood idly by whilst his companion and fellow missionary, Brother Hugo, had vainly attempted the impossible. It would have been a great achievement to have converted the mighty Yngling ruler of Sweden to the faith of the White Christ, but something had told Gerard that the attempt was foredoomed to failure, and that another, greater destiny than Hugo's useless martyrdom awaited him. That, he consoled himself, was what had kept him hidden. That was what had made him let Hugo rush unaided into the face of certain death.

Even so, he had followed the riders as best he could, desperately seeking an opportunity to recover his con-demned companion, to atone for the cowardice he had not yet reasoned into a higher purpose. Only when the two columns had joined together, becoming one greater force, had his aching, run-drained lungs gained some respite from their panting labour, allowing him between gasps to draw close enough to witness his fellow Christian's death-agony.

From the cover of the tall grass he had wept fear-silenced tears of rage as the struggling monk was hauled clear of the ground and left suspended from a branch. Even from his concealment, peering between the feet of stamping, strain-ing horses, he could see that Hugo's limbs were twisted and torn beyond repair, that even if he was to achieve a rescue the monk would never walk or use his arms again. His painful travels behind Oli's column had seen to that.

And then, when the tall, gaunt warrior in black had reined in, to send the gleaming length of his spear flashing across the sombre dark of the trees, Gerard had known once and for all that there was nothing he could do to help Hugo any more, that Hugo had received the only help he would ever want. All that remained for Gerard to do, once he had seen Starkadder ride off into the forest to join his lord, was to make sure, in his office as a priest of the White Christ, that the dead man received a Christian burial.

He had plenty of time to think, whilst he clawed the sun-dried earth with his bare hands, whilst he rolled Brother Hugo, eyes staring and tongue protruding, into the shallow depression he had dug, of the puzzles which the last few anguished hours had set him. He would never really know why that weapon had ended Hugo's suffering. He would never be sure if it was an act of simple charity from a heathen with mercy in his heart, intended only to relieve the suffering of a dying man, or if there had been some deeper, pagan significance. Gerard was aware that sacrifices to Odin the Allfather, the chief deity of the pagan pantheon, were conducted by hanging and then impaling the victim with a spear. In all conscience, though, he couldn't tell if this had been an act of mercy or simply the pragmatic opportunism of a legendary viking which had perpetrated an unbidden sacrifice, which was itself a blasphemy against the one true god, but even more so when worked upon the body of one of his chosen followers.

The gaunt man, Gerard knew, he would recognise again. His age, his size, his carriage, proud yet somehow humbled by a power not entirely of this earth, all marked him out as one who would be easily remembered. The fact that he had been the first to show fealty to Oli when the columns came together helped to distinguish him further. It made him an important man. It made him a man to be remembered and reckoned with.

Only later, when the priest spoke with his fledgeling flock upon the lake-shores and hillsides between Uppsala and the Dalalven river, did Gerard learn the name of the tall killer who had ended Brother Hugo's life. Nor did he simply learn the name, for his converts were still close enough to their pagan roots to know and tell him of the legend that was Starkadder. The name itself aroused sufficient fear for them to sign themselves with the cross as they spoke it, to make that sign so like Mjollnir, the hammer of Thor, to defend themselves from whatever evil might dwell in the speaking of the name itself.

So that was Starkadder, Gerard thought, the very personification of all the myths about the old gods and their power. On the banks of the Dalalven, all those months later, it no longer mattered whether Hugo's death had been sacrifice or mercy-killing.

Yet the knowledge he was to gain then was merely to give Gerard a direction, a means towards the end of all his purposing. Even on the edge of the forest, as his dirty, earth-stained hands patted the soil down over Hugo's broken body, he had no need to tell himself of his purpose. Christianity had to be established as the one true religion of this pagan, northern land. Oli, great king though he was, would have to be overthrown or converted, and his young son indoctrinated with the love of Christ. It was Gerard's duty to raise a fervour in the breasts of his peasant followers which would consign the pagan myths and legends to the dusty, forgotten antiquity which was now their rightful place. It was his mission to overturn the pagan ascendancy of the mighty Yngling dynasty, the royal house said to be founded by the gods themselves.

More than anything else, he thought, as he left Brother Hugo in the uncaring sanctuary of that foreign earth, he needed some kind of sign, something which would convince even the most unyielding and obdurate pagan of the White Christ's power over the lives of men. Later, as he watched the waters of the Dalalven rushing down towards the Baltic Sea, Brother Gerard realised what that sign would have to be. Only then, staring at the crystal waters, waiting for the moment when Oli's feeble hold on sanity was broken for ever and the king was precipitated into entire and immitigable madness, a madness which would itself threaten the stability of the ancient ruling dynasty, did the brown-haired priest realise just what it was he had to do.

It wasn't by chance, he knew, that he had come north to

spread the work of the White Christ into the bleakness of the viking north. Nor was it simple accident which had spared him and taken his brother missionary into the ragged folds of a painful death, perhaps even damning his soul in the very moment of its release from his tormented body. No, Brother Gerard had been spared because there was work for him to do, work which had to be done to ensure the White Christ's triumph over the mythical gods and creatures of the northern realms.

He would never see those pagan gods to test their reality. He would never venture through the massive mountain pillars which divided the realms of men from Trollheim, the abode of the dwarfs. He would never meet them, and he would consequently never believe in them. He would never know the reality or otherwise of the creatures he was to work so hard to dispossess.

In that place, at that moment, Brother Gerard unconsciously dedicated his life to one simple aim. As he stood before Brother Hugo's unmarked grave and stared towards the forest, into which King Oli's column had long since vanished, there came the stirrings which would later grow into an ambition, the stirrings which led him in his service of an alien god to join the ranks of those who, like Angantyr's daughter Hervara, were governed by a single irrevocable desire.

If he never did anything else in the service of his god, he knew he had to do this one thing. One way or another Brother Gerard, the Christian monk from the foreign shores of England, must lead the ancient, accursed warrior Starkadder to his death.

And in that, the Norns had already decreed, he had his part to play.

In the kingdom of the dwarfs

CHAPTER ONE

Gifts and prophecies

THE BOY sat upon the shore, the sun behind him, studying the flickering, distant motion of the Baltic waves in the
early morning. He was young and strong, firm-limbed and
bright-eyed, with something of his mother's fair beauty in
his face to balance the dark complexion he had inherited
from his father, Lambi Nef, not to mention the older man's
protuberant nose.

In his ears was the rushing of the waves, and the vigour of
their breaking upon the rocks. There was also the crying of
the gulls, wheeling overhead, scanning the waters for fish to
harvest, screaming to one another as they circled in the
wind. Beneath his feet the earth was still damp with dew,
and his heart sang with the birds of the dawn in a celebration
of youth in springtime.

He was just fifteen and his name was Hather. His lineage
was long and distinguished, for his father, a retainer of Oli
the Great, was from a family that traced its descent from an
early branch of the Ynglings, and his mother was Hervara,
the daughter of the famous berserk chieftain Angantyr.
Today was his birthday, and he was glad to be alive, happy
to watch the signs of new life blossoming and growing
about him after the harshness of winter.

For all of Hather's young life Oli had held the throne in
comparative peace. True, there was always the odd party of
viking raiders to be repulsed, the occasional invasions by

53

foreign mercenaries who rashly believed that they could take his throne, but they always suffered defeat, and their bodies were left on the sand to be scavenged by the wolves or ravens or the ever-wheeling gulls.

Hather held a simple view of life and death. You lived, as his father did, to serve your overlord, the king. Whatever Oli did or said was for the sake of his kingdom, to ensure peace and order in the lands controlled by the Ynglings. At times he might appear to be wrong, sometimes perhaps dreadfully wrong, but his deeds were the deeds of a great king, and it was not for lesser mortals to question the will of one descended from the gods.

Here on his father's lands the workings of the royal court in Uppsala seemed infinitely remote. His father, when he returned for feasts and to visit his family and retainers, was a distant, courteous, correct man, yet one who could still show warmth and love to those dependent upon him. Lambi Nef was a great man in his own right, and his son's ideal of what a chieftain should be. On the occasions when he had travelled with him, occasionally sharing the blood-reddened glory of defending King Oli's realm, he had found his father calm, deadly and an efficient leader in the face of the invaders.

Yes, he admired his father. He was a man to look up to and be proud of. But his mother was something more, someone who bestowed upon him a greater, more pervasive love. Her ears heard his movements through the wooden walls of their hall. Her eyes followed him with their silent glittering when he walked, or ran, or wrestled. They spoke more than her mouth ever could about her love for him, though sometimes, increasingly as his approaching manhood stirred and blossomed, they said things that he couldn't understand, things as yet untasted and secret.

He stood up and stretched his youthful frame, shaking his head in the early breeze, disturbing the plaited locks of his long, fine hair. His build was solid but not heavy, and his eyes shone, even with the sun behind him, ice-blue like his grandfather's.

Rock-still on the shingle, Hather's mother stood and gazed upon her son. He turned, smiling at her approach.

Hervara was yet only thirty. The loveliness glimpsed by a lone fisherman almost sixteen years before had not diminished. Neither had the ineradicable shadow of hatred which so poignantly marred it.

Hervara's face was bright as she studied the strong young man that Lambi Nef had sired for her, her gaze penetrating beneath his belted tunic and wadmal trousers to the firm muscles beneath. It had all been worth it, she thought, worth the years of toiling to push a petty retainer into favour with King Oli, of fighting and fornicating for a success which could only reflect onto Hather. Her son was growing into a man she could be proud of, an avenger.

'This is your birthday,' she said, her voice tinged with the pride which shone from her eyes. 'I have a gift for you.'

He had seen the bundle in her hands. It was long and thin, wrapped in that fine shimmering stuff called silk which the more adventurous traders brought back from the south. Some claimed that it was made by worms, but that was just a silly story. Hather had watched worms. All they did was eat earth and shit it out again.

His father had taken him along on the last two raids Oli's men had conducted against invaders. On the second he had snatched up a fallen sword and hamstrung one of the mercenaries. The deed had won him praise and renown from King Oli's victorious forces. He had shown himself a man, even if some childishness still remained. 'He has earned a sword of his own,' Lambi Nef grunted at the victory celebrations. 'We must find my son a sword.' Now, as his eyes studied the bundle of shimmering fabric, Hather knew already what it was.

He looked up into the beauty of his mother's eyes, seeing in them a love which had not diminished with his vanishing childhood.

His breath caught in his throat and he gulped to clear it. 'A sword, Mother?' he asked. 'My own sword?'

She smiled at him, her face showing pride and delight at his eager guess. The little boy was fading with every day that passed, left behind by the young warrior who was Hervara's future. He was strong and, by his own proof in

55

battle, brave. He was also, in his mother's eyes and those of the daughters of Oli's court, beautiful.

'This is something more than just a sword,' she replied, the emotion in her voice keener than the screaming of the gulls. 'This is your grandfather's sword. This is Tyrfing.'

She extended her arms, holding out the silken bundle for him to grasp. He stepped forward and took it from her, then squatted on his haunches and began to pick at the thongs which held the precious wrapping in place.

'Handle it with caution,' Hervara urged. 'My father Angantyr once told me that the blade bears a deadly venom. The finest cut will be fatal, so take care, my son.'

He pulled the silk away and studied the fateful gift. The wrapping caught the breeze and fluttered some feet along the beach, to lie still, discarded. It had journeyed a thousand miles to blow forgotten on a foreign shore, insignificant now that the dwarf-forged sword had been lifted from the folds.

'Tyrfing?' Hather demanded, studying the hilt, wrapped with gold wire and worked with metal depicting the deeds of mythic heroes.

Carefully he drew the blade from its bronze-banded leather scabbard and held it high, saluting the dawn sun as his mother had saluted the night on the Isle of Samsey all those years before. The blade, greased with refined bear's fat, glistened in the early light, catching the red of the sun, as though it dripped blood, the blood of the dead King Svafrlami, the blood of Angantyr himself.

'Tyrfing,' he breathed, the beauty of the sword etching itself into his young heart. Here was a blade from the shadowed depths of legend. Here was a beauty, unlike but equal in intensity, to rival his mother Hervara's. Here, raised in his hand, greeting the dawn of his fifteenth birthday, was a weapon that any might be proud of.

He slid the blade back into its scabbard and slipped it through his belt. For a few moments he looked intently at his mother. Then he embraced her, pressing her still-firm breasts against his chest, feeling in their kiss something more than the love of son and mother, feeling a fire that presaged a life he had yet to live.

And Hervara herself, now feeling little more than contempt for the man she had married, fought against answering to that fire, crying inwardly for the youth she had never known, the youth that her hatred had burned away.

They walked back from the sea together, hand in hand, towards the stockaded hall which Lambi Nef had raised for them, in the province his wife's guile had won from Oli the Great. Hather's father had no illusions about his own worth. He was a fair warrior; he had to be to have reached the age of forty-three in Oli's service. But he was basically a simple man, uncomplicated by immoderate lusts, shunning the elaborate and deceptive plans for advancement that were hatched, sometimes stillborn, by the other retainers. He suspected that his wife Hervara had been, in the early years of their marriage, Oli's mistress. It was the only reasonable explanation for the sudden preference and advancement that the king had shown him. But he did not know, and what he did not know he was content, in his dark stolid way, to ignore. Perhaps Lambi's two most notable characteristics were an unquestioning loyalty to a king who wasn't interested in him, except in times of need, and a complete absence of curiosity.

Lambi Nef was away from his estate, at the royal hall in Uppsala beyond the mountains. He had promised to try and return for his son's birthday, as there was no fighting and little statecraft for him there, but Oli's government could often be tedious, and a messenger had reached their lands the day before, saying that he expected to be detained for at least another week.

There were things about Oli the Great's rule that Lambi Nef, and some of the king's other principal retainers, were growing to dislike. Oli had lived a long life and was now in his early seventies. Nobody could call him senile, but his growing awareness that he would not, as his captain Starkadder seemed to do, live for ever, was gnawing at his mind. As a result his rule was becoming increasingly trying and tyrannical for his subjects. Peace at home was preserved, but only by a repressive barbarity which some believed even Odin must abhor. The slightest word against Oli might be repeated to the ageing king, and earn the critic

the bloody and painful death of the blood eagle, or imprisonment in a dank, freezing dungeon dug out of the earth
beneath the timber palace, for whatever remained of a
shortened and miserable life. Some, in whispers, said that
Oli the Great was dead-in-life, that the darkness of the grave
had already claimed his spirit.

Hervara and Hather returned to Lambi's hall and were
served a breakfast of goat-cheese, bread, butter, honey and
milk by their servants. Hervara ate little, merely sitting at
the trestle opposite her son, studying the young man with
an interest intensified by his sudden fire of eagerness on the
beach. He would be a fine man. He was almost ready. And
with Tyrfing in his hands he could do what Hervara herself
was too weak to do, what no woman in the north, not even
the cruel beauty Rusila, for many years the most feared and
lovely pirate in the entire north, could do. For this one time
the implacable Norns had written in her favour. Her son
would win his fame. He would become the man who killed
Starkadder.

Hather ate with the hunger of youth, calling to the servants
to bring more whilst his mother simply picked at her food.
He felt no terror of the future, no fear of failure or defeat.
Any that might once have grown in the corners of his mind,
sprung from the tales of defeated vikings, had been scythed
down by the blow that hamstrung an older opponent in his
youthful triumph. He was invincible. Like Starkadder, the
man he was to kill, he could not die. He would live longer
than King Oli, and win more glory and more wealth. And
his mother would be Queen beside him.

When he had at last eaten his fill, and the servants had
taken away his own board and his mother's, he pushed back
the bench and stood up from the table, Tyrfing in its
scabbard still stuck through his belt.

'Where are you going?' Hervara asked. 'It's still early,
Hather. I thought we might go riding. Would you like
that?'

He smiled down at her and nodded, warming her heart.
They were, and had always been, close. They spent as
much time as possible in each other's company, she telling
him tales of the heroes of years gone by, of the deeds of

58

her father Angantyr, of the early kings of the Yngling dynasty, he listening, absorbing, learning the tricks of those heroes and then going off by himself, practising the arts of war with a small javelin and a wooden sword. That was how he had won his early fame, from the tales his mother told.

But she had never spoken to him of Angantyr's death. He did not yet know of that fatal battle on the plain at Roliung where his berserk grandfather had fallen – not even Hervara knew the full story of that death, or the part that the accursed weapon Tyrfing, which now nestled against Hather's body, had played in his dying – but he would know quite soon.

Yes, they were close, mother and son, but there was one who equalled and, in Hervara's eyes, rivalled her for Hather's affection. Perhaps one day she would have the old crow killed. But not yet. There was no need at present for Hather to feel the unhappiness that her death would cause him. When he was older the time would come, whilst he was away fighting.

'Let us go riding in a little while,' he smiled. 'There's no better way I can think of to pass the day, Mother. But first let me show my present to Tisti.'

Hather was never to know how his words wounded her, how the pang they caused hit deep into Hervara's being, tainting her pleasure in this long-awaited day. Old Tisti had come to Lambi Nef's household as a necessary evil and had stolen half of her son.

In the early days of her marriage, while Hervara stroked King Oli's flesh into passion and kindled a blaze which would strengthen their position in the kingdom, someone had been needed to look after the baby Hather. Tisti had suddenly been there, brown and wrinkled with an age that was far from being fragile, white-haired and dark-eyed. The indefinable mystery of Lappish blood, thinned but still flowing in defiance of both nature and the passing years, ran in her antique veins. Nobody knew where she had come from, or what her name really was. Nor did she enlighten them in any way, save to strip off her coat of furs to reveal wrinkled breasts and stretch-marked buttocks, the irrefutable insignia of her childbearing and her qualification for surrogate motherhood.

Her tongue was sharp and active, so they called her Tisti for want of something better. The name meant 'twitterer', and it suited her.

Yet, despite the care and attention she lavished upon Hervara's baby son, Hervara never liked her. The secrecy, the mystery of her past, conspired to make of the old woman, voluble and yet so taciturn, a baffling puzzle. Had she been simply this then the wife of Lambi Nef might have learned to accept her foibles as the whims of one so old as to be approaching senility. But there was something more, something about old Tisti which reminded her, every time she saw Hather's nurse, of the ancient, shadow-veiled creature who had urged her to take Tyrfing from her father's grave. It could not have been her features, for Hervara never saw the old crone's face. Nor could it have been her bearing for Tisti was, despite her years, less bent, less stooped than that other, darker creature.

Even so, the impression remained, chewing and gnawing at Hervara's memory, striking at those buried fears which had remained with her ever since that day when she had wrested Tyrfing from Angantyr's grave.

Old Tisti had nursed the boy through those early years, giving the infant the warmth of her own body whilst Hervara bestowed her hate-marred youth upon the king. As soon as her efforts had assured their future, and before her husband really had a chance to do more than guess at the cause of their new-found prosperity and favour, she tried to take Hather back from the old Lappish witch. It wasn't to be so easy, however. Hervara's long absences in Uppsala, the traditional seat of the Yngling kings, had served to estrange her child. Eventually, by means of as much care and solicitude as she had lavished upon the satyr-like Oli, Hervara regained Hather's love.

Yet the effort she was forced to expend made her feel cheated. Tisti had set out to steal her son and, though she had won at least a good part of him back, she was still fighting for his heart and the fulfilment of her desire for vengeance.

'If you must show her, do it now,' she told Hather. As she spoke her lip trembled slightly with the stretch of her smile.

Her son grinned back at her. She watched as he got up, stepped over the bench, and walked outside.

He was young and strong. He'd stand as good a chance as any against the ancient Norwegian mercenary. And he had Tyrfing. Tyrfing would kill Starkadder.

Outside the longhouse, in the sunlight, Hather looked briefly about the stockade, as if he found it suddenly unfamiliar, as if the sun blinded his eyes and hid the well-worn path to old Tisti's hut. Unlike the usual Swedish living quarters it was round, and its pointed roof was covered with hides save for the smoke-hole at the top. It stood apart from the quarters which housed the other servants, and away from the outhouses which held the estate's supplies, as if deliberately seeking to preserve the air of mystery surrounding its lone occupant.

The other servants did not dislike old Tisti so much as fear her. Lappish blood, to their superstitious peasant minds, meant sorcery, though that did not stop them sneaking off to her, begging her to consult the runes, when their worries overcame their fears. Tisti did not refuse them. She took the coins they offered and hid them away, perhaps for the old age which had passed her by long ago, and spread her stained white cloth upon the rush-strewn floor. Then she shook the incised slivers of blood-marked yew and muttered her prayers to Odin the all-knowing, god of runemasters, and read the precious sticks, taking her prophecies from the letters cut upon them.

And the prophecies increased their fear of her, and her reputation. If Tisti said it, they muttered in their confusion, it would come to pass. She might be old and feeble, but she had mastered the runes. Only a *volva*, a sooth-sayer, could do that.

Hather shielded his eyes from the low sun lancing across the stockade and studied the old woman's hut. Smoke curled lazily above it from the smoke-hole for a few feet, spiralling lazily in the shelter from the wooden ramparts. Then the breezes caught it and whisked its tendrils into nothing, out of the world of men and into the realms of the gods.

He walked across the courtyard and rapped with his knuckles on the rough planking of her door. For almost half a minute there was no sound from within. Then a voice, deep as a man's but weak with uncounted years, called to him. 'Come inside, little Hather. Come out of the sun.'

He pulled the door towards him, smiling at the way it creaked uncertainly against the frame, rocking in his hand on its worn hinges of plaited leather thonging. Darkness opened before him, blinding as the sunlight, but his eyes sharpened and he picked out the form of the ancient nurse squatting before her fire, her back to him. She did not turn round as he entered the hut.

'How did you know it was me?' he asked.

She laughed softly to herself and continued to stare into the fire. 'Sit beside me, little warrior,' she commanded.

He did as he was told, leaning towards her when she turned to kiss his forehead with her wrinkled, hair-fringed lips. 'I always know when it's you,' she smiled. 'I've watched you grow and listened to the music of your limbs. I know you better than I know myself. Besides, this is your day, my little one. I remember your day. If you need it,' she added, 'I even have a present for you.'

He had heard those words before. He knew what the present was by the worn leather bag that lay upon the old woman's lap, the bag which held the runewands.

'Tisti, I'm not little any more,' he said, reproachfully. 'I'm a man now. I have a man's weapon.'

If the words held any meaning for her the Lappish nurse gave no sign of it. Instead she continued to smile, her face a mask of love and pleasure.

'To me you will always be little,' she replied, her voice surprisingly firm. 'That was how I first saw you, Hather, as a tiny child, a tiny, tiny child in swaddling. The first moment I held you you pissed on me, through all those wrappings. That is why I love you, little Hather. You have never been afraid of me. There can be no room for fear in love. That is why I call you little. No matter how tall you grow, no matter how strong your limbs are or how many men you kill for Oli, you will always be that tiny, pissing bundle I first held.'

She looked at him and laughed softly. Then she continued: 'And yet you will also be the young man you are today, the only child I have watched grow into manhood, the young man I heard singing through the dawn, going down to the sea.

'That is what growing old means, Hather. To watch children grow into men and women, and make more children. To see the children you grew up with wither and die. The world is full of children, Hather. For every man there was once a boy. For every woman there was once a little girl. That is the meaning of time. You sat on the sand this morning and watched the waves beating upon the rocks. Have they not changed, my son? Are they still the rocks they were ten years ago? Or have they worn and changed their shape, beaten throughout the years by the ceaseless vigour of the waves?

'And your mother, Hather, has she not changed? Is she not older, as you are, as I am? That is the price of age, little viking. It shows you the working of time. It takes the strength from your limbs and the wits from your head, but it shows you one of the true mysteries of life. Even while we've been speaking I have aged, and so have you.'

She laughed again, chuckling to herself at the blankness in the blue of Hather's eyes. He heard her words only with his ears. Only with the passing of that mystery called time would he hear them with his heart.

'That's a fine thing in your belt,' Old Tisti grinned, showing the remains of her crumbling, discoloured teeth. 'Is that your present from your mother? Has Hervara given Tyrfing to you at last?'

Hather drew the blade and held it out above the smoking fire, turning the edges to catch the flickering of the flames. 'That's Tyrfing,' he said, proudly. 'Do you like it?'

'It's a fine weapon,' came the cautious reply. 'I like it as much as any woman can like something that takes men's lives. Has it made you a man, or were you one before, even as that tiny baby that I held?'

Hather looked at her crossly and sheathed the sword.

'You're talking in riddles,' he muttered sullenly. 'Tyrfing hasn't made me anything. It's a present. That's all.'

I hope you're right, Tisti thought.

The youth realised that he was scowling at her and forced a smile. 'I'm sorry,' he grunted, rather unwillingly. 'I didn't come here for us to be cross with one another.'

'Nor should we be, little Hather. And nor shall we be. This is a day for you to be happy on.'

Immediately the words left her lips Tisti regretted them. She knew what would happen now, and she also knew that it could take their happiness away.

'Will you read the runes for me?' Hather asked. 'You do it every year on this day,' he added. 'You bring me luck by it. Please, Tisti?'

It was her turn to force a smile. 'If I do this for you every year,' she began, 'and it's brought you luck so far, then I'd better do it for you now, so that your luck can continue.'

Yes, she thought. I must do it. If I have to, I can lie to him. Perhaps the truth will be better another day, when he is not so happy. Perhaps a lie will be better now . . .

No. Tell the truth. Tell him that you've cast them twice already, as you always do. Tell him what you've read in those ancient, Odin–given symbols. In the past you haven't needed to lie, so why lie now? Tell the truth. He's a man now. He's told you so. If the runes fall the same way again tell him what you read. You can't shield him for ever, Tisti. Better that he know now. Tell the truth.

Her fumbling fingers untied the leather thong which held the bag closed. She set it down beside her and wearily got to her feet. On the other side of the circular hut, beside her bedding, stood its only piece of furniture, a heavily carved chest of age–dark oak. Tisti crossed to this and opened it, taking the stained white cloth from its night-shrouded depths. Then she came back over to Hather and spread the cloth on the ground where she'd been sitting. Crouching beside it, opposite the youth, she lifted the leather bag above her head.

'Allfather, you gave us the runes,' she chanted, her old voice swelling and growing until it echoed from every rafter in the hut. 'You gave us the runes so that we who know

might see, even as you have seen. You won the runes in nine
nights of torment, stuck with your own spear, Gungnir,
upon the sacred world-tree, the ash Yggdrasil. You saw the
runes in the depths beneath you and snatched them up, as
the skalds have told. You know their meanings and their
lore. Let me read them now. Lift for me the veil of the
future. Let me see the will of the Norns, as I speak your
words . . .

'Wounded I hung on the windy tree
For nine long nights;
Wounded by a spear, offered to Odin,
Myself to myself.
None knows from what depths spring the roots
Of that ancient tree.

None brought me bread or drinking horn.
Groundwards I gazed and cried aloud,
Snatched up the runes, then fell at last.'

As she spoke the last four words Tisti slowly turned the bag
in her hands, letting the age-darkened slivers of yew tumble
down onto the spread white cloth. Still staring upwards,
her eyes fixed on the sky glimpsed through the smoke-hole,
she tossed the bag aside and fumbled on the cloth with her
fingertips. Three times they touched a runewand, and each
time she took the wand, without looking at it, and set it to
one side.
'Put the others back in the bag,' she ordered Hather. He
hurried to obey her.
'Is the cloth clear?' Tisti demanded.
'It is,' he replied.
Her eyes still locked onto the smoke-hole, Tisti carefully
picked up the three pieces of yew she had kept apart and set
them down upon the cloth in the order that she had picked
them up.
'Allfather, help me to read aright.'
Only then did she bend her neck downwards again and
look at the runes she had chosen. Even the most rapid of
glances was sufficient to tell her that there was no element

of chance in the casting, that the runewands had fallen the same way for the third time running.

Tell him the truth, her conscience prompted. Don't lie to him. That would be stupid, and it could later bring him to harm.

Tell him what you see.

She picked up the first of the three slivers, caressing its worn surface with her wrinkled fingers. 'This is the rune *Othil*,' she began. 'It signifies an inheritance, Hather. In your case it probably means the sword Tyrfing which your mother has been so quick to give you. On its own it means nothing, but together with the other two runes it will reveal whatever future that blade will carve for you.

'This is the second rune. Its name is *Thurisaz* and it has many meanings. And it is a dark rune to read,' she added. 'It's first meaning is a giant or demon. In relation to the first rune it indicates that your inheritance, Tyrfing, comes to you with some evil attached to it. If you are to profit by that inheritance you must first find a way to rid it of its curse . . .'

'A curse?' Hather interrupted. 'Tyrfing is accursed?'

'Let me finish,' the old woman snapped.

Hather bit his tongue and watched as she set the second rune down beside the first, then gently, almost lovingly, took the third. Her eyes strayed from the symbol cut into its surface, flitting across to where Hather sat waiting for her to continue, the fingers of his left hand nervously plucking at the gold wire wrapped about Tyrfing's hilt.

His eyes stared back at her, asking the question his lips dared not yet speak. His heart was beginning to pound uncomfortably and a tight, sick feeling was forming in the pit of his stomach.

Is there a way, Tisti? Does the third rune tell me how to take Tyrfing's curse away? Does it?

She knew what he was feeling, what he was asking. She smiled at him across the silence of the little hut, hoping that the smile carried some comfort with it. The silence grew about her smile, thick with Hather's impatience and the old Lapp's doubts.

Tell the truth, she commanded herself again. Lies can only harm him more. He must know what to expect, or all my years of loving him, caring for him, will be as nothing.

Besides, it's not so bad. It could have been a darker rune than this.

She took a deep breath, a breath which shook her withered frame, filling and expanding it until there was no room left for the doubts and the unquiet silence. Then she said: 'The third rune is called *Raido*, little Hather. It is Thor's rune and it means that you must do Thor's work. It signifies a cart, or a journey. In your case it means that there is a way to lift the curse from Tyrfing, but that in order to find it you must start upon a journey.'

He looked at her with blank confusion written across his young face. 'But . . . where am I to go?' he demanded. 'Do the runes tell you that?'

Tisti shook her head, then turned her seamed features away. She didn't want her baby to see her surreptitiously wipe the forming tears from her eyes. When she looked back she replied: 'No, Hather. The runes don't tell me that. But perhaps the curse will tell you.'

The silence crept back and settled around them.

She studied Hather's face, but his eyes would no longer meet hers. The world about them, for those few moments, was a dead thing, killed by the power of the runes. Only the faint crackle of the fire, the chattering of a sparrow perched upon the nearby wall of the stockade, and the faint sound of their breathing bespoke any kind of life.

And then there came the raucous, unmistakable cry of a raven wheeling overhead.

Old Tisti smiled grimly to herself. Now she understood. Now she could face the terrible truth that she had sought to hide from herself throughout the years of Hather's child-hood. Today he would become a man, for today he had become a pawn in that great and fateful game which the

67

gods played with the lives of men. In the crying of Odin's raven, in the reading of Thor's rune, in the giving of the sword Tyrfing, fate had pushed Hather onto the gods' *tafl*-board. Now he was become both man and plaything.

Whatever Tisti knew of the playing of that game she had always harboured close within herself. She had never spoken to any of what she knew, of that secret knowledge which could be found only in the crisp white wastes of Lappland, drawn into the shamans from unwilling deities by strange, bloody ceremonies, the eating of strange fungi and the ritual drinking of the urine of those who had eaten that fungus. In those secrets and their keeping lay the key to whatever power she possessed, and she could not reveal them, not even to help or save the young man who was almost her own son.

But what she could do for Hather she would. She could make him draw out from himself and from those around him more of the story behind his past, and his future. She could fuel his curiosity until it became a fire which would burn its way fearlessly into the future the Norns had written for him.

'What has your mother told you of the sword?' she asked at length.

'It was my grandfather Angantyr's weapon,' he answered slowly. 'The edges are poisoned and the merest scratch will kill.'

Tisti's eyes glittered darkly. 'And the rest? Has she told you the rest?'

The youth looked puzzled. 'What else is there?' he asked.

For a moment she was ready to answer his question directly, but that would be breaking the rules she had made for herself in guiding Hather. The answers were not hers to give. Not yet.

So she said only, 'So famous a sword, your sword, and you do not know its story?'

'I know that Angantyr took it from a dead king.'

'She must tell you the rest, little warrior.'

He looked at her, the deep blue of his eyes suddenly accusing. 'Do you know it, old nurse?'

She nodded and stood up. Now that he had grown so far

68

towards manhood it was the only way that she could look down upon him. 'Yes, my son, I know it. But it is not for me to tell you. Only your mother, the Lady Hervara, can do that. Speak to her first. Let her tell you the full story of Tyrfing and its curse. Then come back to me, and I'll tell you how you can defeat it, and where your journeying will take you.'

His eyes travelled up her ancient frailness. His mother filled him with a fire, a pride in his destiny. She exhorted him to be a man, so that he might take the revenge she herself could never wreak. But Tisti, this old and wrinkled woman from the wildness of the Finnmark wastes, for all her rambling mystery and mastery of runes, saw back in time, beyond the strength of youth back into childhood. And she also saw forward into age, into a time to come, beyond her span of years.

'And Starkadder,' Tisti added. 'Ask her to tell you about Starkadder.'

Starkadder.

He knew the name, of course. Everyone knew the name. The first time Lambi Nef had taken him across the mountains to Uppsala, Hather had seen a tall, gaunt figure in King Oli's hall, dressed completely in black, except for the shimmer of polished metal and a torque of silver. Even the rings of his mail were blackened, like the leather of his boots and the gauntlets which the day never saw him remove. Wisps of silver hair strayed out from beneath the hood of his heavy black travelling cloak, pulled up as it was over his uncrested helmet of black iron, and deep-sunk eyes smouldered grey like winter ice. His face was bronzed by too many suns, yet pale like the sickness that comes with poison. Hather had never seen a face like it, and secretly hoped that he never would again. The old fighter stood almost a head taller than any other man there, and was shunned by most of them.

Starkadder.

Hather's father had started to tell him something of the strange viking's legend, of how he had been blessed by Odin and cursed by Thor, becoming both a legend and a monster in the north. Once Lambi Nef had hinted at how

Starkadder had killed twelve berserks single-handed, but had fallen strangely silent before the tale was done, almost as if he had remembered something about the story that he did not want to repeat.

'I'll ask her,' he heard himself say to Tisti. 'I'll ask her about Starkadder.'

As he stepped from Tisti's circular hut, built to the same shape as the little temple with its images of Odin, Thor and Frey, which his father and their steward Thorkel Tongue tended as priests for the estate, he saw Hervara waiting for him beside the entrance to their longhouse. A servant held the reins of two of the sturdy little ponies they used for ordinary riding.

Hather returned his mother's distant smile with one of his own and jogged across the courtyard to where she waited. Tyrfing's hilt pushed against his stomach with its unfamiliar bulk, reminding him of the talk that he had just had with Tisti, and of the one he had yet to have with his mother.

He took the reins of one of the ponies from the servant and held them whilst his mother mounted. Hervara had changed out of her dress of pale green linen into a tunic and wadmal trousers, like his own except that they were reinforced with leather inside the thighs.

He mounted beside her, feeling again the new thrill of burgeoning manhood as he studied her lovely features. Even in such shapeless clothing the Lady Hervara was a woman to desire, lovely as an ice palace but far more dangerous.

'Where shall we go?' she asked, the smile persisting. It was not so much a question as an invocation in a ritual of pleasure. They had ridden together throughout the days of Hather's childhood, and he knew the answers by heart. Along the beach. To the standing stones. To the bridge, to the mouth of the river, to the foot of the mountains. To the place where the snows are last to melt.

'Let's go to the foot of the mountains,' he replied.

Her reply was to set her heels to the pony's flanks and ride towards the gate. He followed, feeling the breeze tug at his plaited hair, feeling it press the folds of wadmal to his skin. The day was still young, and there would be joy ahead of them.

The sentries watched them ride off along the stone-paved path between the fields, and swung the gates shut again. Inside the stockade life would continue without them. They might not be there, but the cleaning, washing, cooking and repairing did not know that, and the servants knew their mistress well enough not to want to displease her. There was a dark streak buried in the heart of the Lady Hervara, and it was better for all of them to leave it there.

They galloped past the working peasants and Hather waved to Thorkel Tongue, who sat his horse on a ridge above the beach. For the present there was a young day to enjoy, and the foot of the mountains to be reached. Later there would be time for the questions he had to ask. Later, when they had dined and the long fire blazed in the darkened hall, he would ask his mother about Tyrfing. Later, after they had drunk mead from the gold-mounted horns, she would tell him why the sword carried a curse and an odour of the grave.

She would tell him all she knew. She would even tell him about Starkadder, and unknowingly send her son on the journey foretold by Tisti's runes. And only then, when he had made that unhallowed quest, would Hather be able to travel the weird which the Norns had written for him. Only then would he know his place in the gods' great game.

CHAPTER TWO

Towards the gates of Trollheim

THEY SAT in the firelight late into the evening. Son and mother, together with Thorkel Tongue, had celebrated Hather's birthday well. Now, as the ageing steward rose from the trestle and staggered away through the flickering shadows of the hall, Hervara looked at her son, puzzled by his sudden silence. Moments before they had been merry. Now with Thorkel's departure, Hather felt memory flood back like the waves of an incoming tide.

'Have you enjoyed your day?' Hervara asked. Her voice was soft and, somehow, no longer maternal. Some of the braiding in her hair had come loose, and fine wisps shimmered like beaten gold in the uncertain light from the long fire. Her dress was tight, pulling her breasts into a strong, moulded shape that told more of her missing youth than of motherhood. Hather felt the same disturbing stirring that had pursued him on the beach in the dawning, and after his visit to old Tisti, and he knew that Hervara felt that stirring too.

Hather stared into the fire. The flames and embers changed their shape before his unseeing gaze, becoming dark eyes set in a wrinkled face. Wisps of smoke formed the age-white hair, and its gentle crackling was the voice of the witch-nurse.

72

'She must tell you the rest, little warrior.'

He blinked and looked away. Then, unwillingly, he stared back at the long fire. Old Tisti's face was still there.

'So famous a sword,' crackled the embers, 'and you do not know its story?'

Again he looked away, but the face did not vanish. Instead it was stamped in fire upon his mother's, breaking with its own spell the unholy sorcery of her beauty, stripping away her loveliness to reveal the festering hatred beneath.

'Well?' Hervara asked again, her voice tainted with the seductive languor which had won their wealth from King Oli. 'Is my son content?'

It was unnatural that such a voice should issue from his nurse's lips. Hather began to feel unease. Perhaps another horn of wine would work to banish it . . .

Suddenly Hervara sensed his disquiet and sat up in her seat. She had no way of knowing what troubled the young man. All she knew was that something invisible had come between them, threatening the effect of the most powerful weapon she had. The feelings were there. She knew that. She had worked subtly throughout the day to nurture them, to bring them to an incestuous fruition. But now something had gone wrong.

'What is it?' she demanded sharply. 'What's the matter?'

Tisti's face began to waver and dissolve, its work finished. Again Hather saw the features of his mother, the Lady Hervara, but their beauty was marred by her frustration, and the fires which blazed within her eyes were more powerful for vengeance than for love.

'Tell . . . me . . . about . . . the sword.'

Hervara sat back. The voice was her son's, yet something had forced him to speak those words.

'I've told you already,' she smiled. The smile was forced. 'It was my father's. It belonged to the great berserk chieftain Angantyr. What more is there to tell?'

'The curse,' Hather muttered. 'Tell me about the curse.'

And then it was Hervara's turn to hear the voices in the fire. All the years of watching her son grow into manhood, the years of nursing her hatred to keep it alive and fresh, fell away from her. Her heart fluttered at the words, then began to pound in wild abandon, threatening to rob her of breath, to burst from her chest and fill her mouth with pulsing terror, to flood her very spirit with the acid taint of fear. Once more she was a child, younger than the son who sat by her, a child who stood among the blue and smokeless lights of the corpse-fires on the Isle of Samsey, in the dark time of the moon. Once more the thrilling, hollow boom of the voice from the grave-mound rang in her ear, echoing across time the warning uttered by her father newly dead.

'Let Tyrfing lie here, my daughter. Let its curse end here, in the depths of the earth, with me . . .'

'I need it for my son.'

Hather was chilled with fear. His mother was talking to the shadows, her features twisted with a nameless terror.

'Mother?'

Sweat beaded her forehead, matting the wisps of loose hair, dulling their colour, running down into her wide-staring eyes. She'd not heard Hather's question, for she wasn't there in the hall with him any more. She was still on Samsey Isle.

Hather repeated his demand, this time with a greater urgency in his voice. 'What is it, Mother? Tell me.'

Her breasts heaved within the tightness of her dress, swelling as she gulped in the tainted air which swirled amongst the corpse-fires. She leapt up, the lacings of her robe torn loose and the girl, Hervara, stood bare-breasted in the flickering light. She reached out for something that wasn't there, her face pleading, imploring the shade of her father to tell her what she had refused to hear before.

'The curse,' she whispered.

Hather stood up and walked across to her, grasped her face firmly in his hands and forced her to look at him. But her eyes, for all they stared, saw nothing. Then she fell limply forward against his chest, pressing those staring eyes into his tunic, seeking to blind-fold them with the cloth, knowing that even if she clawed them from her skull, the vision would haunt her still. She needed darkness in her mind, darkness to quench the corpse-fires of Samsey. Finally, as the threads of the wadmal touched her still-wide eyes, she blinked and began to feel the cleansing power of tears.

Hather stroked his mother's hair, comforting her as if she were a frightened child, telling her that it was all right, that it didn't matter, that whatever she'd seen in the firelight was just a waking dream.

He did not try to guess at the horrors she had seen, the dread she had relived. He knew only that her madness had something to do with Tyrfing's curse, and that the mystery was about to be unfolded. He held his mother in his arms until her sobs died down and she lifted her pain-wild eyes to his. The breasts which had suckled him as a babe were hard against his tunic. He bit his lip until the blood came, but his own hardness would not die.

Thrusting his mother from him, Hather sat down again and drained a horn of mead which Thorkel Tongue had left upon its stand. The half-prophecies of Tisti's runes, the half-promises of Hervara's beauty, everything had to be grasped in this moment, and known.

The fire crackled and muttered against the cloaking silence, and Hather waited.

'What about the curse?' he asked at length, his voice sullen, his features set in a heavy scowl.

The corpse-fires were fading from Hervara's eyes and her breath was quieter now.

'I . . . don't know,' she whispered to the flames.

'You *must* tell me,' Hather repeated.

'I don't know!' she yelled, wild-eyed, her hair flying wildly and loosely about her naked shoulders. 'I don't know about the curse! Angantyr holds that secret in the grave!'

'Then tell me how you got Tyrfing from your father.'

This was what Hervara had dreaded. For a moment the cold blue flickered again in her eyes. Then she said: 'Angantyr took the sword in battle.'

'That's not the answer I want, Mother,' Hather said tensely. 'Who did he take the sword from?'

'It belonged to a king called Svafrlami. My father disarmed him in combat and killed him with his own sword.'

'The sword will kill its owner? Is that the curse?'

'No!' Hervara shouted. 'Tyrfing did not kill my father!'

'Then how did he die? You must tell me. I know he met

an honourable death in combat, but that's all you've ever told me.'

Hervara rose uncertainly to her feet once more, her hair wild and tangled, her face streaked with tears, her eyes ablaze with fury. Many a viking on a raid had forced women who looked as she did, lovely and tormented, but if Hather had taken one step towards her at that moment she would have torn out his eyes.

'Starkadder killed him!' she spat.

The figure of the old warrior, black-helmed, forbidding, gaunt as a lightning-blasted tree, black as his deeds, rose before Hather's eyes. Everything, he knew suddenly, even the unfinished story told by Lambi Nef, was about to fall as surely as Tisti's runewands into a pattern for him to read.

'Starkadder,' Hather repeated.

Hervara stretched her arms out to him, the fingers clawed to grasp him to her. 'Hold me?' she whispered, begging, suddenly a little girl again.

'So how did you get the sword?'

'Does it matter? You have Tyrfing now. It's yours.'

'It's accursed!'

She sighed and dropped her arms. 'It was buried with Angantyr on the Isle of Samsey, she muttered. 'I took it in the glimpses of the moon.'

'You stole it from your father's grave?' Hather demanded, chilled suddenly. 'Is that it? Did he curse it before he yielded it to you?'

'He gave it to me,' she replied, her fingers twitching. 'I called out to his spirit in the dark of the moon and he answered me. He answered me and gave me Tyrfing for you. It was not he who cursed the sword. My father would not do such a thing. He told me of the curse, but he didn't tell me what it was.'

She looked up, her fingers stretched out to him, stroking lightly, strengthening the firmness beneath the cloth. 'Believe me, my son,' she whispered. 'That is the truth of it.'

He felt her touch and was unable to think of anything else. His eyes began to glaze as his breathing grew deeper. He felt he must surrender to that incestuous caress, to the

76

control by which Hervara had shaped his life until this moment.

'I love . . . you,' he whispered in return, arching himself on the seat to bring her closer.

Her hands lifted and went about his neck. 'Then hold me,' she cried. 'Hold me, Hather, comfort me.'

'I love you,' he repeated, his voice stronger, his hands reaching up to grasp her wrists. 'And yet you give me an accursed sword,' he added, his voice now almost a snarl, his grip breaking her embrace. 'Why, Mother?' he demanded, stressing the last word, growling it to make it clear that he understood what she was trying to do. 'Do you want me dead?'

'No!' she howled, trying to regain her hold, 'I want you to live! I want you as you are now, young, strong, alive. That's how I want you, to love me, to comfort me, to do what my father couldn't do. You must do what I don't have the strength for.'

'And what is that?' he demanded. The hardness had died and he was clear-headed now.

'I want you to avenge my father! I want you to kill Starkadder!'

He leapt up with a choked cry of rage, using the strength of his arms to hurl Hervara from him across the floor. She fell back heavily and stared up at him, supporting her body on her hands, her breasts hanging free of the torn dress. Her hair hung loose and golden in the firelight. She was panting and her wounded eyes pleaded for his understanding.

That is how a tortured she-wolf must look, Hather thought.

'Do it!' she snapped. 'Do it! Anything you want is yours, but kill him!'

He strode towards the door. Her hand reached vainly out to stop him, to hold him through the distance widening between them. 'Where are you going?' she called helplessly. 'I love you, Hather. Come to me. I love you!'

'I'll be back,' he called over his shoulder.

And then the Lady Hervara, wife of Lambi Nef, was alone with the firelight and her thoughts. She shivered, for her vengeance was not yet within her grasp, and seemed still

77

uncertain. The years of plotting and scheming, the years of waiting for her son to be a man, all seemed to hang in the balance. She had used her body shamelessly to win favour from Oli the Great. She had bribed and cajoled and seduced to raise Lambi Nef to his present position, one where she could truly be the Lady Hervara, one where her will could be respected and obeyed. And she had stood between the worlds to win the sword Tyrfing from her father's grave.

But now she was alone. Whilst Hather crossed the court-yard towards old Tisti's hut, Hervara climbed down off the trestle and pulled the torn edges of her dress together. Then she filled her mead horn from a jug. Once she had drained it she began to feel calmer and stronger, so she repeated this action several times.

'I've been waiting,' Tisti chuckled. 'I knew my little warrior would come to me.'

Hather pulled the door closed behind him and sat down in front of the old woman's fire. His face was long and troubled, and he suddenly felt very, very tired.

His Lappish nurse stared at him across the flames. 'Do you know the nature of the curse now, Hather?' she asked him.

He shook his head. If it would not have betrayed his new-won manhood he would have cried with self-pity and bewilderment.

'But you know something of Tyrfing's story? Of how Angantyr pulled it from the corpse of Svafrlami? Of how your mother took it from her father's funeral mound? Do you know that?'

'Yes,' he sighed. 'I know that.'

'And now you want to know the rest, so you come to see me, you come to see old Tisti. Is that it?'

He nodded mutely.

'Then listen to me, Hather. I'll tell you what I can of the truth of it all. There are some things I cannot tell you, but I'll tell you more than your mother, the proud Lady Hervara, did.'

Her smile was wicked as she spoke, but it was not evil.

'Here's a story, little Hather. It's not a fable, so hear it and remember. Once there was a king. He was a proud man, and his soul was filled with greed. He sought to surround himself with the best of everything. His retainers were as fine as peacocks. His halls were decked with rich and foreign hangings to hide their wooden walls. His tables groaned with fine food, served on gold and silver plates. He drank his mead from eurochs' horns, edged with precious metals. He had everything, almost.

'And yet he was not happy. His queen was firm-breasted and white-limbed, his daughter was lovely, but he was not happy. He had everything a man could wish for, yet he sought something more.

'His name was Svafrlami. He was a skilled fighter, and he kept himself fit for battle by duelling with his men. One day he was fighting with one of his captains, and he lost. That, for Svafrlami, was unheard of. He never lost. If ever it looked as if the king were tiring his men gave ground, but this day they had no chance to do so.

'The truth of his defeat was that his sword broke. It was a fine sword, little Hather, forged by a master swordsmith and inlaid with precious stones. It weighed no more than a feather in the king's hand and could cut an ox in half with just one stroke. But it shattered on his captain's blade.

'Naturally this misfortune made King Svafrlami most unhappy. His sword had been the best and finest sword his kingdom could produce, but it had not been good enough. So Svafrlami decided that his next sword should be better than the ones which mortal men created. Now he had heard the legends, the stories of gifts made for the gods. He had heard of the golden boar Gullinbusti, which the dwarfs made for Frey, and he knew that even redbeard Thor's hammer, Mjollnir, was of dwarfish craftsmanship. And so he sought for one who knew the lore of sorcery, one who might stand between the Midgard world of men and the Trollheim abode of the dwarfs, and open the very gates of Trollheim for him. Can you believe it? Did ever any man have Svafrlami's proud conceit?

'Well, he found the man he sought. A one-eyed man came to his court, wrapped in a traveller's cloak of light blue wool, and with a great hat pulled well down to cover his face. Old One-Eye knew the spells, but he warned King

Svafrlami that the dwarfs would not give up their treasure to a mortal. Even so, the king would not be warned, and insisted that the one-eyed man should chant the spells, and open the gates of Trollheim for him.

'And so it happened as he had desired. He passed through the gates and entered the court of Dvalin, the dwarf-king. And there he saw a sword he desired for his own. "What is its name?" he asked King Dvalin. "What is that fine sword called?" And Dvalin replied, "Its name is Tyrfing. That is what my sword is called."'

She paused and looked at Hather. The youth sat entranced by her story, still as stone.

'So Svafrlami asked him for the sword, and Dvalin laughed at him. "A mortal with a dwarf-sword?" he demanded. "Go and play with yourself, Svafrlami. You shall not have Tyrfing. No mortal shall have Tyrfing."

'But Svafrlami was not to be put off. He waited for his chance and, when it came, he stole King Dvalin's sword whilst the dwarf-king slept. Now, Dvalin noticed the theft as soon as he awoke, and he and his dwarfish army pursued the fleeing Svafrlami. But they were too late. One-Eye earned his money well, and held the gates of Trollheim open long enough for Svafrlami, with Dvalin and his dwarfs upon his heels, to escape back to Midgard. And even as the great Trollheim gates closed in the dwarfs' faces, Dvalin hurled his curse upon the thief.'

'And the curse?' Hather demanded. 'What's the curse, old Tisti? What is it?'

She peered at him from the depths of her dark eyes and smiled. 'That is the one thing that I cannot tell you,' she replied. 'Only the one-eyed man can tell you that. Only he and Svafrlami heard the curse, and Svafrlami is long dead, killed by Angantyr.'

Hather fought to keep his brain from whirling. To hear so much, and yet to hear so little. It was unbearable.

'Do you believe in the dwarfs, little Hather?' Old Tisti asked.

'I . . . suppose I do,' he stammered. He was confused that the question came after the story about Svafrlami and the dwarf-king instead of before it.

80

The old nurse nodded and returned her gaze to the fire. 'They all suppose they ought to,' she mocked. 'You are clever enough to know that's not what I asked you, little Hather. Do you believe what I've just told you about King Dvalin? Do you believe in the Norns? Urd, Skuld and Verdandi? Do they mean anything to you?'

He struggled to recognise the trap she had set for him and to free himself from its foils. 'They are as real as the gods,' he replied, allowing a degree of indignation to edge his words. 'It would be akin to denying Odin to dismiss the Norns and the dwarfs as superstitious gibberish. I may not, dare not, do so.'

She continued staring silently into the fire whilst she weighed his words. There was a stiffness in his words which suggested he was reciting something learned by rote, vaguely remembered, rather than stating a sincerely held belief. There was also, implicit in her question, something which suggested her own faith was adopted rather than inborn.

'That will make things easier,' she sighed. 'Belief is a valuable tool in the hands of those who know how to use it, Hather. Still,' she added, deepening her smile, letting it grow and strengthen until it had almost transformed her wrinkled-parchment features, 'in this case there is no choice other than to believe. Even I, an old crone from the snow-spattered forests of Finnmark, know that three realities are beyond all dispute. One of them is the gods. Another is the Norns. And the third is the dwarfs. We may believe or not in the giants as we choose. We see them so little, and they are so easy to explain when we do, that they play no part in our lives. The dwarfs we see equally rarely, yet their power is all the greater for their secrecy, for being hidden from us.

'They have their own reality, little Hather. Oh, I'm not saying that they're real, as you might understand the meaning of reality. There is a cloud, an uncertainty about things rarely seen or understood, which makes men doubt that they really exist. Such a cloud masks our understanding of the three orders of being I have mentioned. The gods are rarely perceived, as are the dwarfs and the Norns, but they may still be real for all that.

81

'Listen to me. Hear me, for the sake of your self and for the sake of your sons as yet unborn. Dismiss nothing. Keep an open mind. Hold your beliefs and doubts to yourself alone. Make no mistake, little Hather. You will meet dwarfs and, though you may not see them or know them in any other way, both gods and Norns will be close by you in the days which are to come. Such is your weird, little viking, such your destiny and your purpose. You many not remember my words in the days which lie ahead of you, but they will go with you none the less. With the holding of Tyrfing, with the ownership of that marvellous, cruel sword, comes both a duty and a fate which you may not avoid, even if you so desire. You are a piece in a game, little Hather, and that game is one which may only be played by the gods, the dwarfs, and the Norns.'

'Then . . . what must I do?' he asked.

'You must be a good little warrior, my Hather. You must do what your mother wants you to.'

'Kill Starkadder?'

'Perhaps. But before you can do that you must understand the nature of the curse upon Tyrfing. And if the sword is not to betray you, as it betrayed Svafrlami and your grandfather, you must have the curse lifted from its blade.'

'And how shall I do this?'

Tisti chuckled again. 'You know the answer to that,' she replied. 'I've told you twice already, once in my tale and once this morning, in the runes. You must seek the one-eyed man. Only he can help you now, for he is the one who knows the curse. And more. He is the one who can open the gates of Trollheim.

'He must open the gates for you. He may know the curse, but only the one who placed the curse may lift it. That is the journey you have to make, little viking. That is your weird. Before you can kill Starkadder, and perhaps that is also in your weird, you must take Tyrfing back to the court of the dwarf-king, Dvalin. You must do that, or you might as well die now. The curse has been passed to you with the sword, little Hather. It is already upon you now, even as we speak. Only King Dvalin can take it from you.'

She studied his face in the firelight. It was so tired,

82

so lined, so old for one so young. The gift which had brought him joy in the morning now bowed him down in the night.

'Do you doubt the truth of my words?' Tisti asked, gently.

'No,' he replied. 'It is the truth. I must do as you tell me.'

'Then may the gods travel with you and be kind to you.'

He stood up and walked to the door.

'Where should I start my quest?' he asked, a lost, lonely little boy frightened of the dark future before him.

'Ride across the mountains,' Tisti answered. 'Let your journey be towards Uppsala. One shall come from there to help you, one who seeks the lifting of a curse even as you do. Search together, for the one-eyed man can help you both. If you succeed, then one of you may live. But if you fail, little Hather, then the curses will destroy you. Both of you.'

He left her there beside her little fire. In the courtyard, waves of pain and torment flooded over him. He might save himself the quest; he might give Tyrfing away, or throw it in the sea. But it was too late now for even that to save him from its curse. It would taint his life and shape his future, whether he kept it or not. It had a power beyond that of mere possession, a life of its own which could blight that of its keepers.

In the longhouse his drunken mother was struggling from her seat. Hather felt a sudden loathing for her that was stronger than her own hatred of Starkadder. It welled up from the depths of his being, overwhelming him with its potency, blackening the day which had dawned so brightly, flooding his memory with bitter bile.

He remembered the gentle touches and the smiles. He remembered the stirrings she had sought to foster, to encourage. He remembered her beauty, and her ugliness. And he remembered Tyrfing.

It was her gift to him, her curse. He was nothing to her, a lump of clammy clay for her to mould into the instrument of her revenge. That was all. The years, the caresses, the love, all meant nothing now. It didn't matter that her gift, won from Angantyr's grave-mound, was the blighting of

83

his youth, even as her father's death had blighted her own. All that mattered to the Lady Hervara was that he should kill Starkadder for her, not even for himself.

His mother. She felt no love for him, nor for herself. Only hatred. All-consuming hatred. Well, he'd do what she wanted. He'd do everything she wanted. And more.

He strode in through the door to their longhouse, loosening his clothing as he went. He passed through the anteroom, casting his tunic from him, and into the hall. Hervara stood swaying, grasping the columns of his father's high seat for support. Her eyes were dulled and her lips were moving in wordless speech. Her hair, so long, so fine, hung loose and unconfined about her face and shoulders. The fastenings on her dress no longer held, and only those bare white arms flecked with the firelight, raised to grasp the columns, held it up.

And Hather, in his fear and in his anger, felt the hardness growing anew. It grew, strengthened, forcing him to halt long enough to strip off the encumbering trousers, long enough for him to expose the manhood which Hervara had tried so hard to encourage.

For a moment she smiled, and as she did so her face held traces of that indomitable beauty which had so enchanted Lambi Nef and King Oli the Great. Then the beauty fled, pushed out by fear, forced from her by the consuming knowledge that this was not to be a union born of love but something else, something much darker and more brutal.

It had been her last weapon in the war of persuasion she had been waging for all of Hather's young life. Yet now it had become a weapon in the hands of another, keener, more potent, and it was turned against her.

As she had used others, so Hervara knew that she herself was about to be used.

She tried to back away from her son, relinquishing her hold upon Lambi Nef's high seat. Her dress slipped to reveal her breasts, their nipples proud with lust despite her frenzy of fear. Her hands clawed instinctively at the fabric, snatching it up, pulling it back into place, covering herself again.

She tried to speak, even to scream, but the sound wouldn't come. There were no words left to her. Nor was there salvation or reprieve from the punishment she had devised for herself.

Hather reached out, pulling at her dress with vicious fingers. The fabric rent further beneath his grasp, ripping and tearing until there was nothing more for him to shred away from Hervara. Her fists beat against him, her nails tore claw-like at his flesh. It made no difference. The pain only spurred him on, fanning the fires of contempt burning within him, fires which they both knew would only be quenched by a greater shame.

'No, Hather, stop!' she commanded. 'You must not do this.'

She was panting with the useless effort of fighting him off. Hather didn't bother to reply. Nothing mattered to him any more except his hatred and despair. That was all that Hervara had left to him, that and the promise of their day together, a promise she might bitterly regret but now had no power to unmake.

A lifetime had taught Hervara to know when to submit. There was nothing left to her but surrender. She hugged him to her, pressing her nakedness against his own, inviting what she could no longer avert. She sought his lips, her tongue tried to prise them apart but they were set grim, unyielding. Hather pushed her down, onto his father's high seat, and forced his way inside her.

His eyes bulged sightlessly, rolling upwards until only the whites showed through their slitted lids. He strained against her, hurting both of them, desperate for an unholy fulfilment.

Then, as suddenly and violently as it had begun, it was over. Hather threw her from him, hurling her from Lambi Nef's defiled high seat, casting her down amongst the embers and charred rushes which had spilled about the long fire.

'It . . . was never meant to be like this,' she whimpered.

Her son groaned and the groan became a howl which echoed about the rafters of the longhouse. 'How else could it have been?' he snarled. 'Starkadder stands between us, where your hatred has placed him. That's all I am to you, isn't it? The one who can kill him for you? Oh yes, I'll be the instrument of your revenge, Mother. But I'll do it for my sake, not for yours. I'll do it to rid Tyrfing of the curse you gave me for my birthday gift!'

He looked down at the humbled woman, naked on the floor beside the fire. She was still young, still lovely, probably lovelier than he had ever seen her because all the pride and hatred had been washed away by self-pity. Hervara was sobbing violently, and for a moment Hather thought of taking his mother in his arms to comfort her, to banish the darkness of the years that had brought them both down to this. But he did not do it.

'I must go,' he said.

She held her breath to choke back her sobs. 'Go?' she gasped. 'Where are you going?'

'To lift the curse on Tyrfing. To save myself from my sword.'

He started to gather up the clothing he had scattered about the longhouse.

'Must you go . . . now?'

Hather threw back his head and laughed mirthlessly. 'Should I stay?'

Some of the old fire returned to his mother. 'This is that old witch Tisti's doing. Can't you see that she's taking you away from me, Hather? Can't you see that?'

'If she is,' came the cold reply, 'she's doing it to give me to myself. I'm not your plaything, Mother. I can live and breathe for myself. You wanted me to be a man, a warrior, someone who could do your killing for you. Well, that's what you made me. I proved it to my father when he took me into battle. Now I've proved it to you as you wanted. I hate myself for it. I hate myself because it's made me feel ashamed. But what has it done to you, Mother? Are you ashamed? Are you crawling across the floor to find your rags? You don't care for anything but yourself and your vengeance. And that's another reason for my going. To be free of you!'

'Is . . . there . . . nothing I can say or do? To make you stay?'

'You've said and done enough already. Goodbye.'

Hather saddled a horse and took provisions from the storehouses. Only when his mount was loaded and tethered in the courtyard did he go back to the longhouse, into his father's bed-closet.

He was strong for his age and his limbs were thickly sinewed like Lambi Nef's. That was useful, because it meant that his father's old mail-surcoat fitted him quite well. He also found an old helmet of beaten bronze and a baldric to hang Tyrfing from. Finally he selected a worn but serviceable travelling cloak of russet wool that would keep out the night chill.

Hervara still lay amongst the spilled ashes, staring empty-eyed at the fire. If she heard him pass through she gave no sign. Nor did her sightless gaze waver, or her body tremble, as the sounds of the horse's hooves and the sentries opening the gate in the stockade came to her through the wooden walls.

The witch-nurse, supporting herself on a strangely carved staff of blackened yew, hauled her aged bones from the circular hut and stood beside the gate, watching Hather leave. He didn't look back at her, but she had not expected him to. She had played her part, as had his mother the Lady Hervara, in preparing him for what he had to do. There was no need for looks, or words, any more.

And Hather, on his fifteenth birthday, already battle-hardened and a man, rode away, alone in the darkness of the night and the deeper blackness of his thoughts. Had he not been told of Tyrfing's curse he would have divined it now. In the brief space of a single day he had lost his innocence and contentment, perhaps for ever. He had raped his mother, and now he embarked upon a quest that would take him across the mountains, through lands he had never seen, to the very gates of Trollheim. It was an awesome, a frightening future, but it was his, and only death could take it from him.

He rode on through the night towards the dawning. By the time the rosy eastern light had stained the peaks before him he had passed the foot of the mountains and begun the climb towards the pass.

He had started alone, but in time he would find a companion, someone to share the dangers of his quest. Old Tisti had promised him that. One would come to him, accursed as he, to ride beside him. Then he would not be the only one who travelled towards Uppsala, looking for the one-eyed man. There would be two of them.

And afterwards, when he had found the one-eyed man and pleaded with the dwarf-king Dvalin, he might find it in his heart to forgive the Lady Hervara and even to do the thing she wanted.

The way was clear. First, he must seek the one-eyed man, then go to Dvalin, then kill Starkadder.

He began to wonder what his companion would be like. Possibly it would be a warrior, more seasoned than himself. Perhaps it would be a boy, or even a woman. Probably, he thought impatiently, with the luck that had beset him so far, it would be an old, old man who needed even more care and guidance than himself.

Thus Hather rode and mused. By mid-morning, with the sun bright in his eyes, he had entered the pass between the snow-topped mountains, a broad, green valley rich with game and bright with the flowers of spring. There were pools and rivulets of crystal water, and even the occasional small steading where he might find shelter for the night.

Towards noon he dismounted and watered his horse beside a stream. The day was fine and warm, and its kindly beauty began to mellow the bitterness of his thoughts. He laughed to himself as he realised that there was still peace and gentleness in the world, but he also cried to himself when he realised that he was not a part of it, merely a swallow passing through, a fly on the face of a mountain.

'Towards Uppsala,' old Tisti had said. 'One shall come from there to help you . . .'

To help. So it had to be a warrior. Or someone like Tisti, someone who knew runes to ease the way and guide his uncertain steps. But there were the other words as well.

'If you succeed, then one of you may live . . .'

Only one? He should have asked which one. And yet he knew that it had to be him. He had to survive, to go on living. Tyrfing would be truly his once he had entered

88

Trollheim. The sword would be his by right, he would have earned it. But he also knew that it had been given him for a purpose. It was his grandfather's sword, the sword of Angantyr, and with it he must avenge Angantyr's killing.

With the help of Tyrfing he would kill Starkadder. With the help of Tyrfing, and the one who was to come.

CHAPTER THREE

The court of King Oli the Great

LAMBI NEF was fighting to keep disgust from showing in his face. Whenever he dared, whenever he could be certain that King Oli's piercing gaze was not upon him, he stole a glance at those about him. The younger retainers, those who had grown up in a time of peace and prosperity, stood with bitten lips and eyes wild with anguish. Some gaped, wide-mouthed with terror. Others clutched their spears and used them for support, struggling to keep their feet, struggling to force the rising vomit down.

The older ones, the hard men like himself, who had seen many times the cruelties of war and the bloody reprisals wrought upon a captured enemy, bore the sight with less unease. Yet even their features showed disgust, not with the execution, but with its familiarity. Most had learned the art of letting their eyes rest on the far distances, of stopping their ears against the tormented howling of the victim, but the horror of the scene still struck deep into every one of them.

Only one man took pleasure in the sight. King Oli leaned forward eagerly, his fingers twitching upon the arms of his high seat as the blood and the demented ululations seared him with unholy pleasure. A man stood beside him, slightly apart from the king and from the others, his face void of all expression, narrow and aloof in his night-black cloak.

In the centre of the courtyard, before the king's royal hall, a horizontal beam had been set up upon supports as high as a man. Both the beam and the supports were brown and sticky with use, and it seemed to Oli's men that hardly a day passed by without some grisly ritual killing. That this man, held in Oli's dungeon for months for just this purpose, should have lasted so long was testimony both to his strength and to the craft of Oli's executioner. Now, as the last rib was severed from the spinal column in a fresh spurting of blood, the screams became a coughing, wheezing, gurgling, choking whine. The executioner tore back the rib-cage in the bloody pageantry of his trade, exposing the straining lungs beneath, and the prisoner erupted in a spray of blood and vomit, shuddering and twitching like a dying eagle struggling from the eyrie. For an instant his breath hissed and bubbled, then he collapsed, only his bound arms on the beam keeping him upright.

'And so, my friends, another traitor dies the death of the blood-eagle,' Oli smirked, tossing a silver coin to the blood-drenched executioner.

To look at, Oli the Great was still a handsome man. His features, though fallen with age, still revealed something of the clean lines of his youth. His mouth was strong, and his nose aquiline. His hair, once flaming red, was a strong yellow-white, matching the long beard that flowed down over his gorget. His build in recent years had become heavy, and his movements less certain than they had been throughout the glorious protection of his kingdom. Oli's most remarkable feature, though, was his eyes. They were neither large nor small, neither protuberant nor deep-set, but they possessed a formidable strength, and few could meet the gaze of the ageing king. Whilst others might disturb those who faced them by the blueness or greyness of their glare, King Oli's eyes disturbed by their very blackness. The irises were dark, as dark and nighted as the pupils, so that the eyes looked like dull stone, black set in white. No feeling ever showed in them.

The grisly spectacle was over. Soon the body would be removed and thrown with the others beyond the walls of the royal enclosure. No matter what the victim's former rank, no matter how humbly his family might entreat the hard-eyed king there would be no burial, save that done piecemeal by the carrion-eaters.

The massed warriors stood in silence, awaiting the king's dismissal. Starkadder eyed Oli warily, trying to see into the decaying mind of the man he had served for so many years. The tall Norwegian in the black armour was probably the only man at the court of whom the king had ever shown any fear. Although they had never spoken of it they both knew the truth about the battle on the plain at Roliung. Oli had wanted the ageless mercenary dead, not because he was a threat to Oli's rule, but because the king could not understand the old man's apparent ability to defy both time and death. It was not natural. It savoured of sorcery and witchcraft, and witchcraft had been known to destroy kings.

The attack, of course, had failed. Oli had had little faith in it when he arranged it, through his agents. If Starkadder had been an ordinary mortal, even one of the heroes such as Sigurd or Hadding, then he could not have stood alone against Angantyr and his berserks, and would never have been able to kill them all while himself remaining unscathed. That he could do so was reason enough for Oli to fear the old man, a reason to keep him in his service, if the story of the curse were true.

The third betrayal, Oli knew, was the one that would signal Starkadder's death, his release from the curse that bound him to the lands of Midgard. Yet it was also the thing which the invulnerable Norwegian dreaded more than anything, not because he feared death or injury – he had faced both too often to feel any terror of either – but because he feared the act of betrayal itself. There was no knowing that his end would follow quickly upon the third betrayal, and that meant there would be time for the horror of shame and guilt which had already consumed him twice before.

And so, reasoned Oli the Great, Starkadder was the one man he could truly depend upon to work his will. The old mercenary's fear of the betrayal was stronger than the ageing monarch's fear of being betrayed. Whatever his feeble, faint-hearted popinjay retainers might plot or devise, Starkadder would save him, though Oli doubted that there was any among them capable of even looking him straight in his odd, disquieting eyes, let alone bringing about his fall.

'The execution is done,' the king proclaimed, suddenly wearied by his thoughts. 'Learn its lesson well, my friends. There can be no disloyalty in this land if we are to safeguard the peace which grants our families safety for their lives. Remember that.'

Lambi Nef suppressed a snort, hiding his mouth by scratching at his moustache. Safety for our families, indeed. Is that why Oli keeps his only son a prisoner in a stronghold in the north? So that he's safe? Safe from whom? Himself? Or from the old man's fear of the day when his tyranny would be broken and his miserable life finished for good? Well, perhaps that day was nearer than Oli thought. He turned to walk back to his quarters. As he did so he felt, rather than saw, the black forbidding figure which remained alone, looking at the mutilated remains of Oli's latest example. Lambi Nef did not care to look at him. There was no knowing where Starkadder's allegiance really lay. That was what set him apart from other men, even more than the legendary curse which armoured him against death and the passing of the years. If he knew, if he could be sure, then he might find a useful ally for himself and his fellow conspirators, but without that knowledge he dare not approach the mercenary, lest his action betray them all.

Lambi Nef walked away, smiling grimly to himself. The blood-eagle executions were indeed an example to them, but the example merely signalled caution, not restraint.

From the corner of his deep-set eye Starkadder watched the chieftain leave the courtyard. He had lived too long in a violent, distrustful world not to know something of the retainer's thoughts. There was a wariness in his bearing, a watchfulness in his eyes, which bespoke a hidden unease. Whilst men rarely spoke to Starkadder, there were few things that the ancient killer didn't know. Not by sorcery or witchcraft came his knowledge, but by instincts and senses sharpened to a deadly edge through two hundred long years. The hero Sigurd Fafnisbane might have known the language of the birds, but Starkadder knew the language of the face and the body and of the pumping heart which gave them life.

He had seen Lambi Nef's uneasiness in others at the court. He had not bothered to count, but there were probably about a dozen of them altogether. Some, like Vithin of Limfjord and Thokkar of Leire, were Danish mercenary captains, whose help would only be assured by substantial payments in gold. But others, like Lambi Nef and Atyl Cod of Bravalla, were native-born Swedes who were worried about the future of their homeland, men who saw Oli's age-borne madness as a weakness and a threat to the strength of the ruling house, men who wanted to bring Oli's son Omund out of his enforced imprisonment in the north and set him upon his father's throne before Oli destroyed the power of the Yngling dynasty.

And then there was a third kind of conspirator, the native Swedes who saw advancement in the gratitude of the liberated Omund, the petty chieftains who would attach themselves like leeches to their new king, only to take his wealth and, eventually, to depose and supplant him in the fulfilment of their greedy ambitions. These were the men that Starkadder despised. They were moved by neither the gold-bought loyalties of the mercenary, nor the steadfastness of the honest men such as Lambi Nef and Atyl Cod.

As he stood in the sunlight, wrapped around with the darkness of his cloak, Starkadder felt a deeper blackness clutching at his heart. There was a discontent abroad in the court of Oli the Great and, if the court was a mirror of the land, throughout the whole of Sweden. Sooner or later either the conspirators or the king would have to be destroyed, and his long, long life had taught him that he could not expect to escape his part in that destruction. Yes, he knew of the conspiracy, so the slaughter of the plotters would constitute a betrayal. Yet he also served the king, and a part in Oli's death was something he feared even more than the curse which still enfolded him.

Watching his shadow fade as the sun passed behind a cloud, he shuddered. Perhaps a horn or two of that pale Frankish wine from the south would help.

Starkadder walked back to the longhouse he shared with Thorvald Brotamad, Gisli of Sogn and some other Norwegian mercenary captains. He seated himself at one of the trestles and sent a servant for wine and a horn. The man returned quickly, as frightened of Starkadder as he was of King Oli himself. As he was pouring the third horn Thorvald strode importantly into the hall. He was a tall man, only a few inches shorter than Starkadder, and twice as broad. His face was almost hidden by a thick thatch of glossy, blue-black hair and beard. The beard, however, was uneven and grew only in patches on the right where a broad ugly scar ran, caused by a side-swipe with a war-axe which had laid the jaw open to the bone. Thorvald Brotamad, Thorvald the Disrupter, was well named. He delighted in goading others, and his fighting skill was known to be such that few men challenged his swaggering manner.

He sat down opposite Starkadder and eyed the old man mischievously. 'Getting drunk so soon?' he asked, an edge of menace in his voice. 'What's the matter, old man? Losing the stomach for the blood-eagle, eh?'

Starkadder's hollow gaze wandered the breadth of the worn, creaking leathers that Thorvald wore at court instead of mail. 'Go and piss yourself, Thorvald,' he replied calmly.

With a bellow of outrage Thorvald Brotamad sprang to his feet, knocking the bench over behind him. His hand touched the hilt of his sword, then froze. The point of Starkadder's own sword was pricking the flesh beneath the mercenary's beard.

'Want me to cut the other side to match?' the ancient Norwegian smiled gently. 'I will, if you don't get out and leave me in peace.'

The mercenary snarled warily, but his hand dropped away from his sword. Starkadder lowered his blade, allowing Thorvald to back away, out of the longhouse. When he had gone Starkadder sheathed his sword and returned to his seat.

'One day I'll kill you!' Thorvald Brotamad's shout came from the courtyard, but the old man only smiled and poured another horn of wine. It would take more than a blustering bully to carry out that threat.

He continued drinking through the morning; but long years of mead and winter beer had hardened him against drunkenness, and the pale Frankish wine had little power to dull his wits.

Whilst the life of the court went on around him, Starkadder pondered. He could betray the conspirators or join them, support Oli or betray him. Both choices held the same appalling promise for the accursed viking, for both meant he would have to join one side or the other. Only as the wine began to mellow his distress did he see that there was another choice for him, a choice which might yet save them all. Slowly a plan began to take shape in his mind.

Towards noon he hauled his weary body to its feet and looked about him. This had been a good place, even despite men such as Thorvald Brotamad. Perhaps he could stay here for a while yet and enjoy something of the peace and contentment that was the right of old age, for others.

He tried his feet and found them reasonably steady. He tested his tongue, softly, to himself on a particularly tortuous and kenning–laden skaldic verse. His speech, he decided, was understandable. So much the better, for what he had to say. It probably wouldn't go down too well, but he had to give it a try.

Starkadder left the longhouse and approached King Oli's private quarters.

He found Oli immersed in a large wooden bath, its sides decorated with panels of beaten gold bearing the Odinic wolf and raven motifs that were the right of members of the Yngling royal house. In recent weeks the king had suffered from a skin complaint which nothing but the warm, oiled waters of his bath could ease for any length of time. Only Starkadder and one or two other trusted retainers were allowed to see the monarch other than at the times appointed for audience, and Starkadder reflected that this privilege might well be withdrawn from him if Oli didn't like what he had to say.

And Oli wasn't going to like it. The ancient Norwegian had no doubt about that. His fear of being overthrown was the cause of King Oli's regular 'examples' to his court. He knew that he was getting old, and that a younger man could supplant him easily in the people's hearts, but the throne was his whilst he lived, and no one was going to take it from him.

The king dismissed his servants.

'Well, old friend,' Oli smiled, wearily, briefly allowing the discomfort of his affliction to show on his worn features, 'have you come to kill me?'

Both men knew that it was only half a joke, but Oli, for all his years and creeping madness, still retained something of the valour of his youth. Some said that a sword, greased to protect it from the water, lay ready at the bottom of his bath.

'Not this time,' Starkadder replied, as he always did.

Most of the times when he gave that reply King Oli could hear a trace of humour in his voice. This time, however, there was none, and the king felt that, whilst he was in no immediate danger, this interview might not be altogether to his satisfaction.

He forced some of the forbidding darkness back into his gaze and shifted his body painfully in the bath. 'Whatever it is you've come to say,' he grunted, 'you'd better say it.'

Starkadder looked back at him. The old mercenary was probably the only man at court who was not afraid of Oli's eyes. 'Yes,' he nodded. 'It's best said and over, King. You know what's going on here as well as I do. You know that your men either hate you, or fear you, or both.'

'That's nothing new,' Oli snapped. 'Come to the point, Starkadder.'

'Then here it is. You must give up the throne to your son.'

The words were said calmly and without any hint of threat. For some moments they lay heavily upon the silence. Then, with a wordless roar of demonic fury, Oli erupted from his bath and threw himself at the ancient Norwegian, his clawed hands seeking for Starkadder's throat.

Before the hooked fingers could touch the old man's windpipe, Starkadder had seized the king's flaking wrists. 'Haven't you learned yet?' he asked, calmly searching the

97

black depths of Oli's eyes. 'You cannot kill me, King Oli. Not even Angantyr and his berserks could kill me. Or had you forgotten?'

The king struggled briefly against the imprisoning grip of Starkadder's unyielding fingers, then gave up and allowed himself to be held.

'All right, Starkadder,' he said, resignedly. 'I'll listen to you.'

'I don't want to hurt you,' the mercenary continued. 'You know that. But others might. For all our sakes, Oli, including your own, let a younger man take the throne. Set Omund free. Let him learn at your side the craft of kingship. Then give him the throne. No harm shall come to you. I promise you that.'

'I'll . . . think about it.'

'That's not enough. Do it, Oli. There's still much you can do for your country and your people, but you need their love as well as their obedience. No man can rule by fear alone. You have to show wisdom. I'm not saying that you have to give the order for Omund's release today, or this week, or this month. But set it in your heart as a course of action worthy of a great king.'

Starkadder loosed his hold upon the king. Oli stepped back a few paces and stood frowning, uncertain and dripping water. The two old men held each other's eyes across the space between them.

Oli gestured to a stool nearby with a richly embroidered garment upon it. 'Will you hand me my robe?' he asked.

Starkadder moved to obey. As he did so the king, moving with surprising speed, leapt across the chamber and snatched a war-axe from its mounting on the wall. With the hoarse shreds of his battle-cry upon his lips he swung the heavy weapon at Starkadder's neck.

The blow never fell. A sudden spasm racked Oli's decaying body, sending the weapon crashing from his pain-knotted fingers. Starkadder simply picked up the robe and slipped it about the old king's quaking shoulders.

'You're not well, King Oli,' he observed. 'Think on my words.'

He led Oli to a bench beside the wall and sat him down. A

jar of wine and a Frankish glass goblet stood on a small table; he poured some of the wine and set it to the king's lips. Only then did he leave the chamber, summoning Oli's attendants as he walked out of the king's quarters.

Starkadder returned to his longhouse and sent his servant to saddle a horse and obtain some provisions. The king had chosen not to listen, not to consider the advice offered to him. Oli the Great would follow his own course, even if it led him to ruin and brought him to a tyrant's death. Well, he'd tried. Word of his attempt would already be spreading through the royal hall. He'd tried, and he'd failed. Now there was only one course left open to him.

The old mercenary went over to a rack on the wall and selected a spear. The one he took was of strong, dark wood, rigid in the shaft but unlikely to shatter. On the bright metal of the spearhead the single word *sterki*, strong, was inscribed in runes.

He set the spear beside the entrance and tied his bedding into a roll, putting it beside the weapon. Then he examined his shield, noting with grim satisfaction the dents and scratches in the blackened metal cladding where enemy weapons had fallen harmlessly upon it.

Now he was ready. All he needed was a horse.

He was still waiting when Lambi Nef approached him. Of all the men at Oli's court Lambi Nef was perhaps the closest to the old mercenary's alien heart. True, his wife had won him most of his advancement with her whoring, but Lambi used his position well, for the good of his people, and was no faintheart when it came to fighting. He was a simple, honest man, and his honesty would probably destroy him. The retainer was not slow to notice the spear and bedroll, nor to guess what these preparations meant.

'You don't have to leave,' he began, unsmiling.

'I've no choice left,' Starkadder replied. 'I expect you've heard that I've been to talk to the king?'

The retainer nodded. 'Some rooms have thin walls and nosy servants beyond them,' he said, his voice innocent of humour. 'You know of course that no other man here dare talk to the king as you did?'

'My curse has its uses,' Starkadder said, ruefully.

'Oli tried to kill you, didn't he?'

The mercenary sighed deeply. 'I know what you're going to say,' he began. 'If Oli tried to kill me then I'm not bound to him any more. That's it, isn't it?'

'It is. It also means that you know why I've come to you.'

Starkadder laid a hand upon Lambi Nef's shoulder and searched the retainer's eyes. 'I'm not your man,' he said at length. 'I can't do it, Lambi Nef. That's why I have to go.'

'One hundred pounds' weight in gold.'

Despite his resolve a low whistle escaped the Norwegian's lips. 'That's a high price for a killing,' he muttered.

'It can be higher, Starkadder. You know the risk that I've taken in approaching you. I'm not alone in this. We can pay more. You're the only man here who won't lose his nerve when Oli turns his eyes on you.'

Slowly, determinedly, Starkadder shook his head. From the corner of his eye he saw the servant leading his mount across the courtyard.

'You're the only man who can do it,' Lambi Nef urged him, his voice almost pleading. 'He must die! Before he kills us all!'

'Perhaps. But not by my hand.'

'It will end your curse, Starkadder. It will free you. And the gold will help you live out your life in peace. You'll never want. I promise you that,' he added, his voice dropping to an urgent whisper. 'You can't just ride away. You have to kill Oli, for all our sakes!'

'I'm sorry, Lambi. I'm truly sorry.'

He picked up the bedroll and the shield, set the spear under his arm, and walked away across the courtyard.

Lambi Nef watched him climb into the saddle and turn the horse's head towards the gates. From the shadow cast by the eaves at the further end of the longhouse other eyes also watched, the eyes of Thorvald Brotamad.

For a little while Lambi Nef watched as Starkadder rode slowly away. Then, pulling ruefully at his long nose, he made his way back to his own quarters. Thorvald watched the retainer, noticing his disappointed slouch. The mercenary captain had not been close enough to hear their conversation. The fact of Starkadder's leaving was enough for him.

As Thorvald turned away, smirking to himself, Lambi Nef stopped and glanced briefly around the compound. Having satisfied himself that those watching eyes, felt rather than seen where they lurked in the shrouding shadows, were no longer with him, he changed direction. He knew only too well that Oli regarded Starkadder as a threat, and that meant that the king would either try to have the old mercenary killed or brought back to Uppsala as a prisoner. Even though Starkadder had refused Lambi's offer he was still, in the chieftain's opinion, the only man who could bring the mad king's murderous regime to an end.

And that meant that Starkadder would have to be protected.

Thorvald Brotamad made his way quickly towards the king's quarters. After a brief delay he managed to talk his way past the sentries and enter the royal presence. Oli, now dressed, sat alone in his private room, emptying the goblet and refilling it from the jar. As Thorvald entered he turned the full power of his forbidding eyes upon the nervous mercenary.

'This had better be worth the interruption,' he snarled, his speech slurred by the wine. 'What's so important that it can't wait for an audience, Thorvald?'

'Starkadder's gone,' Thorvald Brotamad replied, averting his eyes.

Oli sat up, and his shrunken form seemed to gather size and strength. 'Gone?' he thundered. 'What do you mean, he's gone, man? Gone where?'

'He's . . . gone, sir. He's left the palace.'

'Alone?'

'Yes.'

'Armed?'

'To the teeth.'

King Oli nodded to himself. Though he could not begin to tell what was worrying him he felt something in all this that could prove dangerous. Starkadder's loyalty had been assured, up to that morning, but since their exchange of words the king was consumed by doubts about the old Norwegian's honesty.

'Have you a good tracker in your service?' he asked Thorvald.

The mercenary nodded. 'A reindeer hunter from Bjarmaland. His name's Bolli.'

'Then take him, and as many men as you think you'll need, and set out after Starkadder. Bring him back here to me, Thorvald, and I'll reward you better than you've ever been rewarded before. And if, by any lucky chance, the Norns have written that you can kill him, I don't think I'll object too strongly. In fact, I don't think I'll object at all. Clear?'

'No trouble, sir.'

Oli grinned at the reply. If Angantyr and his berserks hadn't managed to get rid of Starkadder, then a worm like Thorvald was likely to have trouble. A great deal of trouble. He sounded cocky enough, but saying you'd kill Starkadder and doing it were two different things. A chain of burial-mounds stretching across the country bore mute witness to that.

Even so, whilst they might not be able to kill the old mercenary, they might be able to bring him back. And then Oli would see if the curse-ridden Norwegian could defy the blood-eagle.

'Well?' the king snapped. 'What are you hanging around here for?'

Thorvald jumped to attention, then turned to leave. As he reached the door Oli called after him.

'Send my marshal in!'

As soon as he had left the royal presence Thorvald Brotamad did as he was told. Vermund, Oli's marshal, was in his longhouse. As soon as Thorvald had delivered the royal summons he scurried away to find Bolli and assemble his men, leaving Vermund to find the king.

Marshal Vermund Bjarnisson was a seasoned campaigner. He was a small man, but his prowess and energy were widely respected. His hair, once blond, was now a dirty yellow that hung in ringlets around his battered, bearded face. One of his eyes, the left, had long since vanished from his head, spitted on the point of an enemy sword, and a large patch of tooled leather covered the scar and the empty socket. Vermund was proud of this disfigurement. It lent him something of the appearance of Odin the One-Eyed God of battle and warriors. Yet even this seasoned veteran did not dare to stand up against the darkness of King Oli's eyes.

The guards passed him through into Oli's chamber and he stood before the seated monarch.

'You wanted me, sir?' he asked.

Oli nodded slowly. 'Starkadder has left Uppsala,' he began. 'Now, this may simply mean he wants to be alone for a while but, knowing that vicious old bastard as I do, I doubt it.

'This is what I want from you, Vermund. I've sent Thorvald Brotamad and his men after Starkadder. I doubt if they'll be able to kill him, but they might be able to force him to return. If they do, all well and good. If they don't, there's somewhere he might be going. I think you know where I mean.'

Vermund nodded. He'd heard a report of the old viking's conversation with the king as well. Personally he wouldn't have been so foolish, but Starkadder was a law unto himself. There was every possibility that he might strike north and try to free Omund from his captivity. Odin alone knew there'd be plenty of popular support for the boy.

'Send a messenger on ahead to warn the stronghold. Then follow yourself, with a hundred of your best men as reinforcements. If you have to, if it's absolutely necessary, you will kill my son rather than let him fall into the hands of Starkadder or any other rebel leaders. Is that understood?'

Vermund swallowed hard. This was butcher's work, not a soldier's. But he nodded, because those black eyes were upon him and he did not dare to say no.

King Oli the Great dismissed his marshal and settled back in his seat. This was not the day he'd planned for himself. Since the execution things had not been going smoothly at all. If only Angantyr had finished the job he was paid for, all those years ago . . .

Vermund Bjarnisson held strictly to his orders. The messenger was sent and his men prepared for their journey. Now it was time to leave.

The sun had sunk low in the mountain-screened west, staining the snowy caps blood-red. Thorvald chafed at the frequent halts his company made for Reindeer Bolli to examine Starkadder's tracks. Even so, the tracks showed that the old killer was riding slowly, sparing his horse. This meant that, if they kept riding through the night, they should be able to overtake him by mid-morning the following day.

Thorvald tugged at his beard, mildly puzzled. The sunset was on his right, so they were following Starkadder south. There was little that way except more mountains and the province ruled by Lambi Nef. Why hadn't the old bastard turned north, towards the stronghold where Oli kept his son?

And Starkadder, if he'd bothered to think as he rode, might well have wondered the same thing. The thought of freeing Omund had entered his mind, but he was simply giving his mount its head, letting it take him wherever it chose. There were times in his protracted life when he felt the need to abandon rational thought and exist by his instincts. This was one of those times.

He had tried to convince Oli to step down from the throne in favour of his son. Omund could hold the throne with less violence and anxiety attached to his reign. On the one occasion Starkadder had met the lad he'd seemed a sensible and well-balanced youth, even despite his perpetual captivity. But Oli wouldn't let go, so the plotting would go on. Twice before, the ancient Norwegian had betrayed the kings he served. Perhaps Oli would be the third. Certainly there was a feeling, something in the changing wind, that Oli's end could not be too far off. But Starkadder was not going to betray him. He would not kill him. He would not free Omund. Nor would he betray Lambi Nef and his fellow conspirators. Better that they dealt with it themselves.

104

He spent the night beneath a rocky outcrop, close by a stream which had been swollen by the spring thaw. In the distance was a lake, and the old man's deep-set eyes could just make out the water fowl upon its surface. Everywhere there was the new life of the changing seasons. Everywhere but inside Starkadder.

Yet, why south? True, it was easy riding, following the roots of the mountains. But there was more to life than ease, or giving your horse its head. Why south?

The only answer that came to him was one that he did not entirely understand. He was naturally glad to be free of the oppression and bickering of Oli's court, but he could not free himself of the feeling that he was being guided. For two centuries Starkadder's life had not been his own. He was both the servant and the plaything of the gods. Such was his curse. And, since he was not entirely his own master, since he knew that Oli's death was drawing nearer, since he felt the dark purposes of the Lords of Asgard stirring deep within him, he did not question the path he was taking. What will be, he reasoned with the resignation of one who knew his life to be governed by the immutable decrees of the Norns, will be. Whatever the purpose of this journey, I shall know it soon enough.

Odin would know. At times during his overlong life Starkadder had counted himself privileged to speak with the Allfather. Perhaps this would be one of the times. Perhaps he would see the two ravens circling above him, and hear the howling of the wolves Geri and Freki in the distance. Perhaps the one-eyed god would come to him and tell him what he had to do, and what his purpose was.

So he slept, but Allfather did not come to him in his dreams. He woke in the morning, but the ravens were not wheeling overhead. He saddled his mount and set off once more towards his unknown destination, and the grey, shaggy wolves were not crying in the distance. There was nothing to hinder him, and nothing to guide him.

Reindeer Bolli raised his hand and Thorvald ordered his men to halt. The tracker pointed to a dark shape in the distant morning, a shape that, though enlarged by its long shadow, was still little more than a speck to untrained eyes.

'That's him?' Thorvald Brotamad demanded, checking his rearing mount.

Bolli nodded. 'That's him,' he grinned. 'That's Starkadder. You could be on him in little more than an hour.'

CHAPTER FOUR

At the meeting of the streams

HATHER CLEARED the long pass and came out on the other side of the mountains. Had he known that he was so close to the plains again he would have pushed on that bit further and left the pass before making camp for the night. Even so, it was a refreshing surprise to find the plains again before him. His journey would be easier now.

As he turned north the early sun mercifully left his eyes, and his long shadow fell over his left shoulder. This was the third morning of his travels, and the youth was starting to feel the effects of spending his days in the saddle and his nights upon the ground.

The thought stirred within him that today, now that the mountains were behind him and he was less than a day's hard riding from Uppsala where his father fretted at the court of King Oli the Great, the promised companion might appear. Yet there were more urgent needs. He had been nowhere near a stream when he stopped for the night, and now needed water for himself and his horse.

As if in answer to his prayers the gleam of running water caught his eyes. It looked close, and he decided to dismount and walk his horse until they had both drunk their fill. The rock underfoot was padded by moss and stretches of scrubby grass, making walking easy and almost pleasurable. Besides, there was nothing to hurry for, not until old Tisti's prophecy had been fulfilled and his companion was with him. Then the days of leisure would be over, as they searched together for the one-eyed man.

Naturally, he had already been looking. 'Have you seen a one-eyed man?' he'd asked, at every settlement he passed. 'Do you know a man who only has one eye?'

Oddly enough, in those days of raids and levies, no one had known anybody, not even an ancient farmer, who only had one eye. They were respectful, naturally, for those at the far end of the pass knew him for the son of Lambi Nef, and those at this end could tell by his dress that this was not just a peasant lad. Besides, that was a nasty-looking sword he carried.

As they neared the water Hather could see that there were two streams upon the surface of the plain. For much of their visible length they ran parallel. Then they crossed, their waters merging in a tumult of running and bubbling amongst their confused and rocky beds. He released his mount and let the horse make its own way to the streams. It bent its neck at the crossing and drank. Hather followed on foot, kneeling to drink upstream of his horse.

He stood up, feeling refreshed after dunking his head in the cold, clear water, and took down a water-skin from his saddle. He pressed the flattened skin beneath the surface and watched the little air trapped inside bubble upwards into the sunlight. When the skin was filled he stoppered it and hung it again on the saddle. His horse snorted and tossed its head. He quieted it with his hands and some soft words.

Then he saw the speck.

He stood beside his mount, watching the speck grow bigger as it approached, watching it become a mounted rider. It was still too far away for him to make out more than its outline, but he could see that the rider was carrying a shield, and probably a spear as well. That meant a lone warrior.

Was this, he wondered, the one who was to come?

Usually an approaching shape grew lighter as it came nearer, but this one remained dark, stirring a dim memory at the back of Hather's mind.

Starkadder had not looked back at the riders his instincts told him were following. He knew that Oli would not simply let him ride out of the royal palace at Uppsala. He knew that there would be some kind of pursuit. It was written by the Norns, and he welcomed it. What was to be, would be, and he laughed inwardly at his own puny efforts to escape the workings of his curse.

He would let them catch up, let them do whatever they wanted with him. Possibly it was a friendly embassy, but the old warrior doubted that. It was not King Oli's way. Well, if they killed him, that would be the end of the curse. But could they kill him?

He looked ahead, to where a single figure stood beside a horse, at the meeting of the streams. Probably it was nothing more than a traveller on his way overland to Uppsala, a pilgrim who wanted to worship at the temple there. Maybe it was a farmer from the south who wanted to beg Frey for a good harvest, or implore red-bearded Thor to be gentle with his rain. But it carried a sword with a golden hilt that glistened on its thigh, and wore a helmet, not a cap. Perhaps it was a warrior, seeking favours from a sacrifice to Allfather.

He laughed again and dismissed his thoughts as vain. After all, he'd learn the answer soon enough.

As Starkadder rode nearer he began to make out the figure's features, to recognise their youth through hard-won lines and the grime of travel. It was a face he'd seen before somewhere, among so many other faces, in the course of so long a life. It was a face set in a scowl, a face that knew his own.

And Hather's scowl became a mask of hatred as the dark-clad rider approached. He had only seen that ancient visage once before, at Oli's court, but it was one that he would never forget. It was the face of the man who had killed his grandfather, and now it was even more than that. It was the reason his mother had given him Tyrfing. It was the reason for his incestuous rape of Hervara. It was the very purpose of his quest.

Starkadder.

Perhaps the Norns had written some kindness into his life after all. Perhaps even old Tisti had been wrong, and there was no need to pass through the gates of Trollheim. Maybe he could kill him now and then throw Tyrfing from him, foiling the curse which had begun to shadow his destiny, leaving King Dvalin to take back Tyrfing if he wanted. And leaving his enemy dead at the meeting of the streams.

Starkadder dismounted a few yards from the water and set down his spear and shield. His horse made its own way forward and bent its neck to drink, leaving the old warrior standing alone, his deep-set eyes studying the vicious hardness on the youth's features.

'Starkadder!' Hather spat.

'You know me?' the ancient Norwegian asked. His voice was soft, almost pacifying, but without any hint of fear. 'I know you, boy, but your name escapes me for the present.'

'You saw me once at the court of King Oli the Great. My name is Hather Lambisson. I'm the son of Lambi Nef.'

Starkadder nodded slowly. 'I remember you now, Hather. You've fought beside your father and won renown in battle already. You have my respect for that.'

'I don't want your respect, old butcher,' the boy snarled back. 'I want your death.'

The old mercenary's eyes twinkled with undisguised amusement, but only for a moment. Then they became veiled with sadness. There were always so many young men who sought to win renown by killing him. Many were silly little braggarts who had nothing but pride and hope to their names, but this one was different. He was the son of a wealthy chieftain and his name was already known for bravery. But for this meeting he would have a bright, respected future.

'We have no quarrel,' Starkadder said. It was both a statement and a command.

He began to walk towards his horse.

'Wait!' Hather snapped. 'You're wrong, Starkadder. We have a quarrel. We have a blood-feud. Do you fear to face me?'

The mercenary suddenly felt every one of his years. He sighed deeply and stopped, turning his head to look at the youth beside the streams. He had determined to ignore taunts and insults, merely setting them down to youthful

110

hot headedness. And yet there was one thing that he could not ignore, one thing that could not be spurned with honour in the northern lands. A blood-feud.

'Who do you claim for this feud?' he asked gently.

'You don't remember?'

They would have to fight, so a guarded tongue no longer had any virtue to it. 'There have been so many,' was Starkadder's weary reply. 'Which one do you want to die for?'

'You killed my grandfather. You killed the chieftain Angantyr!'

He tried to think, to remember the fight upon the snow-wrapped plain at Roliung. He remembered the others he had killed, and their eleven faces fled across his mind. But Angantyr? Had he killed Angantyr as well?

'Defend yourself, Starkadder!'

Hather drew Tyrfing from its scabbard and held it before him, its blade shimmering with light reflected from the water. Starkadder's eyes rested upon the point, then travelled along the length of the sword, noting the fine-honed edge and the golden hilt, then coming back oto the deep chip in the handguard.

Then he remembered.

He saw the blurred arc of his own blade tearing the sword from Angantyr's grasp, watched as Tyrfing flew upwards, only to fall and bury itself in Angantyr's helpless body. And this, stretched across the water towards him, urging him to fight, was that same sword, the accursed sword, Tyrfing.

'Listen to me,' he began. 'This will sound strange to you, Hather, but I did not kill your grandfather . . .'

His words came too late. Hather had already begun to ford the streams towards him, the point of his sword weaving a deadly pattern in the air. If the old Norwegian delayed a moment longer the blade would be at his throat, offering welcome release from his own torment. But after that, sooner or later, it would kill Hather as well.

He quickly drew his own weapon and parried the thrusts. For a young, unscarred fighter the youth handled a sword well. Someone, probably his father Lambi Nef, had taught

111

him the basic skills, and in practice he'd learned a few good tricks of his own. Even so, he was no match for a seasoned veteran, let alone the accursed Starkadder.

Hather's blows were gaining him nothing. The old man's parries were deft and powerful, and the youth soon realised that for some reason of his own Starkadder was only fighting defensively. He aimed a swing at the mercenary's neck as a feint. When Starkadder ducked the blow he twisted his wrists and turned Tyrfing for a downswing that would chop through the helmet into the skull beneath.

But Starkadder's sword rang against his own and twisted along the length of the blade, sending a shock into the hilt which loosened Hather's grip. For a second the two swords lay flat against each other with Starkadder's on top. Then the old Norwegian pushed down on Tyrfing, tearing it from Hather's grasp. The weapon struck the ground hilt first and the mercenary's booted heel stamped downwards, holding it where it fell.

Disarmed, Hather began to back away. His mouth hung open in astonishment and there was sudden fear in his eyes. Starkadder bent warily and picked Tyrfing up in his free hand, curious to examine the accursed weapon which had twice been drawn against him. As he did so a curious thrill seemed to tingle up his arm from the hilt.

Then he began to feel the power of Dvalin's curse. Tyrfing began to weave, gathering strength for its deadly work. Starkadder tried to loosen his fingers about the hilt, to cast it from him, but the same unearthly power which gave the sword its movement held it in his hand. He could not let it go.

He threw his own sword towards the puzzled Hather. 'Take it!' he cried. 'Fight for your life, lad. Cut my hand off!'

Hather picked up Starkadder's sword and parried Tyrfing's first vicious swing. Before he could chop at the old man's wrist he was forced to parry again, and again. Starkadder grasped his forearm with his free hand, desperately seeking to slow the weapon's speed, but the thrilling that ran throughout his frame shook it off with a power he would otherwise have not believed.

112

'I can't help you,' he yelled as Tyrfing swung at Hather's head.'

Once more the youth managed to parry the blow, his sword-arm shuddering with the force of Tyrfing's swing, but he was slowly being driven backwards by Starkadder's reluctant attack. He parried another flashing stroke, but the effort sent his weapon flying away, leaving him defenceless before the accursed blade. He backed and ducked, and the air above his head sang in the wake of Tyrfing's passage whilst Starkadder, his face contorted with his efforts, tried desperately to thwart the sword's intentions, straining to back away and release his unwilling grip upon the golden hilt.

Hather's foot slipped on the bank of the stream and he pitched heavily backwards into the water, falling full-length onto the shallow bed. The slip kept him alive for a moment longer, sending him falling away from the stroke that would have found his heart. But then Starkadder stood in the stream above him, beaded with sweat, groaning aloud as he vainly sought to battle Tyrfing's curse.

Hather had no time for thought, but a flight of memories flashed across his mind. Old Tisti reading the runes beside her fire. Hervara helpless beneath him on his father's high seat. A rocky castle, its roots shrouded in mist, carved from the mountains which jutted from the centre of a lake. A one-eyed man in a blue cloak with a wry smile upon his bearded features. A short, heavy figure, seated on a throne of solid gold . . .

And then his eyes fixed on Tyrfing, raised high above Starkadder's head, poised for a stroke that would split him open and set his blood free to mingle with the running crystal waters, tainting their clarity with the muddy crimson of his dying. Must it all be nothing more than the dream of a boy about to die?

The blade hissed excitedly as it began to cleave the air, flashing down in the arc that would end Hather's quest. Starkadder screwed his eyes shut, determined that he would not watch the blow come down, determined that he would not see Hather die. But the blow had begun, and the youth had no weapon to parry with. It must fall unchecked. Tyrfing must have its deadly way.

113

Hather closed his eyes, ready for death.

The arrow struck Starkadder's wrist just below Tyrfing's pommel, breaking the sword's unholy grip upon his fingers. As Starkadder reeled with the sudden pain Tyrfing splashed harmlessly into the stream beside Hather's prone body.

Starkadder gasped and clutched at his injured wrist. The arrow had passed between the bones of the forearm and lodged there, the bloody point on one side and the rest of the feathered shaft on the other. Somehow it had missed the blood vessels and only a halting trickle flowed from either side of the wound, glistening on the black cloth of the old warrior's sleeve. Hather opened his eyes, bewildered. About them a circle of horsemen, their approach unnoticed in the fury of Tyrfing's combat, was gathering.

Starkadder's eyes met those of Reindeer Bolli as the hunter unstrung his bow. The old man grinned and Bolli nodded, a faint smile upon his lips. Then men were dismounting and binding the old warrior fast with lengths of rope.

Somewhere behind Starkadder Thorvald Brotamad was chuckling to himself. One of his men asked: 'Do we kill him now?' but the captain shook his head.

'No,' he replied. 'We'll rest here a while. Then we'll take our prize back to King Oli. I think he'll enjoy seeing the blood–eagle carved into Starkadder's back.'

The gathering of the mist

THORVALD'S COMPANY rested beside the crossing of the streams until noon, then prepared for the journey back to Oli's court at Uppsala. Starkadder, tired and mystified by Tyrfing's malice, spoke to no one save Bolli, who drew out the arrow and cleaned and dressed his wound. Both men felt that a bond of understanding had grown between them, but it was one that remained unspoken.

Hather told his name to Thorvald Brotamad, and was invited by the captain to return with them to the court. He understood at least a part of what had happened in the course of his duel with Starkadder, and decided to leave Tyrfing where it lay beneath the waters of the streams. He was deeply puzzled by the old mercenary's claim that he had not killed Angantyr, but he did not yet know what to make of Starkadder's behaviour during their fight, and did not approach him for an explanation. He thought instead about the strange flight of images he had seen whilst waiting for the death that did not come. His faith in old Tisti's prophecies was renewed, even though it was Starkadder who had met him instead of the one who was supposed to come to help him.

Reindeer Bolli picked up Starkadder's sword from where it had fallen in the fight and offered it to Hather. The youth refused the weapon, still haunted by the vision of Starkadder wielding Tyrfing. The sword his mother had given him was more dangerous than he had supposed, and it was better that so treacherous a weapon be left beneath the waters of the streams. In time he would find another, but it would not be Starkadder's.

They broke camp and started back the way they had come. The afternoon was sunny, but there was an unusually chill wind for the time of year. Thorvald, in the lead, was cheerful and joked with the riders on either side of him, but his men did not share his obvious glee at the capture of Starkadder, and felt a darkness gathering in the depths of the sunlit afternoon.

By mid-afternoon the wind had dropped, and cold tendrils of grey-white mist gathered about the horses' hoofs on the path beneath them. In the distance the path was clear and unobscured, but the pallid tendrils clung to the riders, weaving themselves together into a strange ground-mist. One or two of Thorvald's soldiers, riding at the rear of the column, had the uncomfortable feeling of being watched, yet when they looked about there was no one in sight.

Bolli rode up the column until he was level with Thorvald Brotamad; his face was furrowed with concern.

'What's the matter, Bolli?' Thorvald snapped.

The hunter reined in his horse and scowled at the captain. 'We ought to stop and make camp,' he grunted. 'A mist is rising. We could lose our way.'

He pointed ahead as he spoke. In the distance, where minutes before there had been only the mountains and valleys, the tendrils of fog were knitting together.

Thorvald laughed unpleasantly. 'You're an old woman,' he sneered. 'We'll not get lost. Besides, there's good gold in this for all of us, once we've delivered the old man to King Oli. I'm not going to risk that by stopping unless we have to. The sooner we get back to Uppsala the better.'

Bolli felt his heart sink at Thorvald Brotamad's words. He reined in his mount and allowed the column to pass him until he could rejoin it at his own place. Thorvald was a greed-blinded fool. There was nothing natural in fog on a day like this, not before evening at any rate. They should stop and wait for the weather to clear. That was the sensible thing to do.

116

Starkadder sat his horse behind Bolli, his arms bound to his sides and his hands behind his back. As an extra precaution against escape his feet had been roped together beneath the horse's girth as well. His captivity had surprised him, but left him unafraid. In the past he'd suffered appalling injuries so often that pain held little to frighten him. And, if he died, it would simply put an end to his accursed existence. But he knew he could not die yet. The third betrayal had not been committed. That meant that he had to live on, to await the full working of the curse.

All around them the mist rose up to their stirrups.

Hather became impatient at so many unanswered questions. He spurred his mount forward until he came level with the prisoner. Then he held out his hand to take the reins from the soldier who led Starkadder's horse.

'It's all right,' he assured the man. 'He was trying to kill me, remember? I'll not set him free. I only want to talk to him.'

The soldier nodded and passed the reins across, then dropped back to the place which Hather had occupied in the mist-hidden column.

Beneath them, though only Bolli and Starkadder as yet knew it, the path was beginning to slope upwards.

Hather looked sideways at Starkadder. The old man was staring ahead, towards the fog thickening in front of his horse's ears.

'Why?' the youth asked.

The old Norwegian turned and peered into his face. Droplets of dew from the mist were beginning to form upon their cloaks and armour. 'Why what, Hather Lambisson?'

'It was as if . . . you didn't want to kill me. Why was that? And you said that you didn't kill my grandfather, but my mother says that you did.'

Starkadder smiled grimly. 'I didn't kill him, Hather. I would have done, but the Norns snatched the chance from my hands. Do you want to know what killed the chieftain Angantyr, young warrior? That did. The sword that hangs at your belt.'

Hather gasped, disbelieving, and reached down towards

117

his scabbard. The gasp became a groan as his fingers felt Tyrfing's hilt.

'I . . . I . . . left . . . it . . . it behind . . .' he stammered.

Starkadder nodded. 'Beneath the waters of the stream. I saw you. But curses are not so easily thwarted, my young friend. That's why Angantyr died. I struck Tyrfing from his hands and it should have flown away from him. It didn't. Instead it turned in the air and plunged back into his body. Forget what Hervara said, Hather. I've told you the truth. That's how Angantyr died. Not by my hand, but by Tyrfing.'

'Then . . . is that the curse?'

Starkadder scowled at the thickening fog. 'That is the curse,' he replied. 'Dvalin cursed Tyrfing that it should cause the death of whoever owns it. I only sought to disarm you back there, until I picked your sword up. I bear you no malice, boy. I'm so very tired of killing. I look forward to death in a way that I hope you will never do. I didn't want to do you harm. But Tyrfing has a life of its own. It tried to use my skill to cause your death. And it has greater powers than that. Turn back, Hather. Turn back to the streams. Lay Tyrfing again below their waters, then ride back here. By the time you rejoin this column it will be back in your scabbard, because it hasn't done Dvalin's work yet. You're still alive.'

Hather placed his fingers about the hilt and began to draw Tyrfing from the scabbard.

'Put it back!' Starkadder snapped. 'You were lucky last time. Bolli was able to stop me. The next time you draw that blade, though, no power on earth will be strong enough to keep it from killing you.'

Hather took his hand from the hilt. He didn't notice that the rising mist had reached the further end of the scabbard. Nor did he notice the heavy breathing of his mount, and the one he led, as they struggled against their sloping path.

In the distance a wolf howled and was answered by its mate. Above the riders, in the thickening gloom of the sky, two dark shapes circled on the tattered blackness of their wings.

Reindeer Bolli felt a sudden urge to spur forward to

where Thorvald Brotamad rode at the head of their company, but he knew that his words would be in vain and fought it back. Instead he slowed his horse, allowing the rider in front of him to fade into the shrouding mist before them, and dropped in beside Hather and Starkadder when they drew level.

'This is something more than a fog,' he grunted. 'The weather's wrong and it's not behaving properly. Fog comes down, and mist doesn't rise this high.'

Starkadder smiled grimly, listening as the wolves howled again, but he said nothing. Then the raucous screaming of the ravens answered the distant wolves.

Hather looked about him, noticing the mist for the first time. 'You're right,' he replied. 'It's too high off the ground.'

Only the sounds of the riders behind and ahead of them told them that they were still a part of the column. Starkadder's horse almost stumbled as a loose stone shot from beneath its hoof and rattled down the slope.

'And there was nothing like this on the way out,' Bolli added. 'No hill like this that we came down.'

'Hadn't you better warn Thorvald?' Starkadder asked, with a tiny edge of malice in his voice. 'He could lose his reward for my capture.'

The mist, terrifying and unearthly, continued to rise. The sounds of the vanishing column of riders began to fade.

Bolli leaned over and whispered to Starkadder briefly: 'This is from Lambi Nef.' He smiled. 'But I'd have done it myself anyway, even without his prompting.' Then he cut the ropes that bound the old man's feet beneath his horse.

As Bolli sat up again he continued: 'Thorvald wouldn't stop even if I could find him in this mist. I don't know what's happening, my friend, but whatever it is I can see the hand of the gods in it somewhere. Will you forgive me that arrow?'

Starkadder smiled grimly. 'It worked my own will, as well as yours,' he replied. 'It was a welcome shot, and I forgive it freely.' Then he turned to Hather. 'You see, lad? There's no feud between us now. You've seen Tyrfing's

119

power. You must know that I've told you the truth about Angantyr's death. So, will you let it rest here?'

Above them a raven cried again, muffled by the writhing fog. Reindeer Bolli held out his knife once again and severed the bonds which held Starkadder's arms and hands. Hather handed the old man the reins of his horse.

Starkadder studied Bolli's seamed face. 'Why are you doing this?' he demanded.

'No man should die by the blood-eagle,' came the answer. 'Something tells me that Oli's reign will be over soon, and that you have a part to play in that. I know your story, Starkadder. There is a power that's keeping you for the days to come. I feared you back there. And I fear you even more now. When I nocked that arrow to my bow I wanted to aim it at your neck, to kill you. But my hands would not hold steady on the shot, for the first time in my life. Then something told me to aim for your wrist, to stop you killing this lad, so that's what I did. Something is guarding both of you. That's why this fog has been wrapped about us. I don't know what it is you have to do, but you'll do it better free. Besides, if you leave the column now, it might just save the rest of us.'

'From what?' Hather asked, puzzled by the hunter's words.

'From whatever is waiting for you in the fog,' was Bolli's reply. 'I'll not argue with gods' or Norns' work. Go on, get away from here, and the gods be with you both.'

Without noticing they had stopped upon the path, but the riders in the column behind them were neither catching up nor passing. 'I almost forgot,' Reindeer Bolli said. He reached down beside him and took Starkadder's sword from a sling at his girth. As he handed it back to the ancient warrior a questioning look came over Starkadder's face.

'I was riding ahead of you,' the hunter smiled. 'Remember? It must have fallen upon the path.'

Starkadder nodded, then pulled on the reins, forcing his mount's head away from the direction of the column. He set his heels to the animal's flanks, then changed his mind and held it still.

'What about Omund?' he asked. 'I know Oli too well.

He'll have taken steps to make sure I don't get to Omund. What's he done, Bolli?'

The hunter took a deep breath and his dark eyes glittered through the mist. He was beginning to realise that the simple act of freeing Starkadder wasn't all that would be required of him. 'As you know,' he began, 'Omund is being held under guard in a fortress just south of the Dalalven, about two days' hard riding from Uppsala. He's heavily guarded, with two or three hundred of Oli's best men around him. As we were leaving to come after you yesterday, King Oli was giving new orders to Vermund Bjarnisson.'

'I know him well,' Starkadder nodded. 'A good soldier. He's loyal to Oli because he is directly sworn to the king's service. But he doesn't like Oli any more than I do. Did you hear what his orders were?'

'I did. He's to take command of the fortress at Dalalven as quickly as he can travel there. He's also to arrange for a further hundred guards to be posted.'

Starkadder chuckled to himself. 'Oli must have been shitting himself in case I decided to go that way. Four hundred men to guard one prisoner, and his own son at that?'

'There's more, I'm afraid,' Bolli added. 'From what I've heard Vermund has orders to kill Omund at the first sign of a rescue.'

The old warrior nodded as he listened. It sounded right. Oli would give such an order. If he'd carve the blood–eagle on men loyal to him because of his own crazed suspicions, then he'd certainly order the death of his son. Omund's only chance lay in the fact that Vermund had been given the order to be carried out at his own discretion. Vermund Bjarnisson was a soldier, not a killer. He was a sound and experienced commander who fought when it was necessary and withdrew only to save needless slaughter. He didn't enjoy spilling blood for its own sake. If the ordering of Omund's death was in his hands, then there was a good chance that the order would never be given. It might be worth the gamble after all.

'What will you do, Starkadder?' Bolli asked.

'As you say, my friend, there's something in this fog that wants us. Until we're free of it none of us is his own master. I might ask you the same question. Will you rejoin Thorvald?'

Bolli shook his head and pulled a leather hood over his cropped black hair to keep out the dampness of the mist. 'That was that I'd intended to do,' he replied, 'but I think that, like many of Thorvald's men, I'm not going to want to face Oli when Thorvald returns without you. The king's not going to be a happy man, Starkadder.'

'So what will you do?'

The tracker sighed and leaned forward in the saddle. 'I'm going north, away from Oli,' he muttered. 'I've had enough of that mad old bastard and his whims. It's time I made my way home for a while, back to Bjarmaland. And you, Starkadder, what do you intend to do now?'

'I've nothing in mind at present except getting out of this accursed fog,' came the reply. 'I've a growing feeling that I'm not my own master any more, hunter. In fact I don't think that any of us are, not even Oli. I left Uppsala because I'd have killed the king if I'd stayed. I don't want to kill him, Bolli. I've turned down a lot of gold for doing the job, and a job is exactly what it is. Besides, he expects me to kill him, and I don't want to give him the satisfaction of being right, I want to disappoint him, and anyone else who might be trying to shape my future for me.'

He sighed wearily and leaned forward on his horse's neck. 'You know my story, Bolli,' he added. 'Everything you've heard is true. I'm grateful to you for your kindness this day. You're too good a man to serve Oli, and I wish you luck, wherever you go. Perhaps one day we'll meet again. And now, farewell.'

He extended his gloved hand and he and Bolli grasped wrists. Only as their fingers locked did the tracker realise that he was holding the wrist his arrow had pierced, yet Starkadder showed no sign of pain. His eyes sought out those of the old mercenary, who read the unspoken question in their depths.

'I heal quickly,' he said. 'It's a small, yet welcome, part of the curse upon me.'

Bolli nodded, released his grip, and offered his wrist to Hather. Starkadder spurred his horse gently and walked it

122

into the concealing mist. Hather was struggling to understand what was taking place around him. His upbringing had left him ignorant of the tangled politics of King Oli's court, and all this talk of betrayals and the authorised murder of kin was contrary to what Lambi Nef had taught him to regard as good and right.

The hunter read Hather's face and grinned at him. 'Go with Starkadder,' he said. 'He's a better man than his legend tells us. I know that now.'

'And . . . what about you?' the youth asked. 'Will you be all right?'

'If I'm not,' Bolli replied, 'then I have only myself to blame for it. You know, it's time I went back to my homeland. I've a feeling that I will never see it again if I don't go now. And feelings like that it's often unwise to ignore.'

Hather nodded. There was something in the quiet sureness of men such as Bolli and Starkadder, men who lived according to their instincts, which gave them a natural advantage over others.

'Then . . . we won't meet again?'

The hunter laughed softly. 'Whatever the Norns have written, we shall do,' he replied. Then he too urged his horse away, echoing the distant, mist-muffled sounds of Thorvald Brotamad's soldiers.

For a moment Hather felt terribly alone in the fog. It wrapped him round like a soft, dank shroud, cutting him off from the world he knew. But he felt blinded by more than fog. He had dishonoured the father he loved by the rape of the mother who had filled him with disgust. Yet that disgust was fading, replaced by a sort of self-loathing. He had met Starkadder and failed to kill him. He was chained to an accursed sword, Tyrfing, and his life was governed by old Tisti's rune-cast.

He was a child trying to be a man. He rode with the man his mother claimed had killed his grandfather, though he now doubted that. This killer, this Starkadder, commanded the respect of men, even those who had tried to kill him. What power not of the gods could make a man like Bolli free the game he had stalked and taken?

123

Hather smiled bitterly to himself. What power beneath the gods indeed? Had he not heard the wolves and ravens through the mist?

He peered about him, seeking in the whiteness the tall, black figure he knew would be waiting amongst the curling tendrils of the mist. He was not disappointed.

For a moment longer he hesitated. It was all so strange, so terrifying. In that moment he knew himself to be in the hands of the gods, even as Starkadder was. And the hands of the gods reach into no man's life without leaving a taste of fear.

For a while they climbed the path in silence, shivering as the clammy fog thinned about them. Then Hather asked: 'Starkadder, where are we going?'

'I think you know where we're going better than I do,' Starkadder's reply came back. 'Wherever it is, I hope we get there soon. This weather may be easing, but I've lost the little warmth my old bones had.'

After that they didn't speak for a while. Hather knew now that the old Norwegian was the companion that Tisti had promised him, and that they were fated to ride together. Somewhere ahead of them must lie the gates of Trollheim and the audience with the dwarf-king Dvalin. Perhaps somewhere in the mist-shrouded future lay the lifting of Tyrfing's curse.

Starkadder, for his part, did not think a great deal about their journey. He had heard the wolves and the ravens. He had known the power of the curse upon Hather's sword. And he knew now that, sooner or later, he would fulfil his own bane with the killing of King Oli.

The mist thinned enough for them to see twin peaks looming out of the greyness ahead of them. As they drew closer the fog rolled back from their path, forming dense banks to either side, banks from which solid walls of mountain rock rose sheer and unscaleable into the twilight sky which brooded purple overhead. The cliffs looked like a vast gateway, opened for them to pass through.

Between the massive flanks of rock Hather could see a scene which he already knew. On the other side the ground fell away, sloping downwards towards the shores of an endless lake. The water itself showed black and unfriendly through clear patches in the haze which masked its surface, a haze which thickened into a dense shrouding towards the centre, a shrouding which hid the base of a jagged, jutting rock from which a rock-hewn castle soared, evil and proud. It was solid, so solid, with its towers and ramps and archways. It reared blackly upwards, intricately carved with monstrous gargoyles in a fashion which their viking eyes had never seen before. Its heights stabbed unevenly at the deep purple of the evening sky, and dark and tattered shapes flapped about its spires on lightless wings.

Starkadder urged his horse forward, into the rocky entrance, but it refused to move. So he dismounted and tried to enter on foot, but there was a thickening of the air which, though yielding at first, forced him gently but firmly back. His brows knitted together above his deep-set eyes and he drew his sword. The blade rebounded from the unseen barrier and flew from his fingers to clang against the darkening rocks.

A cloak-wrapped figure stepped from the mist beside them, bearing a burning torch which cast a shadow at its feet. Its face was hidden beneath the brim of a broad hat, and it was chuckling softly to itself.

'I think you need my help now,' said the one-eyed man.

CHAPTER SIX

Through the gates of Trollheim

AT THE first flashing of the torchlight, before the strange figure had uttered its first word in a deep, amused tone of voice, Starkadder retrieved his sword and stood ready to use it. Hather, his surprise-widened eyes never leaving the blue-cloaked stranger, slowly dismounted and stood beside his companion.

From beneath the hat's low brim a single eye glinted at them, its expression unfathomable. Nor did the mouth give any clue as to the one-eyed man's intentions, for it lay hidden beneath a thick tangle of grey beard.

Neither of the travellers spoke. The youth was still wonderstruck by the glimpse of the castle beyond the invisible gates, the castle he had seen when he lay waiting for Tyrfing to kill him in the water at the meeting of the streams. Starkadder's deep eyes, the torchlight flickering in them, were staring down at the strange figure, not quite as tall as himself. In one hand it held the torch, now raised to cast a wide circle of light about them. In the other it bore a staff of blackened yew-wood, a staff with runes cut along its length and stained darker than the wood with blood.

'Are you Allfather?' Starkadder demanded, his voice as well as his words betraying uncertainty.

The figure laughed softly. 'Many have asked me that,' he replied. 'It's about the only advantage I can think of to having only one eye. Perhaps I am a part of Allfather, Starkadder, as indeed we all are.'

'You speak like a fool,' the old mercenary grunted. 'Or a sorcerer. How do you know my name?'

'Everyone knows Starkadder,' the one-eyed man replied, his beard twitching in token of a smile beneath it. 'After all, my ancient friend, you've lived quite long enough for your legend to spread throughout the north. And you, young warrior,' he added, turning slightly towards Hather, 'you are the son of Lambi Nef. I've been waiting for you.'

This statement did nothing to quiet Hather's unease. 'How did you know I was coming?' he asked.

'Old Tisti told me,' came the smiling answer. 'We are of a kind, you see, that old witch and I.'

He inclined his head towards Starkadder and looked at the naked sword in the ancient Norwegian's hand. 'Put up your weapon,' he urged, still smiling under his beard. 'You have no need of it here just yet. I mean you both no harm, and you should not mean harm to me. You need me too much for that.'

'Then . . . you are the one who helped King Svafrlami?'

'I am, Hather. My name is Harbard, and I and I alone held open these gates of Trollheim for that unhappy man. You see, none of us is his own master. All that is to be has been written by the Norns. Even Odin himself must follow their decrees. The only difference in his case is that he sometimes knows what they have written, and deigns to tell those who serve him. That, young man, is the true secret of prophecy.

'You blame your mother Hervara for giving you the accursed sword that hangs at your side,' Harbard continued. 'Indeed, some of the blame is hers, but you should not think of her too badly. She only obeyed the decree of the Norns, as did Svafrlami when he took Tyrfing out of Trollheim and into the lands of men. That is why I helped him, because there was work for that sword to do. And there is still work for it to do, Hather.

'Hervara took the sword from Angantyr's burial mound, in the glimpses of the moon. She obeyed the prompting of

127

the Norns then, and she obeyed them also when she passed the blade to you. Now you will obey in turn, like a *tafl*-piece moved upon its chequered board. You will not see the strategy of their play, but you will none the less move as they direct you. That is why you're here.'

'Then these,' Hather ventured, gesturing towards the rocky pylons which towered before and above them, 'are the gates of Trollheim?'

Harbard nodded. 'They are. And beyond them, rising from the lake like a broken fang in the mouth of the Midgard Serpent, is Trollheim itself. When you are through the gates, go down to the shore of the lake. As I knew that you were coming, so does King Dvalin. You will find a boat there waiting to take you to the dwarf-king.'

Starkadder turned towards the apparently passable gateway and prodded it once again with his sword. Again the weapon flew from his fingers. He faced the one-eyed man again and scowled at him.

'And how are we supposed to get through there?' he demanded.

A twinkle of amusement came into Harbard's single eye. 'With a key,' he smiled. 'There is a lock upon those gates. You cannot see it, but it's there all the same, as surely as if it were forged from iron.'

'And where is this key?'

'In my hand, Starkadder. Here.'

Harbard held out the staff of blackened yew, walked calmly into the centre of the narrow gateway and laid it upon the ground, its ends touching the rock-faces on either side.

'The gates are open,' he grinned, 'and Dvalin is waiting for you.'

'How do we get out again?' Hather asked.

'The same way, young warrior. Don't be afraid. I'll be here, waiting for you. Only you and Starkadder have moves to make upon this board, at this time. The rest of us, myself, Dvalin, even Oli and Lambi Nef and Reindeer Bolli, can only wait for you to make those moves.'

'And if we don't?' Starkadder snapped. 'What happens then?'

128

'You have no choice,' Harbard smiled back. 'The Norns are the players of this game. We are merely the pieces.'

Starkadder nodded slightly and turned towards the pylons. He strode determinedly between them, stepping over the staff of yew-wood, and the invisible gates of Trollheim did not stop him.

Hather hesitated for a few seconds, then followed the ancient mercenary through the open gates. On the further side he turned and looked back. Harbard stood watching beyond the threshold of a massive archway cut from the living rock. To either side of the arch huge doors of iron-bound oak strained to close upon the staff.

The one-eyed man watched their progress down towards the lake. As the figures of Hather and Starkadder dwindled into the darkness, that of Harbard seemed to grow in stature. He walked across to where the two horses awaited the return of their riders and whispered into their ears. They remained calm and untroubled as grey shapes with hungry amber eyes padded silently out of the mist and nuzzled at Harbard's legs.

'Leave the horses be,' he muttered, stroking the wolves' shaggy pelts. 'Starkadder will find you food before too many days have passed.'

His voice was tired and strained. The irony which had sharpened it before was gone with the passing of the old man and the youth through Trollheim's gates.

He looked up to the darkened sky. Two ragged shapes circled there, watching their master on the ground. Somehow both the ravens and the wolves divined his thoughts. Somehow they knew how he dreaded what was still to come, even more than old Starkadder dreaded the third betrayal. And yet they accepted it, because they had to. Allfather had read the decrees of the Norns. He had no power to change those aweful runes, to thwart the destiny that they proclaimed and save the Yngling dynasty from dissolution and decay. The long years of waiting were done, and only the doing remained.

CHAPTER SEVEN

Tyrfing

STARKADDER SCRIED the surface of the lake, seeking to probe beneath its troubled surface. Their approach had shown the two companions that this was something more than water, and that the haze which hung about its surface was more than ordinary mist. In places, away from the shore, the liquid bubbled and spat into the air, its wicked droplets scattering the mist, Here, where they stood, there was no such bubbling, simply a swirling of iridescent currents.

Hather's gaze was obsessed by the rock-hewn castle which towered above the milky haze of the lake. He had known craftsmen, of course, who worked wood and metal in intricate patterns of animals and trees by way of ornament and decoration. But they did nothing like this. They built in wood and carved in wood or bone. Roughly shaped stones and monoliths were set up to bear runic inscriptions, but stone was not used for building. Palaces were collections of longhouses arranged within a stockade or embankment. Some longhouses had two storeys, but never three. And yet here, in the kingdom of the dwarfs, there rose a building of stone set in the centre of a lake, a building which rose storey upon storey in spires and turrets, its walls carved in nightmare shapes festooned with the forms of unknown, mythic beasts.

The mist that clung to the rock parted to reveal to

130

Hather's straining eyes a gateway carved in the shape of a serpent's open mouth, with twin stone fangs, each the length of a man, jutting down towards the shimmering water. Then, between the fangs, he made out a dim, unlit movement and, very slowly, a shape began to glide towards them.

'Starkadder!' he called, his voice echoing strangely back from the encircling mountains.

The old man left his puzzling over the unnatural-coloured, swirling liquid. He too saw the parting of the haze and the shape which slid closer to them across the bubbling lake.

'It's the boat,' he grunted.

It was indeed a boat, and yet, like the dwelling beyond, it was one such as they had never seen before. Its prow and stern were high, like those of a viking longship or trading vessel, but they were intricately carved into writhing pyramids of strange, forgotten creatures, beings with serpent-tails and peculiarly bent legs. Some of them were finned or bore strange frilled crests about their necks, and the head which surmounted the prow had some of the features of the traditional viking dragon, but without horns or ears, and with flattened nostrils.

A dim lamp burned amidships, shedding enough light as the vessel drew nearer to show the watchers on the shore that it was made, not of planks, but of blocks of fine-joined stone.

'A stone boat?' Hather demanded in amazement.

Starkadder nodded. 'The lake isn't water,' he explained. 'I don't know what it is, but wood would rot in it in no time at all. I don't like this, Hather. I don't like this at all, but I'll not turn back from it now.'

Hather held his silence, knowing full well that there could be no turning back now, even if they had a choice.

The boat touched the shore and a small head appeared above the salamander-carven prow. In shape it was more or less human, but rounder, and the faint glimmering of the evening light reflecting from its unnatural baldness matched the lambent flickering in its bulging eyes. The head was followed by shoulders and arms that were stunted and

131

foreshortened. Hands with talon-like nails gripped the stone sides of the vessel.

Starkadder felt his young companion's unease and laid a reassuring hand upon Hather's shoulder. The old mercenary had lived so long in a world where the gods, Norns and dwarfs were real that he could hardly know the shock which such a discovery might be to the boy.

All Hather's doubts about the myths and legends which the travelling skalds had told beside the longhouse fire were vanishing before the haze of the lake which guarded Dvalin's castle.

'Stay there,' the dwarf squeaked, its voice high as a bat-squeal. 'Don't get wet or you'll never get well again.' The little creature chuckled, a sound which chilled even Starkadder and brought up the hairs on the nape of his neck, and reached down inside the boat to bring up a flat length of worn stone. Its edges were polished and the broader sides bore a criss-cross cutting so that whoever walked across it would not slip. Hather knew that it must weigh several times more than a large man, but the tiny figure in the boat handled it easily, sliding it out across the gunwale until the end came to rest upon the shore.

'Come aboard, servant of Tyrfing,' came the dwarf's high-pitched voice. 'And you, old killer. Come aboard, Hather and Starkadder.'

The old warrior held Hather back and walked ahead of him up the stone gangplank. The dwarf reached out a clawed hand to help him into the boat, and as Starkadder took it a thrill of revulsion shuddered through his frame.

'It's all right, Hather,' he called back. 'If it takes my weight it'll take yours.'

The youth stepped onto the length of stone and the dwarf scowled at Starkadder. 'Do you question dwarfish craftsmanship?' he demanded. 'Do you mistrust the work of those who made Thor's hammer and the necklace Brisingamen which Freya paid for so delightfully?'

'I mistrust all that I don't understand,' came the old man's reply. 'And I don't understand stone boats and lakes that aren't filled with water.' He held up his hand to help Hather, who stepped down into the boat.

132

The dwarf continued to scowl as it hauled in the gangplank and stowed it on the deck of the boat. Now that they were aboard they could see that the creature was naked, except for a loincloth held in place by an intricately worked leather belt and a pair of boots almost as tall as its legs. The flesh of the torso and arms was blotched with livid, rigid scars where the liquid in the lake had splashed it.

'Well now,' the diminutive figure grinned, more with malice than with humour, 'we mustn't keep King Dvalin waiting, must we?'

The boat turned, apparently of itself, and started the return journey towards the serpent's-mouth gate in the rock.

'Frightened?' asked the dwarf.

'If we knew how to sail this boat,' Starkadder replied, touching his hand to the hilt of his sword, 'I'd show you what fear really is.'

After that exchange they travelled in silence across the lake. Every so often a tendril of mist crept above the gunwale and lingered in the boat. They saw that the dwarf held its breath rather than breathe in the acrid fumes that floated around the haze and did likewise. Once Hather could not avoid it and he coughed violently and his eyes began to stream with tears.

The gate loomed closer in front of the squirming stone salamanders on the prow, and Hather gazed wide-eyed. The lightless maw was wider and higher than he had at first thought, and the massive fangs, each as long as the boat, were ragged at the ends where they had been eroded by the lapping of the lake. The boat passed between them and a heavy rattling sound began to deafen their ears. As the noise increased, in the distance of the tunnel a light began to grow beyond the outline of an arch.

In a few more minutes they came out into the torchlight and saw that the boat, drawn by chains, had been travelling the length of a narrow canal beneath the castle. Here the canal ended, its stone banks squared off on a level with the sides of the boat. In front of them a massive windlass, wound by she-dwarfs, hauled the vessel to its mooring. It shuddered to a halt as dwarfish soldiers trotted out of the dark and formed a cordon about the winding mechanism, their weapons turned towards Hather and Starkadder.

The boatman scampered up onto the landing-stage, beckoning Starkadder and Hather to follow him, his ungainly gestures indicating that there might be some danger in any delay. They followed him, and the cordon about the she-dwarfs, small lank-haired creatures with lumpish bodies and even uglier faces than the males, closed up behind them as the boatman urged them into a narrow corridor. Hather, looking back over his shoulder for a moment, saw the women leave the windlass and stalk the retreating cordon at a wary distance, their bulging breasts flopping at each step. Then both the travellers and the cordon were inside the corridor, and the last soldier slammed a heavy door in the faces of the scowling she-dwarfs.

'They have a taste for mortal men,' the boatman explained with a vicious leer, 'which is not shared by the objects of their desire. But don't worry yourselves about it. Your escort will keep you safe until you have seen King Dvalin.'

'And after that?' Hather demanded, as they continued along the narrow passageway.

'That's up to the king,' their guide grinned at them, showing rows of sharp and snaggled teeth.

The corridor turned a sharp corner, then ended. Hather and Starkadder found themselves at the bottom of what appeared to be a gigantic well-shaft, except that at its centre, twisting upwards for round upon round, its width diminishing to nothing with its enormous height, was a spiral staircase.

And what a staircase. For the first time since the stone barge had entered the serpent gateway the travellers began to admire the skill of the dwarfish builders. The central shaft and the steps themselves appeared to have been carved from a single pillar of rock. Each step was supported from beneath by an arching bracket in the shape of some mythic creature from a world younger than theirs. The outer edges were decorated with delicate tracery, in places so fine that it looked like the work of giant spiders, and each step was wide enough to take four men shoulder to shoulder, without the outermost being in danger of a fall or the innermost being crowded towards the central column. The staircase stood alone, taller than their eyes could travel, in the middle of the shaft, never touching the sides.

'King Dvalin is waiting for you,' said the boatman. 'Up there.' And he trotted back into the corridor.

Starkadder and Hather looked behind them. Their escort stood to seal the passageway off from them, and the base of the shaft, lit by cressets set about the curving walls, revealed no other way out. Each with his hand brushing the hilt of his sword, Hather and Starkadder walked towards the first step and began their giddying climb.

There were no cressets or torches upon the staircase, but the faint light of evening filtered dimly through irregular windows in the outer wall of the shaft. Sometimes there would be three or four windows close together, but then they could climb several rounds without seeing one at all. Nor were there two windows like each other.

As they climbed Starkadder began to gain an idea of the plan of the castle. The windows were in fact the few gaps between the squirming, interlocking figures which covered the outside of the central tower. That alone could explain their apparently random positions and forms. It also explained why the delicate symmetry and inherent strength of the staircase was not matched in its artistry by the windows.

The climb seemed endless. After several minutes Hather paused and peered down over the edge of the steps. He gave a gasp of amazement at the reversal of perspective. Now the light from the cressets around the base of the shaft was nothing more than the winking of distant stars, and the staircase diminished alarmingly below him, as if he were looking from the hilt down the blade of a sword.

'Keep walking, lad,' Starkadder muttered. 'The sooner we're off this infernal thing the better I'll like it.'

Hather came away from the edge, and they resumed their slow spiral upwards to where the dwarf-king was waiting for them.

At last the staircase came to an end, levelling out into a slightly curving bridge which spanned the distance between the final step and the edge of the shaft. The bridge had no retaining walls, and the old Norwegian knew that if a man fell from it it would take more numbers than he knew how to count before he reached the bone-shattering stone floor.

They crossed the bridge together. During the climb their eyes had become accustomed to the uncertain light of the shaft. Now, in the centre of the bridge, they blinked and fought for balance as a door at the further end opened, dazzling them with the yellow brilliance of the cresset beyond.

The long shadow of a dwarfish sentry wearing full mail and an ornate helmet plumed with bleached human hair was thrown along the bridge towards them. The dwarf carried a spear twice as tall as himself, and his thin high voice ordered: 'This way, mortals. King Dvalin is waiting for you.'

'Well,' Starkadder muttered grimly, 'we've come this far.'

He stepped off the bridge and pushed past the waist-high dwarf. Hather followed, and they found themselves outside the castle, on a balcony as exquisitely and grotesquely carved as the rest of the tower. The balcony was narrow, and ran all the way round the outside of the tower.

Soon the curve of the wall hid the dwarfish soldier from their sight. A few more steps and they saw a high seat of gilded wood, set with precious gems and metals. Beyond the balcony the castle descended beneath them to the mist-wrapped lake, active clusters of bubbles showing through clear patches on the hazy surface. In the distance loomed the mountains, jutting and jagged as the castle itself.

As they edged nearer to the throne, the wind whipping at their hair and clutching at their cloaks, they began to make out a dark shape which waited upon it. Slowly a whitish face appeared, mostly hidden by a heavy hood. Yellow eyes, amber like those of Odin's wolves, smoked in deep-sunk sockets. The seated figure, probably about four feet in height, was dressed in a simple robe of slate-grey. The only decoration or jewellery the travellers could see were the ornate rings which decorated the taloned fingers, fingers that were hooked tight about the arms of the throne.

'I love the air,' came a voice from the depths of the seated figure. It was little more than a whisper, but even that

136

whisper had a greater depth and majesty than that of the boatman or the sentry with the man's-hair plume. 'I love the air,' it repeated. 'It is cruel that I can only take it when the sun has left the sky.'

Dvalin rose and looked at them. His features were sharp and spare, and the fires that burned in his amber eyes held flickering malice. He studied Hather and Starkadder for some moments, then raised a clawed hand and rubbed at his firm, beardless chin.

'I envy you,' he sighed, 'and it is not wise to arouse my envy. Still, there's nothing to be done about it. It's simply a fact of life that men can live in the sunlight, but dwarfs are turned to stone by it. Did you see the decorations about these walls as you approached?' he asked, sweeping a bejewelled hand out across the balcony. 'Did you think that they were carvings, Hather? Did you think that, old Starkadder? Did you perhaps wonder at the skill which fashioned them?

'Not so,' he continued. 'These shapes are the shapes of the condemned, of those who have transgressed against my rule, and the rule of my forefathers. We set them there in the hours before the dawn, and the sun is their sentence. It turns them into stone, my friends, into the finest carvings you have ever seen. It would do the same to me, if I came up here during the hours of daylight. Do you see the shapes?' He gestured upwards, towards the dark, tattered stains which wheeled and circled about the jutting tower. 'Those are their spirits, and the guardians of this place. They hope that by their service they may one day be returned to their bodies and know true life again. They are deluded, of course, for what the sun has done no amount of dwarfish magic can undo. But I do not tell them that. I leave them to circle and to serve, hopeless in their hope. They speak to me of things they learn. They saw you pass through the gates of Trollheim, and told me. When they see you leave, if they see you leave, they will tell me that as well. But you've not come to this place to listen to my mumblings, have you?'

He began to walk around the balcony. Hather, shivering with a chillness that was more than just the wind, drew his cloak close about him and followed. Starkadder glanced up at the turret roof of contorted, calcined bodies, then walked after them. Somewhere, a long way away beyond the mountains, a wolf was howling to the night.

'You've come to see me about Tyrfing,' Dvalin resumed, not pausing in his short-strided walk about the turret. 'You want me to lift the curse it bears, do you not?'

Hather nodded, then realised that the dwarf could not see the gesture. 'Yes,' he said, in a voice so small and quiet he could hardly believe it was his own.

'And what then? It becomes just another sword in the Midgard lands of men? Or shall you fulfil the destiny that has been written for you by the Norns, and kill the man who travels with you?'

'I . . . don't know.'

Dvalin suddenly stopped and turned back towards him. 'Neither do I, young Hather,' he grinned. 'What do you have to say about it, old Starkadder? Are you to be killed by Tyrfing?'

The old man's pale eyes glittered in the twilight. 'The Norns have written what is to be,' he growled. 'No power in the realms of man, nor in Trollheim, nor even beyond the walls of Asgard where the gods mark out their games with men, can alter what the sisters cut in runes as they sit beneath Yggdrasil at Urd's Well. The problem is, King Dvalin, that they don't tell me what they write, so how should I know what Tyrfing is destined for?'

The dwarf-king studied Starkadder's face with his yellow eyes, and his grin slowly faded, giving way to an expression of surpassing sadness and pity. 'You're a wise man, Starkadder,' he said. 'Your lives have not been all in vain. There is a blood-feud between this youth and you, yet you have learned to travel together, and are even friends, though you may not yet know as much. That sword,' he went on, gesturing to where Tyrfing hung at Hather's side, 'was made for me. I helped to craft it, as did the other three who worked with me on the necklace Brisingamen for the lovely whore-goddess Freya. She paid a fearsome price for her bauble, old man. We were repulsive to her, as we are to you. No, do not protest and seek to use words to flatter me. I know that we have no beauty in the eyes of men and women of Midgard. Yet she wanted Brisingamen, and she agreed to pay our price. It hurt her, you know. The four of us had her for a night. In the dawning, of course, we were gone, and she had her necklace. When we left she was clutching it in trembling fingers, and moaning with the pain of sating our lust. But that was the price.

'Svafrlami might have bought the sword in the same way, or perhaps in another. You see, we have no love of men, Starkadder. We neither love them nor wish to show them kindness. They are not our kind, and never will be. As I said before, we envy them the sun. Well, the goddess Freya whored with us for Brisingamen, but King Svafrlami would do nothing to have Tyrfing. True, he offered us gold, but what use is gold to a race which is master of the hidden places of the earth? We have more than enough of that yellow shit, Starkadder, and we told him so. Now, had he chosen to service a dozen or so she-dwarfs, he might have asked for Tyrfing and been given it. But, you see, they're revolting, even to us. So he stole the sword from me. He stole it and fled back through the gates of Trollheim. He stole it with my curse ringing in his ears, and he has since learned that a dwarfish curse is not to be ignored.'

Dvalin broke off and cupped his hands to his mouth, calling a single name out into the night.

'Svafrlami!'

A dark shape, something between a bat and a herring, flapped through the sky on tattered pinions and perched clumsily upon the rail of the balcony. Its form seemed to alter with every passing moment, and the only constancy in its darkness lay in sad, red eyes which burned within the shapeless head.

'Enough,' said Dvalin, almost gently, and the enslaved spirit of the dead king flapped wearily back into the night.

'You've made your point, Dvalin,' Starkadder growled, 'What's your price for taking the curse off Tyrfing?'

The dwarf-king eyed the old mercenary strangely. 'An astute question,' he observed. 'But the answer is not so easily had, my friend. Listen to me now, and I'll try to explain something that I'm not even certain of myself.

'For Tyrfing to be stolen from me at all the deed must

have been written by the Norns. It must also have been written by them that you and this young man would come here tonight, bringing the accursed weapon with you. I knew that you would come, long before my shapeless sentinels could tell me of your coming. I knew you would come because there is a game that the Norns are playing with us all, even with me, old Starkadder.

'Think back, young Hather, to the runes old Tisti read for you. Tell me what they were.'

'The first was *Othil*,' Hather began. 'She told me that it signified inheritance, and stood for the sword Tyrfing. The second was the rune *Thurisaz*, and told of your curse, King Dvalin.'

'And the third rune? What was that?'

'*Raido*, the journey-rune.'

Dvalin nodded to himself, his eyes studying the fine, grey hairs on the back of his hand. 'You were to come to me for the curse to be lifted. What were you to do then?'

Starkadder answered for him. 'He was to avenge his grandfather, Angantyr. Hather's mother, Hervara, believes that I killed Angantyr. She did not know that his taking of the sword from Svafrlami's corpse had transferred the curse to her father, and that it was Tyrfing which killed him, not I. Though I would have done, if your blade hadn't beaten me to it, Dvalin.'

'And now, Hather? What are you to do now?'

'I don't know any more,' came the weak reply.

'And if I lift the curse from Tyrfing? Will that be the next move in the game which the Norns are playing? And you, Starkadder, do you know what you must do next?'

'I do, King Dvalin. I've tried to fight it, but I know what I have to do.'

Dvalin stared at the old man. Then he said: 'Yes, I believe you do. Your own curse is drawing towards its end, old Starkadder. You will betray King Oli, even as this boy's father seeks to betray King Oli.'

Hather's eyes widened and he stared at the dark-clad dwarf. 'My father?' he asked. 'Lambi Nef is to betray the man he serves?'

'That was not what I said,' came the curt reply. 'I said that

140

he *seeks* to betray King Oli the Great. Seeking is not doing, young viking. You may look for gold, yet die a pauper on your quest. And you, Starkadder, will you put Omund on his father's throne?'

'It is his by right of inheritance.'

Dvalin sighed and turned to look out over the lake. 'So the game shall be played out,' he whispered to himself. 'This is a cruel world,' he continued, his voice stronger again. 'And the cruelty is not all of your making, or of mine.

'You asked me for my price, old Starkadder, for taking my bale-words from Hather's sword. Oh yes, it's Hather's sword now. I no longer lay any claim to the weapon. But tell me, young viking, are you willing to surrender Tyrfing for a while, in order that the curse can be lifted from it?'

Hather worked his tongue inside the dry cavern of his mouth. Once the spittle was running and he was sure of his voice, he replied: 'I will do what has to be done, King Dvalin.'

The dwarf nodded. 'Brave words,' he replied, 'for one who knows that my price may be terrible. Yet you have come here with a companion, Hather, and it is of him that I shall ask it. Give the sword to Starkadder. Now.'

'And what am I to do with it, Dvalin?'

'Nothing that you have not already decided to do, old killer.'

Slowly, carefully, distrustful of the weapon's power, Hather drew it from its scabbard and handed it to the ancient mercenary, holding it by the blade with hands wrapped about with the edges of his cloak. Starkadder took the proffered hilt and held the sword point down whilst he drew his own blade and passed it to the youth. Once the exchange was completed he sheathed Tyrfing in his own scabbard, then looked up at Dvalin with pale, suspicious eyes.

'Very well,' he grunted. 'We are ready, King. What now?'

'Do what you have to do, Starkadder. Then the curse will be broken and you can return Tyrfing to your young friend. The Norns have already decided what we all must do, but if you hold Tyrfing until your weird is played out your own accursed destiny will keep the destructive power of the sword in check.'

Starkadder smiled bitterly. He too was beginning to recognise the power of the Norns in his overlong life. Now he began to understand the strange promptings which had taken him to the confluence of the streams and his meeting with Hather. Now, at last, he understood why the youth had been saved from Tyrfing's blows. But Dvalin must spell it out in full. The old man was going to have that much satisfaction.

'Tell me, King Dvalin. Speak plain. Tell me the price you ask.'

The dwarf-king returned his smile. 'You shall be the last person Tyrfing kills by way of the curse, old killer. Once you are dead Hather, if he is still alive, may take back his sword without fear of meeting your fate, or Angantyr's, or wretched Svafrlami's.'

'Am I to become one of your shapeless flying servitors, then, Dvalin? Is that it?'

Dvalin began to laugh. It began softly, almost musically, from the depths of his short, grey-robed body. Then it grew and swelled, bursting out into the night in a raucous cacophony that sent the shapes flapping and screaming away from the tower. Hather felt the acid taste of fear burn at the back of his mouth, but Starkadder, if he felt afraid, stubbornly refused to show it.

They waited for the laughter to die away, and for the dwarf-king to continue. Dvalin slowly shook his head. 'Oh no, Starkadder,' he chuckled. 'Not that. Only Svafrlami deserved that. Your torment shall come in other ways, as shall my own. Tell me, Hather,' he asked, 'do you know the full story of this man? Do you know why Starkadder is feared and shunned by so many of the bravest men? Listen to me, boy. I'll tell you the truth in this matter. I'll tell you about Starkadder.'

As he spoke his eyes remained fixed upon the black-clad warrior, watching for the effect of his words. 'There is a giant in his ancestry, Hather. One of his forebears was an eight-armed giant who lived beside a waterfall. His name was Starkad, and he carried off the daughter of a chieftain

142

who was a priest of Thor. Well, the chieftain invoked the god's aid, and Thor sought out Starkad at the waterfall and tore off six of his arms. He left Starkad to die there, and took the chieftain's daughter home again. But she was already pregnant by Starkad, young Hather. The giant had forced himself inside that lovely virgin and deflowered and defiled her. She later died in childbirth, giving birth to Starkadder's mother.

'Now, you doubtless recall that Odin and Thor are father and son. Yet there is a rivalry between them. You know what the skalds sing, that Odin takes the chieftains who die in battle, but Thor has to settle for the thralls. When Starkadder was born Odin knew that the giant blood in his veins would make him a mighty warrior, and he promised that Starkadder should live for the length of three men's lives and become the greatest warrior in Midgard, and the most renowned of all men. Thor heard this promise and remembered the rape which had conceived Starkadder's mother. So it was that he countered Odin's benison with a curse of his own. This was his bale-speech, that for each of Starkadder's three lives he would commit an act of treachery against one he served, and that these acts would take from him the love of the people, and replace it with their fear and abhorrence.

'And so it has been, Hather. Starkadder was brought up at the court of a king called Vikar, and they were boys and played together. When Vikar took the throne he made Starkadder the chief of his bodyguard. For many years, until both were old in the reckoning of men, they fought together and Starkadder served Vikar well. But then the betrayal came. It was time for Starkadder to make a sacrifice to Odin, and Allfather made it clear that only Vikar would do as the victim. And so it happened. Starkadder convinced the king that it would be a mock sacrifice, that the noose would not tighten, that he would stand upon firm wood, and that the spear would be nothing more than a weed that would brush his skin. The idea amused Vikar and he agreed to go along with it, believing that it would help him to win favour in the eyes of the god. And it did, didn't it, Starkadder? It did indeed, because the noose suddenly tightened, and the log beneath the king's feet crumbled, and the weed became a sharpened stake, and Vikar died . . .'

'But not through my doing!' Starkadder snapped. 'The noose was too flimsy to take his weight and the log was firm when he stood upon it. As for the weed, I uprooted it myself . . .'

'Yet Vikar died, old killer, and his blood is upon you. You knew that Odin is noted for his betrayal of those he loves the most. He must love you very much, Starkadder!

'Such was the first betrayal, Hather. Starkadder betrayed King Vikar. Perhaps it was because Odin betrayed him in turn, but the deed speaks for itself in the eyes of men. The second betrayal was no less a thing than the first, and it cannot be laid to Allfather's doing, can it? Oh, you covered yourself as well as you could, Starkadder. After your years of serving Frothi you betrayed him to his enemies, even though you later urged his son Ingel to kill them and even joined in their slaughter at Ingel's feast. Vikar was an indifferent king, but Frothi was a good, a noble man. Why did you do it, Starkadder? Can you tell us that?'

Hather followed Dvalin's gaze to the face of the ancient mercenary. Starkadder's features were drawn, and his eyes were filling with tears.

'It had to be,' he croaked. 'You say that Allfather cannot be blamed, and you are right. But Thor played his part. He promised me freedom from his curse in exchange for Frothi's life. King Frothi was not called the Peace-King for nothing. He built a good life for his people, and made them rich through peaceful trading. Ingel was a wastrel. He taxed his subjects into poverty and strife. War followed Frothi's peace. Thor knew that it would. That's why he tempted me. But you're right, Dvalin. I should not have done it. I should have known that once Thor had his way he would forget me. And he did,'

'Two betrayals, Starkadder,' the dwarf-king replied. 'One more and your curse is ended. And you have my word that with your life the curse I placed upon Tyrfing will also be over.

'That is my price, Starkadder. The third betrayal. You have already told me that it must be done, so do it. Kill Oli the Great. Not for Odin, and not for Thor. Do it this time for the peace it will bring to you, for the final, fatal peace it can bestow. And to lift my curse from Tyrfing.'

'So you seek to use me as well, King Dvalin?'

The dwarf nodded. 'I do, Starkadder. I seek to use you even as the others have done, even as they use Hather and Oli and Dvalin. Even as they used Svafrlami and Angantyr. Even as they use Hervara and Lambi Nef and thousands of others.

'Do you imagine for a moment that any of us has a choice? Are you really so stupid after more than two hundred years? We do as we're told, Starkadder,' Dvalin continued, his expression serious and his voice calm and level, without malice, and with perhaps a trace of self-pity. 'You have no choice any more. Tyrfing is yours now, until you die. Use it to kill King Oli. However, if you'll take a word of advice from a creature that you and all your race loathe, you'll free Omund first.'

Starkadder smiled grimly, then nodded. 'That's good advice, Dvalin. And you're wrong about us loathing the dwarfs. Loathing is too simple a word, and it's not the right one. We don't understand you because you're not human, and what we don't understand we fear. We envy your wealth and pity you for living in perpetual darkness. We also envy your skill at crafts. But we don't loathe you.'

Dvalin smiled back. 'Perhaps I was also wrong to call you stupid, old killer. You're a wise man in your way, and a brave one. You should have been born a dwarf, Starkadder. Then we might have been friends.

'And you, Hather Lambisson. Go with your friend. Help him, until the last betrayal separates you for ever and the curse is gone from Tyrfing. Leave me now. Let me sit up here alone until the first red taint of dawn is in the sky and the warning stiffness comes upon my limbs. Learn well from this man beside you, and, if the Norns have written it so, you shall one day be a great fighter and a chieftain. You see, my shapes tell me many things that they learn from many places. Whatever you may think of the Lady Hervara, your mother, she is a brave woman. She stood before her father's grave-mound in the glimpses of the moon to win

Tyrfing from the earth and the dead. Perhaps you can no longer love her, but for her strength alone she deserves your respect.

'Go now, both of you. There's no difference between us. We are all the playthings of the Norns.'

The dwarf-king watched them bow and turn away. The interview was over, and as they followed the curvature of the balcony, back to the doorway where the single sentry waited, Dvalin went back to his throne and sat down. In his mind he followed them down the spiral staircase and along the corridor to the canal beyond.

There was a great deal more I could have told them, Dvalin mused. But it was not mine to tell. Is it the Norns that still our tongues, keeping back words that might be spoken? Is it the cutting of their runes that makes us what we are? Or is there something even beyond them, as they are beyond Freya and Thor and Allfather? Something that directs their hands, even as they direct our lives?

He looked out over the misted lake, his amber eyes sweeping the peaks of the mountains in the distance. For the first time he began to pity the tattered blackness which was all that remained of Svafrlami.

So that was Starkadder, he thought. That was the mightiest warrior in the north, the man most shunned by men. There is a surprising greatness in him. Perhaps that is why I could feel an unspoken understanding between us.

And so King Dvalin sat upon his balcony. The shapes came unbidden out of the night and spoke to him, and he listened to their words before dismissing them. To man it would have been a scene from a nightmare, but to the dwarf-king it was the only life he knew.

'Will it be over then?' he asked aloud. 'Will the Yngling dynasty truly fall with Oli?'

His mind travelled back through the perpetual darkness of his days to the words a shape had brought some time before. He had been sitting alone, as he was now, and the shape had come with its message. It told of strange men in brown robes who carried before them a sign that could have been Thor's hammer, but was not. They spoke in southern lands of a new god, a god not of Odin's race, nor of the

146

Vanir race which Freya and her kin belonged to. He had difficuty in remembering the name, for it was foreign to his ears, but he knew that it was more than just a name. It was the death-knell of the Lords of Asgard. It was a sound that would close the gates of Trollheim for ever, and bring the fire-giants sweeping into Asgard at the Ragnarok, the twilight of the gods. It was a name, spread by the brown-robed men, that would destroy them all.

And have the Norns written that as well? Is there nothing left to watch for, save the ending of my world? Oh Freya, I enjoyed your body and your agony. I enjoyed the firmness of your nipples and the sweaty rivulets amongst your pubic hair. Now memory is all I have. Shall this too be taken from me, or will he leave me with no more, no less? He's coming for us all. I know that. His brown-clad minions are spreading his name even now, and soon it will reach even to the gates of Asgard, and beyond. Then the old gods will die. Then Odin and his kin will fall. Then I shall be left to face his wrath, for he will not be a friend to such as I . . .

He sighed to himself, and with the sigh the name came flooding back. A new god, from the south. A new god who will change the old ways, who will govern the reigns of future kings, once the Yngling dynasty is gone. For the Ynglings had ruled in the north for hundreds of years, and they were the first and greatest of all who followed the ancient faith. With their fall this Jesus will gain his foothold in the lands of Midgard, and the world ash-tree, Yggdrasil, will shudder before the sign which is almost Thor's hammer, but not quite, will shudder and fall.

Is this truly what the Norns have written?

CHAPTER EIGHT

The closing of the gates

HATHER AND STARKADDER descended the spiral staircase to where the soldiers waited to escort them along the corridor to the canal, acting as a cordon, keeping the ugly leering she-dwarfs at a distance whilst they boarded the stone barge. It took prompting jabs from the cordon's spears to set the repulsive creatures on a second windlass, one that took the chain from the one it had first been wound to, and send the boat out through the serpent gate, across the bubbling surface of the lake towards the shore.

The boatman said nothing, and for much of the slow journey his eyes swept the darkened sky, studying the shapes that wheeled and circled overhead. As the barge neared the shore one shape, one that had hovered all the way closer than the others, flapped down and settled on the salamander-carven prow. The boatman seized a spear and jumped forward, ready to prod it back into the air, but Starkadder called a warning, and Hather took the spear and snapped it across his knee. The boatman, terrified by this display of force, cowered in the stern, his eyes darting from side to side.

The shape quivered, rearranging its form as it sighed. Only the eyes remained constant, the red, pitiful eyes that they had seen up on the edge of King Dvalin's tower.

'Do you know me?' it asked, its words no more than a voiceless whisper in the night.

148

Hather nodded. 'You are . . . King Svafrlami?' he asked.

'All that is left of him,' came the whispering reply. 'I am forced to serve Dvalin, but I bear him no loyalty.'

Even Starkadder, hardened and inured to adversity as he was by his own centuries of suffering, found himself awed before the pitiful remains of a once-great monarch. 'We cannot help you,' he muttered sadly. 'There is nothing that we can do to help you.'

The shape nodded, its eyes dimming before they brightened once again. 'No,' Svafrlami agreed, 'there's nothing you can do for me. Yet there's something I can still do for you, Starkadder. And for Hather too,' he added.

The dwarfish boatman suddenly lurched forward again and made a grab for the broken spear. On the balcony upon the grotesque, gargoyled tower, Dvalin smirked to himself with silent mirth and Hather stamped hard down onto the dwarf's foot and pushed him roughly back into the stern of the stone barge. Then he picked up the pieces of the spear and threw them over the gunwale. They splashed into the lake, and the haze cleared for a moment as fragments began to bubble and fume.

'Stay there,' Hather ordered the dwarf, 'or you're next!'

The boatman cowered and obeyed. He knew all too well what the lake would do to fragile flesh.

Starkadder studied the bright-eyed darkness of Svafrlami carefully. 'Go on,' he said. 'Tell us how you can help us.'

'Let me give you a word of caution,' the shape whispered. 'You may think that Dvalin has told you the truth. Indeed, Dvalin may believe that he has told you the truth. But has he told you everything? For your own sakes I urge you to beware the sword. Beware Tyrfing, Starkadder. Beware Tyrfing, Hather. Beware the dwarf-forged blade.'

'But tell us why,' Hather begged, bewildered.

'Don't trust King Dvalin,' Svafrlami hissed. 'He may not even understand the meaning of betrayal . . .'

Before he had finished Svafrlami uttered a loud and discordant shriek. His black wings began to beat against the misted air and his taloned feet loosened their grip upon the stone prow. For a moment he hovered, his eyes blazing mutely at Hather and Starkadder, then he rose up and was gone, indistinguishable in his faceless agony from the other tattered shapes which winged their way about Dvalin's lake-bound castle.

The dwarf-king smiled grimly at the shape's sudden departure. Distance was no impediment to his communication with his servitors. He'd heard Svafrlami's words and, in his way, had understood them. Now, Dvalin thought to himself, was the time to test the players of the game. Now was his opportunity to probe the other forces which were threatening to control the destinies of his visitors. There might not be another chance before the game drew to its fateful end, so it had to be seized before it escaped.

When the gates close, he determined. That will be the moment.

The stone boat reached the shore of the lake. The dwarfish boatman, glowering at the treatment he had received from his passengers, made no move to push out the boarding slab. Starkadder, grinning, picked it up from where it lay on the floor of the barge and set it in place. For all its bulk and apparent weight the old mercenary found it surprisingly light.

'You go first,' he commanded the enraged dwarf. 'Once we're safely off you can board again.'

The dwarf made no move to obey, but a little gentle prodding with the point of Hather's sword soon convinced him that obedience was in his best interests.

They disembarked and the boatman scuttled back up the boarding slab. Only when he had given the signal for the she-dwarfs to move to the inbound windlass, and the stone barge was safely out upon the lake, did he let the travellers know exactly what he thought of them. As his oaths faded into the mist Hather and Starkadder exchanged smiles and walked towards the arched gateway between the mountains.

From his throne upon the balcony King Dvalin watched them go, little more than fly-specks in the darkness. As they neared the gateway the dwarf-king called his sentry over.

'Give the order,' he began, 'for them to pass the gates in safety. Then close the gates. For ever. When that is done destroy the shape known as Svafrlami. It can now be of no further use to me.'

The companions stepped through the archway to where Harbard awaited them, torch in hand. 'Have you accomplished what you wanted?' he asked.

'As close as we can,' Starkadder replied.

'Then I'll allow the gates to close.'

On the balcony King Dvalin nodded to himself. It was time.

The one-eyed man stepped forward to pick up the blackened yew-wand. As he did so it suddenly began to bow in the middle under the pressure of moving rock. Before Harbard could touch the staff it had bent almost double, the flexibility of the wood permitting an acute curve which might have been impossible with almost any other material. Then, with a loud cracking, it split, splintered and shattered as the mountainous walls were forced together.

High above in the darkness, silently, a mere fragment of the cliff face began to split away. The earth was Dvalin's element, and the dwarf-king knew how best to use it, even though the fragment weighed more than a full army together with supply wagons and cargo ponies. Gradually, with a stealth belying its enormous bulk, the rock swung outwards, like a door on well-made hinges, the deeper blackness of the cracks about it widening in the night, its rain of sand and pebbles lost in the greater confusion around the shattered yew-wand and the ruined gateway.

Harbard cast a wary eye upwards, then he sighed. 'Everything changes,' he muttered softly. 'Soon nothing will be the same any more.'

Let Dvalin make his moves, the one-eyed man thought to himself. He has few enough of them left. He'd already lost the game before he began to play.

On the balcony King Dvalin's smile widened yet further, splitting his thin, sharp features almost in two. With deceptive slowness the detached portion of rock began the early, slithering phase of its descent. Directly in its downward path Starkadder and Hather watched the closing of the gates of Trollheim.

151

The archway on the inner side of the gates buckled and crumbled before the onslaught of the moving mountains. Dvalin's smile persisted, even in the certain knowledge of his failure, but it was a smile without humour, even tinged by sadness.

The falling fragment gathered speed. Its slide became a rush, then it came completely away and, gathering speed, began to bounce wildly down the side of the mountain.

Hather looked up and a speck of cascading stone bit into his eye. For a moment the stinging pain and sudden blindness obliterated all trace of what he'd seen. Then, with a cry, he thrust out blindly towards where he last remembered Starkadder having been. His hands caught the ancient warrior slightly off-balance. With desperate force he threw himself at the old Norwegian, hurling both of them from the path of the descending boulder.

They fell together in a heap at the same moment as the fragment shattered and sharded on the ground. The dust engulfed them briefly, shrouding their bodies with a gritty mist.

Harbard nodded grimly. Somewhere a wolf was howling and twin ravens screamed hoarsely into the night. The breath caught in Dvalin's throat, making his utterance, inarticulate as it was, fall somewhere between a gasp and a sob. As the last of the dust settled around them Hather rubbed his watering eyes clear and blinked as he stumbled back onto his feet. A strong hand reached out to steady him.

'You saved my life,' the old man said grimly. 'Should I thank you, Hather, for doing me such a service? Yet your motives were good, and I think perhaps I should.'

He didn't expect the youth to understand just how weighty a burden his life had become. No one who hadn't experienced the weight of centuries and the horrors of self-recrimination which followed his ordained betrayals could fully understand.

Besides, the ancient mercenary thought, could he have acted in any other way? Would he have been allowed to leave Starkadder to a fate other than that which had been decreed for him?

He took Hather's face in his hands and stared into the

youngster's rubble-reddened eyes. 'Thank you, Hather,' he whispered. 'I owe you for what you've just done.'

He suddenly wanted to laugh, realising even as he spoke that his tongue and words were being guided by others than himself.

Hather shook his head. 'I repaid a debt,' he replied. 'You saved me from Tyrfing when first we met. Now we're equal and our debts are cancelled out.'

'No,' Starkadder responded. 'I was powerless at the meeting of the streams. It was Bolli who saved you from dying and me from killing you. I still carry a debt to you. You thought of me in the same moment as you thought of yourself. For that alone the debt goes on. How or when I shall repay it I don't know, but it shall not go uncancelled. Before I die, Hather, before I'm finally free of the curses which control my destiny, I shall find some way in which I can repay your kindness.'

If you're speaking for me, he asked the answering silence, why can't you find me better words? This boy has shown a love for me which I may never be able to repay, yet you make me give him promises of payment.

Give me the chance to do what I've promised. Let me have that much satisfaction before you've done with me. They were your words, Mother Skuld, not mine. Now you owe me their fulfilment as I owe their fulfilment to Hather.

No answer came to him through the levelling dust. But then, he hadn't really looked for one.

'Perhaps we had better move away from here,' Harbard remarked.

And Dvalin, watching from his tower, consoled himself with the thought that sooner or later everything had its appointed end. There were other, less imposing entrances to Trollheim, tunnels and caverns that might be used by the dwarfs without ever men discovering them. No more mere mortals would pass through the gates of Trollheim, though. No more would enter, no matter how brightly the symbol of the new god Jesus might gleam upon their brown robes. Let Asgard fall if it must, Dvalin thought. Let Allfather fight his last battle with the fire-giants and leave Jesus the mere pickings of his mastery. That was as it might be, but

153

no one would ever enter Trollheim from the world of men again.

He sat upon his balcony, the gargoyle-forms of dead servitors crusting the tower above and beneath like barnacles upon a rotting sea-bed hulk. His taloned fingers dug deep into the arms of the throne, the knuckles white with unease at the failure of his test.

Hather and Starkadder still lived. Whatever had saved them had taken their lives almost beyond the scope of his powers. But there was still Tyrfing, still the dwarf-forged blade which might work his will in the fated days to come.

Now I know what you have written, you Norns, he thought. I know the runes that you have cut, Urd Verdandi, Mother Skuld. You have written of the end of the Yngling dynasty which Starkadder once served, and of the end of the ancient faith it enshrines. I don't know why it has to be, but you desire it, and that in itself must be reason enough for such as we. Allfather has served your decrees well throughout the ages of his dominion. He's given his son Baldur to your whims. He's betrayed his followers because he fears your power and influence, seeking to take them to himself to use against you if he has to, to fight a last fateful battle against the power you exercise so remorselessly. This new god, this Jesus, will seek even to destroy you, Norns. It's in his nature, in the all-consuming fire he's bringing up from the south. So, why have you opened the way for him? Why have you doomed Oli and his son? What is it in them that makes the fall of the Yngling dynasty so certain?

There came no answer to his unspoken questions. No tattered, red-eyed shape flapped out of the night above the lake to bring him the Norns' response.

'I'm powerless now,' he said aloud. 'I can't do more than I have done.'

Tyrfing was all that remained to him, and the dwarf-king knew it. Tyrfing, and the waiting for the darkness which finished every changeless, torpid day.

I climb the stairway to this balcony when the sun goes down. I sit here. I listen to my shapes, and I watch.

That's all.

154

He sighed. The shapes flapped on about him. The silence stiffened.

King Dvalin, alone, lost forever in the darkness of himself, continued his musings.

You know, in one way you're kind to me, you Norns. Urd, Verdandi, Skuld, all kind. You make it so easy for a dwarf to die. Each night I shall come here. Each night I shall sit here on my balcony and watch the progress of your play. Each dawn I shall hurry back into the darkened recesses of my realm before the stiffness in my limbs turns them to staring stone. You see, I know you now, in my way. I know what you intend. And I know that there shall come a day, quite soon, when I shall have seen and learned enough.

On that day I shall not return to the tunnels and caverns below. On that day I shall accept the redness of the dawn. Oh yes, the time shall come, you Norns, you gods. I may not know the night before, when I ascend the stairway, but I shall know before the dawning.

And the next night, when the sentries come, they will find me here. Just another carving on the castle of my forebears.

Yet even turned to stone I shall be smiling.

The politics of destruction

CHAPTER ONE

The king's marshal

Whilst Thorvald Brotamad's triumph was being turned
to bitter failure by the mysterious mist which covered
Starkadder's escape on the return journey to Uppsala,
Marshal Vermund Bjarnisson and his columns were
approaching Oli's fortress on the banks of the Dalalven.

The fortress, its longhouse barracks clustered within
earth-mounded, palisaded walls, stood close by the river on
the Uppsala side. Stretched about like a giant horseshoe
bulking against the quays and jetties on the waterside, were
the huts and booths of the artisans and tradesmen who
served its needs. Whilst the fortress was their livelihood
they were only allowed within its walls when summoned to
carry out given tasks or receive orders.

To the ordinary people of his kingdom Oli the Great was
remote and unknown as a god. They scarcely ever saw him,
and all that they heard or knew of him was whispered in the
hushed voice of rumour. That in itself was quite sufficient to
change respect to fear, even in the most far-flung settle-
ments of his lands.

The villages along Vermund's route had looked deserted
as his column of three hundred men rode past. Fires still
smoked, it was true, and work appeared abandoned outside the sun-bright wooden homes. But no curious faces
appeared in the doorways or peeped out at the soldiers from
behind the walls. No children toddled naked in the empty

159

alleys between the wooden huts. Only the flocks were to be seen, grazing with the stoicism peculiar to domestic animals, and once an aged hound opened its toothless jaws to bark at them, almost with indifference.

The marshal closed his single eye in thought, allowing his mount to pick its own way, unguided along the northward-leading track. It was a sign of the times, of rumour and uncertainty if not of actual fear, that the common people no longer came to watch the soldiers of their king pass by. Behind Vermund rode fifty mounted warriors, tall and proud, if dusty, on their short-legged war-horses. After them came the foot-soldiery and the supply wagons, rumbling behind the oxen on solid wooden wheels, and the laden pack-horses, hung with bundles of arrows and javelins and led by grim-faced men in metal-studded leather jerkins.

They're scared sick, afraid of the Court, afraid even of the common soldiery. A sign of the times, Vermund thought. A sign of the times of King Oli the Great. King Oli the butcher.

Then another thought came to him and he opened his eye to watch in silence as the bulk of the fortress drew nearer. People can only get so scared before they begin to be brave. The first step is fear, and that's the step they've taken. The second step is something more courageous, and that's the step they've yet to take.

Rebellion.

Behind the palisade above the curve of the rampart, the tiny shapes of armed defenders began to appear, coming to watch the long noisy snake of the column wind across the plain towards the southern gate. What would they do, the marshal asked himself, if the fortress were threatened? What would they think of the order he had been given by the king himself? And his own men, what would they say to the murder of young Omund, the king's own son, at the hands of their commander.

Fear. Courage born of fear. Rebellion.

Unlike the villages they had passed, the town was crowded with people who gathered, curious, to stare at them from the ends of the horseshoe. Vermund didn't know any of them. He didn't need to. Yet for the first time

160

he looked at them with new eyes, seeing them as something more than just people, seeing in the tools they held and the staffs they leaned upon the weapons which might one day clear Omund's path to the throne, if the young prince lived that long.

As he rode up to the massive wooden gates of the fortress he raised his hand in a signal for the column to halt. He nudged his mount forward until it entered the cutting in the defensive embankment which gave access to the gates, then looked up at the faces and weapons lining the palisade.

'Fetch Askel Sigurdsson to the gate,' he ordered. 'Tell him that the king's marshal is here.'

Two of the soldiers broke from their positions on the rampart and disappeared. When they returned they brought with them a short, heavy-set man in leather-and-plate armour which marked him out as a superior officer. His black hair hung in a plait to either side of his neck and the rest gathered into a bunch at the nape, trailing black and glossy between his shoulder-blades like the tail of a fighting stallion. His dark eyes glared down at the column and his mouth, when he spoke, was entirely hidden behind a full beard.

'Vermund Bjarnisson? Is that you?'

The commander nodded wearily. 'It's me all right, Askel Horsetail. Have your men open the gates.'

Askel nodded, then turned away and shouted the order down into the fort. Slowly, ponderously, creaking on their heavy brazen hinges, the wooden gates swung outwards, each pushed with poles tied to their inner sides which had leather grips bound about their lower ends. Vermund noted with satisfaction that it took almost a dozen men straining hard to move the double-thickness of bound half-trunks which made up each of the enormous doors.

He waved his men to follow, and rode through the gateway, beneath the balconied palisade, into the body of the fortress. Then he pulled his mount to one side and sat in silence as the column wound its way inside, crowding into the open area between the stabling beneath the palisade, built into the depth of the rampart, and the cluster of nearly thirty longhouses which occupied the centre. As the last

161

weary, dust-caked pack-animal straggled within the jaws of the gateway, the men who had stood beside the poles on the inside of each gate were joined by as many others, who grasped knotted ropes hanging down between the poles.

Before Vermund could count beyond ten the gates of the fortress had swung tightly shut.

Outside, with nothing left to see, the people of the little township returned to their tasks, moving back to their work in ones and twos, slowly thinning and vanishing. Soon only a single figure was left staring at the settling dust on the deserted track, staring through green, foreign eyes towards a growing certainty that his time was coming. The man was as gaunt as Starkadder, though only about thirty years old, and the grim light of the fanatic burned in his unquiet green eyes. The brown robe had long since rolled from his shoulders, and now he wore the wadmal breeches and tunic of any other poor commoner. Yet around his neck hung a talisman of gold, almost in the shape of old redbeard Thor's hammer. Almost, but not quite.

If the fortress needs a garrison of that size, thought Brother Gerard, then they must be afraid of something. Or somebody.

The name was never gone from his thoughts or his prayers. Since Hugo's death on the fringes of that distant forest it had sung in his blood, and whispered in his every breath.

The monk turned back to the cottages, knowing that his little flock would be waiting for him. They knew nothing of his ambition, nothing but his words of the power and majesty of the White Christ who had died in the south to save them from such as King Oli. Because they knew nothing, their awe at the magnitude of his feat would be all the greater.

Through all of Sweden the man who killed Starkadder would become a legend, and his words would be listened to all the more readily because of his mighty deed.

The echo of the heavy gates slamming shut was still ringing inside the fortress as Vermund Bjarnisson swung down from his mount and arched his back in a protracted stretch. He swung his arms at the shoulders, feeling the cramped muscles ease and the aches of the journey begin to fade, then waited by his horse as Askel Sigurdsson came striding towards him. They grasped each other's wrists and Askel patted his old friend heftily on the back, laughing at the dust which rose from the marshal's shoulders.

'It's good to see you again, Vermund,' Askel said.

The marshal nodded and grinned back. 'And it's good to see you, old Horsetail,' he replied. 'Still no grey in that black thatch of yours, I see.'

'That's because I live right, my friend, and Odin's still being kind to me. But tell me, are you here as our relief? Have you brought me any orders?'

Vermund gestured towards the longhouses at the centre of the fortress. 'Get your men to settle mine into quarters whilst we have a talk. I'm not here as your relief, Horsetail. I've come for a different purpose. Let's go somewhere where we can drain a few horns without being overheard.'

The dark tone in the marshal's words wasn't lost on his old companion. Askel's features darkened as he led Vermund towards the central building. He called orders to some of his officers, detailing the disposition of the newly arrived soldiery. Finally, he escorted the marshal into one of the longhouses, called for horns and beer, then dismissed his attendants with orders that he was not to be disturbed.

They drained the first horns to Odin, and the second to each other. Then they sat down, either side of a trestle table, with their horns and a pitcher of beer beside them.

'So why are you here?' Askel began, his dark eyes probing the blue depth of Vermund's remaining one.

'On the king's personal orders,' came the reply. 'I'm not here to relieve your men, Horsetail. I'm here to reinforce them.' He paused and swilled down some more of the beer. 'And to take over command,' he added.

Askel pulled at his moustache. 'You're the senior officer,' he muttered. 'I would naturally have deferred to you and expected my men to follow suit. So why does the transfer of command have to be official? Is King Oli displeased with me?'

Vermund noticed the trace of fear which had come into the warrior's voice and thought of the deserted villages and

163

steadings along the line of his march. 'Not at all,' he replied. 'If you had, my orders would be to drag you back to Uppsala so that Oli's butchers could carve the blood-eagle out of you.'

'You're joking, of course!'

'Not at all.'

Askel felt his jaw hang open and had to force himself to close it. 'I'd heard that things were getting bad at court,' he grunted. 'but I didn't know that they were as bad as that. Is it true, Vermund?'

'That depends on what you've heard,' came the reply. 'Though whatever it is you're probably right. Oli's become sick, crazed. He expects even his own shadow to betray him. Executions happen every day and his reign has become a rule of terror for most of those around him. And not only at court, Horsetail. Even the common people are afraid for their lives. Do you know, in all the steadings and villages I passed through on the way here, I didn't see a single person, man, woman or child?'

'But they used to come out and cheer. They loved the sight of Oli's soldiers. They loved Oli. They called him Oli the Great.'

'That was a long time ago, my friend,' Vermund replied. 'Now they're calling him Oli the mad, but they're doing it in whispers in case he hears and has them gutted.'

He finished his horn and refilled it from the pitcher at his elbow. 'Shall I show you how mad he is, Horsetail? Shall I tell you the rest of my orders? It's my duty, you know. Even if he's as mad as a half-castrated aurochs I'm still the king's marshal. The king's marshal, Vermund Bjarnisson.'

Askel Sigurdsson felt a sick, clutching feeling in the pit of his stomach. 'I think you'd better,' he said quietly.

'How's your royal guest these days? Young Omund?'

'Under guard, as are my orders, but as long as he's accompanied he has the run of the fortress. I like the lad. We get on well together. He's rather puzzled by his father keeping him here, but he bears him no ill-will. He almost believes that it's for his own good, to stop anyone trying to kill him.'

164

'Someone like you, or me, for instance.'

'Thor's prick, man! What are you telling me?'

'Exactly what you hear me saying. King Oli has charged me with this mission, Horsetail. If anyone tries to free Omund from his captivity here I'm to have him killed rather than let him escape. There are only two things I've ever seen Oli afraid of, and young Omund's one of them.'

'You're . . . to kill him?'

'If need be. Those are my orders. And yours, too.'

Askel refilled his own horn and drained its contents without a pause. Then he said: 'You'd do it, Vermund?'

'Would you?'

'Give the order or do the killing?'

'You think that's the kind of thing that you can get someone else to do for you? Chances are, even your most trusted man would run you through and surrender the fortress, and Omund, before they'd kill Oli's heir. The Ynglings have ruled Sweden for hundreds of years. The people would deny their gods before they'd give up the peace and prosperity that Yngling rule has brought them. Besides, the legends say that the Ynglings are descended from the gods themselves, that Odin was the first of the Yngling monarchs.

'No, friend Horsetail. I've told you my orders, but only because I've known you well and fought beside you through the years. If Omund is to die, then it's you or I that must do it. If my orders became known they'd topple Oli from his throne and set Omund in his place in the blinking of an eye. Oli doesn't understand that, or he wouldn't have told me to do it. A sane man could never give an order like that. Even a half-mad one would have the lad quietly poisoned and give out that he'd died of some illness. Only a blood-thirsty butcher, such as Oli's become, could issue orders like this.'

'But what's he afraid of? Surely he doesn't expect the people to rise against him? Not if they're so convinced that the Ynglings mean they can continue to live in peace?'

The marshal shook his head. 'The people are starting to wonder about him, and to fear his authority, but I don't

165

think they're ready for rebellion just yet. Make no mistake, though. It won't take much more, or much longer, before they are.'

'Then what is he afraid of? If Omund's one thing, as you said, then what's the other?'

'I'll tell you how I see it, Horsetail. Shortly before he gave me my orders and told me to bring these men north to reinforce you, one of his courtiers left Uppsala without the king's permission. That's what he really fears, that one man. Chances are the men he sent to bring him back have already done their jobs and we'll never need to even think about whether we should obey his order to kill Omund or not. But if they haven't, if they've failed, then we may have to make our minds up sooner than we think. As dangerous men go, the one who left the court is the most dangerous of all. You know him, Horsetail. An old Norwegian mercenary . . .'

'Starkadder?'

'The same. Starkadder. Now, whether his legend's true or not I don't know. I suspect that it is, and Oli certainly must believe in it, since he fears him so much. If it is, then Starkadder has already betrayed two kings, and that means Oli will be the third.

'And now you know as much as I do. So, tell me, Horsetail, will you kill young Omund?'

'What if I say I won't do it?'

'That's your choice. I'm not going to throw an old friend to Oli's executioners.'

'Then you have my answer, Vermund, be you king's marshal or no. I won't take on myself the burden of killing the only heir to the Yngling dynasty. I'm a soldier, not a murderer.'

'Then the burden, and the choice, are mine.'

'Will you do it, Vermund? If you have to, will you kill the boy?'

The marshal stared down at the table before him. The deserted villages, the daily ritual of blood-eagle executions at Oli's court in Uppsala, the figure of the dark-clad, gaunt-faced Starkadder all passed through his mind. Duty and conscience fought a sickening battle within his heart, a battle which threatened to destroy him before it yielded to eternal peace.

Eventually he said: 'I don't know, Horsetail. I just don't know.'

Askel Sigurdsson eyed him strangely, studying the scarred face with its single eye. Vermund Bjarnisson was one of his oldest, dearest friends, but in that moment the dark-haired viking felt that, for all their years together, he didn't know the king's marshal at all.

CHAPTER TWO

Hervara

THORKEL TONGUE's heavy grey brows were knotted above his broken nose as he raised a fist to knock upon the door of Tisti's hut. He rapped gently. It wasn't the way he knocked upon other doors, but he had no fear of those behind them. Old Tisti he feared and respected because she had Lappish blood, and because Thorkel was a peasant at heart.

Lambi Nef's father had raised Thorkel Tongue to preferment, and he had served the family as their chief steward ever since. He had watched his master be trapped by the Lady Hervara, yet he had held his usually ready tongue. He had seen young Hervara brought to birth and rejoiced with the rest of the household. He had reason to know of the affair between Hervara and King Oli which had secured Lambi Nef's position as one of the king's preferred retainers, but he had not believed it to be his place to speak of it to anyone.

The old nurse's sharp tones broke his reverie. 'Come in, Thorkel Tongue,' she called.

He was a tall man, and he had to stoop in order to enter the little hut. Tisti sat, as usual, wrapped in a cloak of skins before her fire. Her position in the household might only be that of Hather's nurse, but there was a power, an authority, in Tisti that the steward knew was more than the equal of his own. That was why she was still here, why she hadn't been sent away once her task was finished.

Once through the doorway he pulled the door closed behind him and walked around to stand in front of the old woman. He looked down at her, wondering when she would look up from whatever she was watching in the flames.

You don't come to see me so often these days, she thought. You want something. I know what you want, Thorkel Tongue, but I'm going to make you ask for it.

'I need your help, Tisti,' the steward began.

'Do you, now?' she asked, still staring into the flickering fire.

'It's two days since the young master left here. There's no word of where he is or who he's with, if he's with anyone.'

'Should there be, Thorkel Tongue?' She looked up, squinting at him through dark, smoke-stung eyes. 'As you say, he's the young master. He's a man now. He has a sword to prove it.'

The steward cleared his throat. 'That's not what I mean, and you know it. You know how he left here. You know how we found his mother the next morning, lying in the ashes of the long-fire in the hall. You put her to bed.'

'I remember.' Tisti was smiling to herself.

'The servants have nursed her since then. The leech has examined her. There's nothing wrong with her, he says. But she's not moving. She has to be fed and her food won't stay down. She just lies there and moans to herself.'

'Yes,' the old Lapp muttered. 'I suppose she does.'

'You can help her, Tisti. You know more of healing both the body and the mind than any leech. I want you to forget whatever's been between you all these years. I know you've not loved her, and she would have sent you away many years ago if it hadn't been for the love Hather bears you. Yet I want you to forget all that. Go to her. Help her. Please?'

'And if I do, what then?'

Thorkel Tongue scratched his grey head. 'Why, she'll get better.'

The old woman smiled at his simplicity. He didn't understand what she meant. He never had done and he never would, and perhaps it was better that way.

'If she gets better, will she stay here? Will she be here alone with her thoughts and the ghosts of whatever has happened between Hather and herself?'

'That's not my concern,' Thorkel replied, trying to muster some dignity. 'All I care about is that the Lady Hervara is my master's wife. If she is sick, and there's something I can do to help her, I am bound by my duty to the family to do so. I think that should apply to you as well. Will you come with me to her?'

Tisti stared up at him for a moment. Then she nodded. 'I'll come with you,' she said, getting to her feet. 'I'll help her for the reason you have given me, because she is the wife of Lambi Nef. I have nothing against him, and I love his son dearly.'

'Good. Don't you want to bring anything with you?'

Tisti shook her head. 'Not yet. Let me see her first. Then we can get whatever we may need.' She paused. 'Are you quite sure you want me to do this?' she asked.

The note in her voice was lost on Thorkel. He simply thought that the ancient Lapp was unwilling to help the Lady Hervara. His simple peasant soul could not see beyond her words, into Tisti's world of gods and conflict. He would never know that she had sat there, waiting for him to come with just such a request, for two days.

'Follow me,' he ordered.

She grinned but said nothing, allowing him his show of authority and dignity. There had to be pride in old age. Without it, without the feeling of being, or having been, somebody, there was no point in waiting for a straw–death upon a sickbed.

She followed him out of the hut and across the courtyard. They passed the vestibule and entered the silence of the main hall. No fires burned there. No maids swept or scattered fresh rushes. There was no need. With the master at court and the young master gone Thor knew where, and the Lady Hervara confined in her bed–closet, no one was using it. The servants had their own quarters and would never presume to use those of their betters.

Thorkel opened the door in the partition wall at the end of the hall. Tisti went through first and led the way to Hervara's bed-closet. She opened the door without bothering to knock and stepped inside.

Hervara lay upon a straw-filled mattress with woollen and skin blankets wrapped about her. She was breathing shallowly and quickly, but was not sweating or showing any signs of fever. Her eyes were closed when the door opened, but they flashed into life as old Tisti approached the bed.

Hervara's lips were forming words, but no sound came. Her skin was unusually pallid, almost corpse-like, as the ancient crone bent over her. The old Lapp pulled back the blankets roughly, ignoring the clutching hands which strove to keep them in place. 'Wait outside,' Tisti ordered Thorkel Tongue. 'Don't go away, though. I'll need you in a moment.'

Hervara's deep blue eyes blazed furiously as the old nurse examined her body, noting the bruises and scratches, and the abrasions about her shoulders where the dress had been torn away. Then she looked lower down, noting the bruised thighs. Her wrinkled hand moved snake-like over Hervara's abdomen and genitals.

'Pain, Lady Hervara?' she asked, her dark eyes glittering with pleasure at the thought.

Hervara struggled and swallowed hard, biting back the threatening cry. Then she croaked the single word: 'No.'

Tisti nodded and smiled. 'I didn't think he'd hurt you badly,' she muttered, no longer troubling to hide her fore-knowledge of Hather's actions. 'Not in your body, anyway. Thorkel!' she called, replacing the blankets.

The old steward appeared in the doorway.

'Go to the leech,' Tisti instructed. 'I want hops from a female plant. It must be a female, tell him. I'll know if he tries to cheat me. I also want wormwood, betony, lupin, vervain, henbane and dittander. And then bilberry, crop-leek, garlic, madder grains, corn-cockle and fennel. About a handful of each. Then have a fire lighted in the main hall and have the kitchen make up some beef broth. Also, send to the storehouse for a tub of sheep's fat and to the dairy for butter. Then get my boiling-bowl from my hut. Half-fill it with the butter and set it on the fire to melt.'

171

Thorkel Tongue nodded and turned to go.

'And as well as the other things I'll need viper's bugloss. And make sure they're all fresh. The dried stuff will take too long to render.'

She turned back to Hervara. 'Get up,' she ordered.

'I . . . can't . . .' Hervara whispered.

'They told me you couldn't speak, either, but your voice seems to have come back. Now stir yourself, Lady. You've lain abed long enough. You have things to do. I'll wait for you in the main hall.'

With a last scowl which left Hervara in no doubt that she had better obey, the old nurse left the bed-closet. Hervara struggled to raise herself upon her elbows, then fell back. Two painful attempts later her hair was sweat-matted and her arms were aching and tingling with the circulation of fresh blood. Taking her weight on the right arm she crooked her left behind her until her hand was spread flat upon the mattress. Then she shifted her weight and did the same thing with her right arm. Finally she succeeded in lifting herself far enough to swing her legs over the edge of the bed.

Hervara sat there for some minutes, looking down past her breasts and groin to her feet. She didn't want to see her nipples or her pubic hair. She didn't want to see ever again any part of her which had been naked to Hather. He was still her son, but he had raped and betrayed her. She loved him still, but he had taken her plotting and wrapped her about with it. She could never look at him freely again.

And where was he now, that fine son? Had he gone to make her happy, to kill Starkadder and avenge the death of her father, or would he betray her in that as well? What might she expect of him, after this?

She took a woollen blanket and wrapped it about herself. Then she tried to stand. The first time her legs refused to bear her and she fell back onto the bed. The second time they bore her a little longer, but still collapsed. The third time, though, she stood upright and did not fall.

Hervara staggered to the open door and out into the corridor. With faltering steps, holding onto the rough-hewn timber walls for support, she reached the partition door

172

and half-stepped, half-fell into the hall. Tisti stood beside the fire where a chair had been set, smiling unpleasantly at her.

'I'll put fire in your veins, Lady,' she smirked. 'I'll give you back what you've lost. I'll give you the will to hate again.'

Hervara studied her tormentor through pain-filled eyes. The old Lapp was wrong. She still knew how to hate. She hated now, hated the old witch who was grinning at her. Yet there was also the invalid's desire to please, the yearning to recover, to fight back from infirmity no matter what the cause. It was the desire which gave a one-legged warrior the will to hold his ground, to learn to fight on one foot and a length of wood as well as he had ever fought with two good feet. She still hated Tisti for all the imagined wrongs of the past, but for once in her life Hervara was glad that old Tisti was there.

'Sit here,' the old woman commanded, pointing to the chair.

There were no walls for her to cling to. If she lost her uncertain footing and fell she would probably roll into the freshly lit fire. Oh yes, Tisti had chosen the place well where she had set the seat. There was no help for Hervara.

She hesitated, looking about her for some means of support and finding none. As she did so the old nurse danced quickly across the room and slapped her face hard. Then, before Hervara could think of aiming a blow in return, Tisti was back beside the chair.

Her face red and stinging, Hervara started across the room. She was half-way to the chair when she fell to one knee. A servant-girl, entering with the beef broth, set it down and moved to help her mistress, but Tisti roughly pushed her away.

'She has to do it alone,' she snapped. 'Help her now and you'll be helping her for the rest of her life.'

Hissing her defiance, spittle collecting in the corners of her mouth, the Lady Hervara forced herself to her feet. A few more lurching steps took her within reach of the chair. Clutching the arms for support she lowered herself into it.

Tisti moved forward to tuck the blanket more closely

173

about her. As she came near Hervara spat full in her ancient face.

The old Lapp stepped back and smiled warmly as she wiped the spittle away. 'That's good, Mistress,' she said. 'You'll beat me yet.'

'You're enjoying this, aren't you?' Hervara grunted.

'It's warming my aged bones better than any fire,' came the reply. 'Now eat your broth. You must be hungry after all that effort.'

The servant approached and began spooning the broth to her mistress. 'Give me that,' Hervara snapped, snatching the wooden spoon. 'I'll feed myself. Get out of here.'

'Better and better,' Tisti grinned. 'This shouldn't take long at all.'

As Hervara finished the broth Thorkel entered with the herbs in leather bags. Behind him came a manservant, balancing the half-filled bowl of butter on top of a small keg of sheep's fat. He set the bowl on a tripod over the fire, then bowed to Hervara and withdrew. Thorkel Tongue set down the herbs and then followed him.

'What's all this stuff?' Hervara demanded, her voice growing stronger every time she used it.

'A simple salve to soothe your sorrows,' came the smiling reply. 'It will do you more good than harm, believe me.'

'The day I believe you will be the day I join my father.'

'Come now, Mistress. You know as well as I do I'm not doing this for you. It's for Lambi Nef and little Hather. And for Starkadder.'

With a furious screech Hervara leaped out of the seat and flung herself at Tisti. Her strength failed her though, and the nurse caught her just before she pitched into the fire. As she set her mistress into her seat again she ordered: 'Stay there. I know what you want to do, Lady, but I also know what you're capable of. You've been through an ordeal which has weakened your body and your mind. I can set your mind straight for you – I'm doing that now – but your body will take a little longer. Don't move out of that chair again until I tell you to.'

The butter in the bowl had melted and was beginning to boil. Using the hem of her dress as a glove Tisti moved it away from the fire and began shredding the contents of the leather bags into it.

When she had done she set the bowl among the ashes to keep the mixture of butter and herbs hot. Then she disappeared behind the partition briefly, to fetch another large bowl and a length of straining cloth.

Tisti carefully strained the impregnated fat through the fabric, letting the brownish-green mess drop into the second bowl. What remained in the cloth she replaced in the first bowl and seethed with milk. From the chair Hervara watched the process carefully, her face creased into a scowl.

Outside the shadows lengthened into late afternoon. Grinning to herself, muttering invocations in her native tongue as she stirred or strained the pungent-smelling mixture, the old Lapp continued her preparations. At last, early in the evening, when the mixture had been boiled and skimmed and strained and boiled again many times over, a clear brown balm remained in the boiling-bowl.

'Take off the blanket and come here,' Tisti ordered.

Hervara, still scowling, hesitated. 'What do you intend to do with that?' she demanded.

'Do as I say, Mistress,' came the implacable reply. The ironic stress on the last word wasn't lost on Hather's mother.

Hervara obeyed. As she stepped naked beside the edge of the long fire her thoughts went back to that time, just a couple of days before, when Hather had taken her. Her head remained proudly erect, but her blue eyes filled with tears.

'I know,' Tisti said gently. 'I feel your pain as well. You may be his mother, but he is my son as well as yours. Still, it had to be. You both brought it upon each other.

'But that's neither here nor there now. All that matters now is to make you well enough to do what you have to do.'

'And what's that?' Hervara snapped.

'I don't know, Lady. Only you can answer that. Now, this will hurt a little. Stand still and bear the pain!'

She dipped her hand into the brownish salve and began to smear it upon Hervara's body. When it touched her genitals it began to sting quite viciously. She flinched beneath the pain, but did not move. She'd show the old nurse who was

175

truly the mistress of the house. There was nothing Tisti could do to her that would make her cry out.

And then she realised that she was doing exactly what old Tisti had expected of her. From a feeble, bed-ridden, self-pitying shell she had become a woman once again. The salve in itself would do nothing for her. But its preparation and application were bringing back her spirit and her determination. As she stood there, flinching beneath the nurse's none-too-gentle fingers, Hervara knew what she had to do. Once this was over, and the muck had been scraped off, she would leave as well. She had to follow Hather, wherever he had gone. She had to do what she was no longer certain he would do for her. The old burning hatred had returned in full as Tisti used up the mixture in the bowl. Hervara was at once Hather's mother again, and the daughter of dead Angantyr.

And now she knew that she could begin to live again. Once Starkadder lay dead she could begin to plan her life anew. With Hather settled at Oli's court she could forget the cloying boredom of her marriage to Lambi Nef and enjoy the youth her desire for vengeance had never allowed her to know. Even those memories of Samsey Isle might fade if her body were in the hands of the right lover.

After all she was a woman, only thirty years old. She was still lovely, an object of adoration and desire, and even wealthy in her own right. There was virtually nothing that such a woman could not accomplish.

The world could still be hers. All that was needed was the death of Starkadder. That death would erase the stain on her father's memory, freeing her to live as she had never lived before.

Tonight, Hervara knew, she would sleep. Early tomorrow she would begin that journey which would take her to and beyond Uppsala, following the path of King Oli the Great. She must still, she reasoned, be capable of some influence there, even if it meant that she had to begin servicing that disgusting old man all over again. At least he'd give her Starkadder in return.

Old Tisti smiled, knowing Hervara's thoughts. Her ancient eyes studied her mistress's anointed body, reading the line of her breasts and the curve of that belly from which Hather had come. Oh yes, there was no doubt that she could persuade Oli to kill Starkadder. The only doubt was whether the gods were yet ready to free him from their *tafl*-board, to permit the death of one who was, as they all were, a gaming-piece in their struggle with the Norns.

And if they gave her Starkadder, if they yielded his life to her desire for vengeance, what would they ask of her in return? Such a sacrifice on their part would have its price. Did the Lady Hervara know that? If she did, was she willing to make whatever payment they might exact?

Yes, Hervara would start out upon her journey, and those who loved Hather, if not his mother, would go with her. Tisti and Thorkel Tongue would accompany her to Oli's court, wherever it might be. It was their right, their duty, to see their part in the playing through to the very end. Besides, Hather might still need them.

And for old Tisti and for Thorkel Tongue, if not for Hervara, that was all that really mattered.

CHAPTER THREE

Thorvald Brotamad

THE SUN was high, shortening the noontide shadows, as Thorvald Brotamad, desperate, dispirited, wondering just what he was going to tell King Oli, rode back through the gates of the royal palace at Uppsala. As he dismounted, giving the reins of his mount into the hands of an attendant, his thoughts were a turmoil of fear and recrimination.

It in no way surprised him that the party he returned with was smaller than that with which he'd left. Others of the men he'd taken, less honourable and courageous than himself, had quietly deserted rather than face the wrath of their maddened ruler after the disappearance of Starkadder in the mist. For several of Thorvald's party it was an easy decision to make, not to be there when Oli started looking for scapegoats. As the mist began to break up and they saw what had happened, silent horsemen had deserted the column. Their companions, faced with the same choice, kept their own counsel about the thinning ranks. One thing that did surprise Thorvald was that Lambi Nef's son Hather, and the tracker Reindeer Bolli, seemed to have gone with them. That made no sense at all, for Bolli's skills made him too useful to execute, and Hather knew too little of Oli's court to be scared away from a meeting with his father.

But Starkadder, the old butcher from Norway, the man they'd been sent to find, was a different creature altogether.

He knew the fate which would have awaited him. Perhaps that knowledge, and the knowledge that, even if only half of his legend were true, he would be condemned to survive even the bloody ritual of the blood-eagle, had prompted his escape. Yet even the stolid mind of Thorvald Brotamad could see that there might be something more, some other reason for his actions. And that was what could cause Oli to howl with demented fear and anger, and to order blood-eagle executions for all his court to see. Not because Starkadder was gone, but because of what his absence meant to the mad, scabrous king who was the present embodiment of the power of the Yngling dynasty.

Thorvald's feet moved and his mind worked as he made his way to the royal longhouse. He walked as one in a dream, both fearing his duty and compelled by it, unwilling to acknowledge his failure yet required, because of it, to do so. Starkadder had seen in him the bully and the bore, not wanting to discover finer feelings in the overbearing warrior who would kill on impulse and rape on a moment's whim. Yet they were there, as they are in every man, though they may be so hidden beneath his outer self as to be all but unnoticeable. He still knew the difference between respect and fear, even if Oli no longer did.

King Oli, alerted by his sentries, awaited him in his bath. The black, pupil-less eyes burned into Thorvald's, reading his report there before his lips could deliver it.

'How did it happen?' the king demanded. 'How did you lose him?'

'In the mist . . . sir,' Thorvald Brotamad informed him. 'When that infernal mist came up he disappeared.'

'Mist? What mist? There's been none here.'

'It came up shortly after we'd taken Starkadder,' Thorvald replied. 'It hid his escape.'

'So he's free, and still alive? Is that what you're telling me?'

The viking nodded slowly.

'Freya's cunt,' Oli breathed. Then he turned his black eyes onto Thorvald again.

'If Vermund Bjarnisson was here you'd be a dead man, Thorvald. Luckily for you, though, he's not.'

'There's something else you should know, sir,' Thorvald, weak with relief at the king's words, continued.

'And what is that?'

'Starkadder wasn't alone when we overtook him.'

'Who was with him, Thorvald?'

'A boy. His name is Hather, the son of Lambi Nef.'

'Is he with you now?'

Thorvald Brotamad shook his head. He'd rather have left all mention of young Hather out of it, but if any one of his men had mentioned the boy, and the word had got back to Oli, he knew he'd never manage to keep his head.

'No, sir. He vanished in the mist.'

'Together with Starkadder?'

'At the same time, though no one saw him go with the Norwegian.'

'Nevertheless, we must assume, until we're told otherwise, that they are together. It would be unwise to forget that they may even now be plotting to do me harm. Tell me, do you find such belief unreasonable, Thorvald Brotamad?'

The viking, knowing the wisest answer, shook his head. Oli thought that perhaps the shake came a little too quickly to be completely sincere, but such ready assent wasn't altogether a bad thing. At least it showed a certain loyalty, an eagerness to please, and, at best, a lack of any rebellious ideas in the captain. And, in a way, Oli decided to himself, the man's return with such unwilling and unwelcome tidings itself showed a loyalty that few were prepared to offer.

'Very well,' the king said. 'Now, this is what you are to do.'

In that moment Thorvald understood that Oli had almost expected him to fail, that the king had prepared himself against the possibility. So that, rather than any sudden impulse or unexpected generosity, was why he was able to keep his head.

'Firstly,' Oli continued, 'you will summon my attendants for me. After that you have my authority to prepare for the court's withdrawal from Uppsala. In my marshal's absence you are to take command of my forces, Thorvald Brotamad.

180

Only a small strength, sufficient to garrison the town, is to remain here. The rest of my forces are to ride with me to the fortress beside the Dalalven where my son is held, and where Vermund Bjarnisson should be awaiting me, if he has any sense at all.

'Do you understand me, Thorvald? You are to see to my departure from Uppsala. I intend to visit my son.'

Oli began to laugh as he spoke the last words. He, at least, found them most amusing, and he knew that Thorvald would pretend to share his mirth in order to confirm the loyalty his return had demonstrated. Yes, Thorvald Brotamad would share the joke, even if he didn't understand it.

Thorvald had heard many laughs from many throats in his time. But never before had he heard one that masked quite such a deadly purpose. Even the howling glee of a maddened berserk in the massed throng of battle didn't carry the same keening of obsessive madness. But he suppressed his shudder and managed to join his own voice to the cackling of the mad king. Then he saluted and walked from the royal presence. With the king's unholy mirth ringing in his ears he sent Oli's haggard-faced attendants in to him, and walked through the vestibule and out of the longhouse into cleaner air.

Oli watched him go, and his smile was evil. Fear was a potent weapon, all right. Fear could make a man like Thorvald stand against a thousand adversaries, rather than face the wrath of one sick old man.

'Soon be over,' he whispered to himself. 'Soon they'll all be dead. Starkadder, Hather, Omund, Lambi Nef, even Thorvald Brotamad. All be dead. All of them.'

And he laughed again.

Thorvald had to pass Lambi Nef's quarters on his way to the main barracks buildings beneath the palisade, sunk into the earthen mound of the outer defences. He remembered the news he'd brought to Oli, so unwillingly, about his retainer's son.

I ought to warn him, he thought. I ought to tell him what I know, what I've told King Oli. I ought to give him the chance to run or stay as he chooses. After all, if his son is with Starkadder, then he'd be a fool to come back here, and I don't think Lambi Nef breeds foolish sons.

And yet, if the boy's not with Starkadder, then the king may well be plotting a vengeance for which he has no real cause.

He hesitated at the doorway for a moment, then walked past it. There was no point in tempting fate any further than he had to in order to earn his pay. It needed but one pair of eyes to see him, one tongue to whisper to Oli that he was conspiring with Lambi Nef, and both of them would die a slow, painful death. Thorvald was happy enough to have returned with his head and kept it, but he was by no means so happy that he couldn't feel some trace of fellow-feeling for the king's retainer.

As far as Thorvald knew Lambi Nef had served Oli long and faithfully, even if rumour did have it that he owed his position to his wife's whoring with the king. Well, if he'd a wife pretty enough to smooth his path, he'd doubtless have used her in the same way. It was really something of a shame that a mere slip of a boy was to bring Lambi Nef down at last.

As a member of the court Lambi Nef would travel to Dalalven with the king. Chances were that whatever Oli had in mind would wait until they got there. Only then would Lambi Nef find out that Oli harboured a grudge against him, and by then it would be too late.

Thorvald, like any other man used to court politics, knew of the plots against Oli the Mad. Lambi Nef could be a useful ally if a rebellion against King Oli succeeded. But Lambi Nef, because of his son, was out of favour, and the chance of Oli's overthrow was still slight. If the king found out that his courtier had been warned then the man who gave that warning was as doomed as Lambi Nef himself.

So it was that Thorvald Brotamad held his tongue. He couldn't see into the minds of others such as Starkadder and Vermund Bjarnisson, and that meant that he had no way of knowing how close Starkadder was to the last betrayal which would set the seal upon mad Oli's downfall. If he'd known of the words that had passed between Marshal Vermund and Askel Horsetail, had he known of the thoughts

182

even then shaping themselves in Starkadder's mind, even had he known that the vengeful Lady Hervara, ready to sacrifice both her husband and her son to avenge the death of her father Angantyr, was riding for Uppsala, then his actions, even then, might have been different. After all, it would be so simple to turn back to Oli's quarters, avert his gaze from those sinister dead eyes, and slice his sword down into the bath, reddening its water with a fatal, fateful stroke. All that stopped him doing so was the fear which stayed both his hand and his mind from the thought and the deed. And perhaps to the back of his mind came a whisper, masked and unheard, from Mother Skuld, telling him that the act belonged to another, telling him that the deed was one for another man's hand to do.

He pushed open the longhouse door impatiently and glared at the startled guard-commander. 'I have been empowered by the king,' he began, 'to supervise the court's withdrawal to the fortress at Dalalven. How soon can the men be ready?'

The commander made a reply and Thorvald nodded, even though he had not heard it. He could ask again if he really wanted to know. At that moment Thorvald Brotamad felt a twinge of fear which had nothing to do with King Oli and his butchery. It had to do with another, darker spirit which, even then, ranged towards their destination, the fortress on the banks of the Dalalven.

Whatever the Norns had written, Thorvald knew, would be. And whatever they had written, he also knew, would come to pass very soon.

CHAPTER FOUR

Hather

THEY CAMPED for the night on the slopes of the mountain, beyond range of the landslide which had closed for ever the gates of Trollheim. Whilst they slept, unperceived either by Hather or by the sharper senses of old Starkadder, Harbard had slipped away. When he awoke Starkadder wasn't surprised to find that the one-eyed man had vanished. He had lived too long and seen too many strange things to believe that the sorcerer was completely human.

By some mystery which Starkadder didn't trouble to explain, they found themselves watching the dawn rise over the distant longhouses and wooden walls of Uppsala. The old warrior said nothing as he saddled his horse and prepared for his journey northwards, but smiled to himself, as if he were enjoying a joke that he was not prepared to share.

Hather, waking to find his companion's preparations well under way, leaped to his feet and struggled to keep pace with the old warrior.

'Are you sure you want to come with me, young viking?' Starkadder asked. He was smiling as he spoke, his smile tinged with both friendship and sadness. Hather hadn't seen such a look before on that gaunt, stretched-parchment face and it worried him. There was nothing in Starkadder's eyes which should have frightened or alarmed him, yet it held a determination behind its gentleness, an unspoken knowledge of the workings of fate.

184

'Where are you going?' Hather asked. 'Are you going to see my father in Uppsala?'

'What would I have to say to him?' Starkadder asked in return. 'That I've tried to thwart the gods and failed? I could tell him that I know at last what I have to do, that I'm ready to do what he suggested. But even that wouldn't mean a great deal to him, for he has to wait for me to do it in my own time. It won't take too long, if everything happens as I intend, but he'd still have to be patient.

'You know,' he added, 'I don't think you ought to come with me. There are things I have to do, and what you don't know you can't tell.'

Hather felt a stab of pain at the old man's words, and his face showed his disappointment. Starkadder reached across between the horses and laid his hand gently upon Hather's shoulder. 'This isn't war,' he grunted. 'This is something worse than war, my young friend. And you are my friend. We have known each other but a little while, yet we have shared adventures and dangers which most men never dream of, let alone live to see. We have learned to trust one another.'

'Then why won't you trust me now, and tell me?'

'Because the knowledge is dangerous. King Oli is a sick, demented old man. He no longer knows or cares about justice. All that matters to him is holding onto his throne, and he's not worried about how he does it. If you go to Uppsala and he even suspects that you know my plans, he'll not hesitate to torture you. You're a brave lad, Hather. You've proved that already. They say few men return with their wits from Trollheim, but you have. I don't doubt either your trust or your courage. What I do doubt – with reason, for I doubt it in myself – is whether you could keep silence whilst Oli's executioner is practising his art upon your flesh.

'You already have enough lies to tell, my young friend. Thorvald Brotamad will want to know how you and I came to vanish in the mist. He's a bully and a lout, but he's no fool and he's Oli's man. He's not close-mouthed like Vermund Bjarnisson. Now, Reindeer Bolli will have said, if he's seen Thorvald, that he was riding ahead of us. That means that

185

you will be the first person to enter the palace who can offer some explanation of my escape. You will say, as we have agreed, that you suddenly saw me cut myself free with a hidden knife. I tried to slip away in the fog and you started after me. You couldn't follow my trail and became lost yourself. You only got your bearings again when the fog lifted, but by that time it was night and you no longer knew which way I'd gone.'

Hather nodded. 'I'll say that if I have to, but I don't like it. It's a lie, and any sort of lie is without honour.'

Starkadder grinned broadly. 'You're right. But whilst Oli lives this whole land is without honour. Even the gods know that. Remember the words of Odin that the skalds have woven into their songs. When you have to deal with someone you don't trust, yet still require his goodwill, tell him what he wants to hear, even if it isn't true. He won't scruple to lie to you, and that leaves you free to tell him any lies you want.'

'And if I see my father? If I go down into Uppsala? What should I say to him?'

'He's your father, and a good man. Never believe evil of all who plot against kings. Some of them, like Lambi Nef, have the most noble aims for their scheming. Tell him the truth, Hather, but don't trust any other ears. Only the lips of the dead can no longer speak betrayal. Remember that.'

The old Norwegian dropped his hand from Hather's shoulder and turned his mount away. He felt very cold and alone. His ancient eyes swept the sky for ravens and the horizon for a waterfall. When at last he saw Mother Skuld again it would not be too soon for his century-wearied bones.

Hather watched him go, his own mind a turmoil of unrest and thoughts and loyalties that did battle with each other. Here was the man he'd come to kill, the slayer of Angantyr, yet Hather had saved his life. The old warrior was probably more dangerous than those who feared him knew. He rode, solitary and deathless, through men's lives and men shunned him. Yet, a few respected him, even loved him, as Hather had learned to do.

Dwarfs, wolves, ravens, all crowded Hather's thoughts

186

A waterfall flowed through a tower made of stone-slaved dwarfs, sad red eyes gleamed balefully through ragged skeins of mist, and Hervara, lovely but evil, hissed for revenge in the hoarsened cackle of an age-old crone. Much had happened in so short a time and Hather, though he had lived through so much, was still only fifteen years old, and needed a moment to think.

Starkadder was leaving him. He was riding away to do what he had known from the very beginning he must do, and leaving Hather high in the mountains alone. He had become as much a father to the boy as a friend, equal to Lambi Nef in his respect and affection. That was why Hather couldn't let him ride to meet his Norn-written fate alone.

'Starkadder!'

The old Norwegian looked behind him, watching with grey, hollowed eyes as the youth swung lightly up into the saddle. A fine young warrior, he thought. He'd be a worthy son for his worthy father, once he learned that life was really little more than a series of random choices and betrayals.

'I'm coming with you, Starkadder,' Hather said. 'I'm not going to Oli's court with a string of lies, no matter how necessary they seem to be. Besides,' he added, 'I know where you're going. And as you said just now, I might not be able to keep it from King Oli's torturers.'

The old man waited for Hather to draw level with him, and studied the boy's face carefully. There was a strength in the young eyes that Starkadder knew could well be of use to him in the coming days, yet that in itself was not enough reason for allowing the son of Lambi Nef to ride with him. He felt the boy's loyalty and affection for him, and in return felt for him something which another, less tortured and less certain of his future than Starkadder, might have called love.

If I'd had a son of my own, he thought, then this is what I would have wanted him to be. Yet I'd take no child of my own along on a journey such as this may prove to be simply for companionship. There must be a better reason than that.

'Very well, Hather,' he began. 'Since you know so much, tell me. Where am I going? And what am I going to do.'

187

The answer could only be a guess, Starkadder assured himself. It wasn't possible for the boy really to know where he was going. Even so, if the guess was right, Hather would have earned the right to ride with him. The old man could lie of course. He could tell Hather he was mistaken, even if he wasn't. But with some people even a warrior with Starkadder's reputation for treachery felt obliged to maintain a sense of honour, and Hather was one of them.

Starkadder tried to hide the sadness in his eyes, hoping that the boy would guess wrong. Yet something inside him, the silent whisper of Mother Skuld, told him that his destiny and future were linked as closely with this youth's as if they had been bound by an iron-linked chain.

'You're going to the fortress at Dalalven,' Hather said, his voice calm and his eyes unwavering. 'You're going to free Omund Olisson.'

The boy's face was alight with intensity, his body strung taut as a bowstring. Then, in a moment which kept faith both with Hather and himself, the ancient mercenary nodded.

'Starkadder,' came the question, 'is it a betrayal to do what you know is right.'

The old Norwegian laughed bitterly at Hather's question. When his cynical mirth died down he replied: 'To you, my young friend, and to me, simply doing what we believe to be right can never be a betrayal. The problem we have to face, though, is that the gods don't always see things in the same way as we mortals do.'

CHAPTER FIVE

The blacksmith

ON THE evening of the third day after the gates of Trollheim had closed behind them, whilst Hervara rode towards the deserted palace at Uppsala and Vermund Bjarnisson played at *tafl* with young Omund, whilst Oli's court, heavily escorted by troops commanded by Thorvald Brotamad, camped a day's ride behind them, Hather Lambisson and Starkadder rode into the little township which nestled against the fortress at Dalalven.

Their shadows were long in the northern sunset which stained the earth with the blood-red of the sun's dying, and their horses were tired. Hather's was lame, having thrown a shoe within sight of the fortress. Ordinarily he would have dismounted to rest the animal, but it was more important that they should reach their destination before nightfall, though neither he nor Starkadder knew what might await them there.

They walked their foam-flecked mounts into the narrow street between the huts and booths occupied by craftsmen and camp-followers. Following the line of the horseshoe they came to a forge, drawn by the failing glow of expiring charcoal and the smell of hot metal which permeated its thatch and timbers. Sitting outside the door, a beaker of beer in one hand and the other clutching a thin, dirty girl in unusually ragged clothes, was a large, dark, sour-faced man with very little hair and a leather apron, who seemed too

189

intent on fingering the girl's breasts with his grimy hands even to notice them.

The girl's eyes were meek like those of a rabbit which has been all night in a trap. They begged for help, for respect and understanding, but held no hope of any. Starkadder reached out and clamped Hather's wrist close as he reached for his sword, and his warning glance held the youth in check.

Then Starkadder said, his voice deadly quiet and his eyes fixed on the girl's: 'Good evening, blacksmith.'

'I'm done for the day,' the man grunted, without looking up.

'Then can you find us somewhere to stay until the morning?' the old mercenary asked. 'We're not fussy. If there's room in your stables, that will do for us.'

'And how do you propose to pay me for my hospitality?' the blacksmith asked, looking up at last. The girl pulled away and fled back into the hovel which served him for somewhere to live.

Starkadder pulled a purse from his belt, took a gold coin from it, and tossed the coin into the dirt at the man's feet. 'That should be enough,' he said, impassively.

The blacksmith bent forward, his bald pate glistening, to pick up the coin. An amulet on a leather thong, a plain, small cross carved from yew, slipped out of his jerkin to hang down about his neck.

'That should be enough, indeed,' he echoed, his dark eyes watching the mercenary's long, gloved fingers tuck the purse, the heavy purse, the jingling purse, into a pouch at his sword-belt.

'Stabling for our horses and food for ourselves. Then, in the morning I'll pay you for your work,' Starkadder ordered calmly. His eyes never left those of their unwilling host, and he laughed inwardly each time the creature looked away. Even the girl, the little whore of a bond-slave, could look him in the eyes better than the blacksmith.

'You don't get the girl for that,' the blacksmith sneered.

'I have no interest in the girl.'

The man laughed, showing stained, ragged-edged teeth. 'I think your young friend has, though,' he grunted.

'Perhaps he knows a high-born harlot when he sees one.'

'If there's a story to be told about her, it can be told later,' the mercenary yawned. 'We've come far today. All we want at present is food and somewhere to rest.'

'Very well,' the blacksmith replied. 'Stable your horses round there.' He gestured to the side of the decrepit building, where there was a lean-to with a badly-thatched roof. 'Then come inside and we'll find something to eat.'

He turned away from them and pushed open the door. Hather and Starkadder led their mounts around the side and stripped them of their harness. They had almost finished when the girl came out again, a heavy yoke across her shoulders with a bucket hanging from each side. As she passed them, on her way down to the river, she stared at them and moved her lips, in some kind of silent warning.

Starkadder felt his young companion stiffen beside him and smiled gently. 'Very well,' he muttered softly. 'You follow her. I'll keep our host busy. And Hather?'

'Yes?'

'Keep your wits about you. She may hate the blacksmith, but she could also be scared enough of him to be setting a trap for us, for whatever he's got in mind.'

'You think so?'

Starkadder grinned and thumped his young friend gently on the upper arm. Hather grinned back, then he took off after the girl at a fast walk.

The old Norwegian tethered the horses and walked around to the front of the forge. He pushed open the battered door without knocking and peered into the dim interior. As his eyes became used to the gloom, with the only light filtering through from the twilight, he saw that the hut was bigger than it looked from outside. At the end nearest the door stood the forge and the blacksmith's tools. Further in, close by the fire-pit in the centre of the floor, was a trestle table with some worn wooden plates and clay beakers, together with a pitcher which had seen better days. At the far end was a raised platform with bedding strewn in disorder across it. The only thing in the house that was not paltry and battered was a strong oak chest, doubtless where the man's few valuables and the household provisions were stored.

Outside the air had reeked of hot metal, but the inside of the forge stank with the rankness of stale sweat. The black-smith sat at the table, striking tinder for the fire and for a single clay lamp which stood among the beakers.

'Well, mine host,' the mercenary remarked. 'Shall we tell each other our names, as we are to eat together?' As he spoke he was looking about him, noting the position of the window, surmising that the ragged hanging just below the dais concealed the door from which the girl had left to fetch water.

'If you like,' came the grudging reply. 'I'm Magnus Gydasson.'

The implication of the name was not lost on Starkadder. Gyda was a woman's name, and any man who bore a woman's name in his surname was as like as not a low-born bastard. Not that there was anything wrong in bastardy, for several Yngling kings themselves had been born on the wrong side of the blanket. In Magnus's case, though, it served to tell that his mother had been as much of a whore as he was trying to make that pitiful serving-girl of his.

'And you, soldier? What's your name? And the boy's?'

'The boy is Hather, son of Lambi Nef. You've heard of Lambi Nef?'

'No,' the blacksmith laughed. 'But I've heard of his wife,' he grinned, evilly. 'And you?'

'My name is Starkadder.'

The words were spoken in a calm, level voice, almost as if he had been remarking on an indifferent weapon, but their effect upon Magnus Gydasson was startling. His coarse, forced jocularity fell away like a mask, and naked panic crossed his features.

'I see you've heard of me,' the mercenary said.

'You are . . . something of a legend, sir.'

But was the legend true? Magnus asked himself. Well, there was one way to find out, and with a purse like that at stake it would be well worth the risk. After all, it had to hold more gold than he'd seen in several years of sweating away at the bellows.

'Tell me about the girl, Magnus.'

'If you want her, she's yours,' he said, rather too quickly.

'I don't want her. My young friend may be interested, though.'

'Where is your young friend, Lord Starkadder?'

'I left him rubbing down the horses,' came the smooth lie in reply. 'Now, the girl. I believe you said that she was high-born.'

Magnus nodded. 'It's true, sir. She is.' Rubbing down the horses, eh? He'd watch to see if they returned together. Let her try to explain that!

'Her father was a chieftain,' the blacksmith continued. 'He was executed for treachery by King Oli. His name was Thorstein of Nerike. Perhaps you knew him?'

Starkadder nodded grimly, the gloom of the forge hiding the frown the blacksmith's words had brought to his brow. An iron hand clutched his entrails into a sick loathing.

'And her name?' he asked.

'Astrid. Astrid, Thorstein's daughter.'

Starkadder had watched her father die. His betrayal of King Oli had been nothing more than to refuse one of the sick king's whims, but it had destroyed him. The man had died the death of the blood-eagle, watched by the entire court, and now the daughter, deprived of her family and birthright, had been forced into slavery to a man such as Magnus Gydasson in a wretched sink-hole like Dalalven. If one thing more were needed to turn Starkadder's hand to the death of King Oli, this surely was it.

'And what does she do for you, Magnus?'

Tyrfing had appeared like magic in Starkadder's gloved hand. It had made no sound, caught no spark of light, as it leapt from the scabbard. It was simply there, drawn, humming for blood.

The blacksmith fell to his knees and spread his arms in an imploring gesture. 'Don't kill me!' he howled. 'Please! I haven't touched her yet. She came looking for food, so I took her in. I haven't had her, Lord. I swear it. By the White Christ I swear it!'

His hand reached for the little wooden cross, which he raised to his trembling, fear-dried lips.

193

'Then see you don't,' Starkadder replied, noting both the oath and the gesture as he slipped the disappointed Tyrfing back into its sheath. 'If I hear that you have, I'll come back from wherever I am and kill you very, very slowly. When I go,' he added, his voice gentle once again, 'I'll leave you some money to take care of her.'

The blacksmith nodded rapidly, then clambered to his feet and kissed Starkadder's hand. The door opened and Hather came into the forge.

'I'll . . . fetch us some beer, Lords,' Magnus stammered, and he pushed past them into the twilight.

Hather watched him hurry up the shabby street, then turned to his companion, his eyes angry.

'Oli had her father killed . . .' he began.

'I know,' Starkadder replied. 'I was there. It's all right, youngster. I feel as you do. She's safe for tonight, and tomorrow I'll throw that worm a few coins for all the "trouble" he's had looking after her.'

'Can't we take her with us?'

'What would we be taking her to? If we can, Hather, we'll come back, I promise you. She deserves better than we can do for her at present, if only for her father's sake. He was a good man, Thorstein of Nerike. His only crime was to be an honest man at the court of a mad king. But where's young Astrid now?'

'Coming back with the water. I wanted to help her, but she said he'd beat her if he found out we'd been talking. She also said that we should be wary of him. She saw how his eyes lit up when they saw your purse.'

'It's ever the way, my young friend. Well, we'll just have to be on our guard tonight. But whatever you do, Hather, don't let our host see that we mistrust him. Just watch what he eats and drinks. That'll tell you what's safe for us.'

'The easiest thing will be if I watch you and follow your lead, Starkadder.'

The old mercenary grinned, more to himself than to Hather. 'In this case it might be best if you do,' he replied. 'But only this once. Always be your own man and read signs for yourself. Never rely too much on anyone except

194

yourself. You'll sharpen your wits and keep hold of your life that way.'

He had barely finished speaking when the girl, Astrid, opened the door with her free hand and set the two buckets from the yoke down on the hard earth floor of the smithy. Magnus Gydasson pushed past her carrying pitchers of cheap beer.

'See to the food, girl,' he grumbled, though there was something careful about his tone which Starkadder caught immediately. The blacksmith was trying to strike a balance between the way he had treated the girl until now, and the way he felt he should address her after seeing the glittering length of Tyrfing.

A devious man, the old mercenary thought to himself. He'll bear watching. I may only have humbled him in private, but the oaf is fool enough to try for revenge, and he won't wait too long for it either.

Dear god, he thought. Dear Odin, I'm so tired.

Since that night when the gates of Trollheim had closed for ever behind him Starkadder had felt the pain swelling inside him. Since he had turned north towards Dalalven, setting aside the inner conflict which had stayed his hand before, it had grown and strengthened like a mouse growing fat by nibbling at his vitals. Now it was real and solid, like the whitened knuckles of a fist driven deep into his stomach.

For he knew what he was going to do and, in the knowledge of his impending betrayal, waiting in the decrepit smithy for a man to kill him whom he could kill without even bothering to draw breath, he saw the true face of the curse which had hunted and haunted him through the ages.

It wasn't the betrayal itself which caused the pain. It wasn't even the berserk rage, the blind fury of destruction which overtook him. That wasn't the thing that hurt. That was only the result, not the cause, only the blood-soaked aftermath of his accursed destiny.

The real hurt, the agony which could only be assuaged with blood, was the foreknowledge. His curse was knowing what he was cursed to do.

'Starkadder?'

There was a little love, at least, in the boy. Perhaps Hather

195

was to be his last friend in the world of men, who would walk with him through the dark days before he could die.

Dear Odin, let it be so.

'I'm all right,' he replied. 'It was simply the ghost of a moment as yet unborn. It will pass. See? It has gone already.' And he smiled at the boy.

They sat down at the trestle table to a simple meal of dried fish, bread and goat-cheese, washed down with water and the ale Magnus had brought from the town. They passed the wooden bowls between themselves, Hather watching to see what Starkadder took and lifted to his mouth, Starkadder watching the blacksmith for some sign of betrayal.

Yet no sign came, and the level of beer in the pitchers dropped as they swilled horn after horn.

Outside, in the darkness, Gerard watched the smithy with death-hungry eyes. He'd heard the word when Magnus fetched the beer. His listening ears, ever alert for scraps of talk which might some time be of use to him, had heard the name he both longed for and dreaded.

Starkadder had come to Dalalven. Starkadder was here.

He hadn't waited to hear the rest. That was enough for him, enough to send him back to his hovel to fetch the bright, bear-greased sword he kept wrapped in wadmal under his bedding.

And he did not notice, intent as he was upon the destruction of a legend, that others waited around him in the darkness.

Had he waited a little longer, paused just a few moments before going to find his weapon, its hilt both a symbol of Christ's cross and a hand-hold for Christ's work in the north, he would have known that others sought to do the work he had marked down for himself. After all, he might have said as he stood sweating with a growing fear of the butcher's work he was about to undertake, it didn't matter in the least who finally killed old Starkadder. All that really mattered, all that had ever mattered since that day on the fringe of a forest in the south, was that the embodiment of the pagan myths should be destroyed. True, it would mean more glory for him and the god he served if the hands that

196

dispatched Starkadder were his own, but the death itself would be symbol enough of Christ's victory.

He listened to the voices, the sounds of eating and the swilling of ale, which came through the mud walls. He hardly dared hope that with each minute that passed, with each horn of ale, the fearsome warrior would become more forgetful, more open to attack.

And Dvalin sat far-seeing on the balcony about the grotesque stone tower and giggled, fed knowledge of the hearts and thoughts of men by the shapes which no longer had hearts themselves. He giggled because, like Starkadder, he too had met and spoken with Mother Skuld. Unlike Starkadder, though, he knew from that meeting most of what was to come. And in that he found a humour he could never share with men, a humour which he knew would some day soon be paid for with his life.

There was nothing wrong with the food. Whether or not his threats had persuaded Magnus Gydasson to show them a more generous hospitality than he had intended, Starkadder didn't know. But there was nothing wrong with either the food they had eaten or the beer that they had drunk in such quantities. All in all it was fine hospitality from a humble smithy, and it warmed the old mercenary's heart, even to the point of beginning to lull away his suspicions.

'A fine meal, Magnus,' he grinned, more for the way it had been shared even with Astrid than for the quality of the food itself.

Their host lurched unevenly to his feet. 'I'll get some more beer,' he mumbled, making his way unsteadily towards the street door.

For a purseful of gold the blacksmith was ready to tempt the Norns. For a purseful of gold he was even willing to challenge the curses of the gods themselves. And this was his signal to the watchers in the night.

Something warned Starkadder. Something forced a hiss from his lips in the gloom, a hiss which warned Hather to slip the thong-loop from his scabbard chape. As Magnus wrenched open the door the old warrior's legs were already tensed beneath him for the spring which would overturn the trestle in the faces of his unknown enemies.

They came out from the shadowed walls and alleys and scrambled in through the open doorway. Others fumbled with the latch of the side-door, forcing it open on its leather hinges. They swarmed, yelling, into the smithy from both ends, the only light the flickering, failing lamp reflected on their weapons.

Hather quickly pushed Astrid to a corner of the room where she could climb onto the platform for safety, out of the scything range of the swinging sword-blades. Then he took his sword in both hands and stood against Starkadder's back, silently invoking Odin and Tyrfing to help him in his need, ready to defend himself and his friend with every scrap of battlecraft he had learned in his short life.

Starkadder faced the main rush from the street door, feet firmly planted apart, sword held with that steady, light, two-handed grip which would enable him to make the deft, skilful cuts which had saved his life time and time again.

I can't die, he thought. Not yet. The betrayal of King Oli is not yet complete.

But I can be wounded. And a wound will slow me down. Odin, can you really be so unkind?

The first took his sword-point in his open, yelling mouth. Before the weapon could stick fast in the palate Starkadder had torn it free and slashed at the shoulder of the second. As the first man went down, choking on his own blood, the second reeled away, his weapon-arm hanging only by a shred of sinew.

Hather swept his sword across a man's stomach, trying to close his ears against the horrified screaming which threatened to deafen him in the confined battleground of the smithy. The next man slashed at his head and the youth only just had time to raise his own blade in a crooked parry.

Gerard saw them forcing their way inside. There was no mistaking their grim purpose. He wasn't alone in wanting Starkadder dead. With a howl growing in his throat he flung himself towards the smithy, his bear-greased blade shining in the night.

'Starkadder!' he screamed.

A dark shape lurched through the gloom towards him, clutching at the blood which spurted from a gash in his thigh. He was Starkadder's third, but Gerard didn't know that. The robber saw the armed priest, sword held high, and raised his own weapon to defend himself. With a grunt which took most of the breath from his body Gerard swung down with his sword, jumping clear of the ground to add force to the blow. The blade turned in its descent, sweeping the man's head clear of his shoulders.

Another robber turned from Starkadder to attack the priest. Before he had gone two steps he twitched violently as the old mercenary severed his spine.

'I don't know who you are,' Starkadder spoke without breaking his swing, 'but you're welcome, friend.'

The sword flew on, trailing dirty droplets in the half-light, and shored through the throat of number five.

Gerard felt a cold sweat break out beneath the matted hair which bestraggled his forehead. This wasn't right. This wasn't right at all. He was killing the wrong men!

But he didn't really have time to think about it. Another blade was streaking towards his eyes, forcing him to duck and weave to one side. He thrust out his sword in a vicious blind jab and Magnus Gydasson stiffened and froze, the point of Gerard's weapon standing out between his shoulder-blades. The others broke and ran, leaving nine of their number dead or dying in the smithy. Hather aimed a cut at the back of a fleeing robber and grinned as the point scored a painful line across the man's buttocks. Starkadder simply sat down heavily, and began to laugh.

Magnus wrenched away from Gerard's sword and turned his bulging eyes towards Starkadder. He tried to speak, but his words were lost in the rush of blood which welled up from his throat. With a noise that was part-cry, part-cough he pitched onto his face and lay still.

Starkadder leaned forward and wiped Tyrfing's stained length on the back of Magnus' tunic. Carefully, with a reverence he had never shown before for any weapon, he slid the sword back into its sheath. His face showed no sign of the effort it cost him to force the accursed blade to accept its confinement.

Hather stood stunned, his mouth open, his tongue clinging to his palate, as if it were unwilling to taste the same metallic fear which rose up from his throat. His knuckles were still white, his fingers wrapped tightly about the sweaty hilt of his weapon and his eyes were wide with horror. The fight was over, and he had shared in the slaughter.

Gerard fought to control the trembling in his limbs. For the first time in his life he knew what killing meant. It was a violent, wanton destruction, a stealing of the lives of Christ's creatures, yet something which, in an imperfect world which had not yet completely learned the virtues and benefits of his master's love, had to be done. To win souls you had to take lives. Besides, they were only pagan lives.

On the stained, blood-muddied earth of the floor, the hand of a dying man reached out to clutch for something that wasn't there. Gerard struggled with the sudden rush which threatened to force itself up from his stomach, a rush which Hather had already felt, and swallowed hard.

They had, between them, killed nine men, including their erstwhile host. Yet not one of them had taken so much as a scratch in return.

Starkadder gave inward thanks to Odin. Gerard groaned, unable to pray.

On the platform Astrid was sobbing with terror. Hather dropped his sword and stepped across the corpse-littered floor to comfort her.

'As I said, friend,' Starkadder began, 'I don't know your name. Otherwise I'd call you by it to thank you.'

It wasn't right. It wasn't fair. Dear Christ, it had all gone wrong. Here he was, within a sword-length of the man he'd sworn to kill, and instead he'd helped to save the old killer's life.

'My name . . . is Gerard.'

'Not a Swedish name.'

The priest shook his head. 'I'm English.'

'Then you have my thanks, English Gerard. My young companion is Hather Lambisson, and I'm . . .'

'Starkadder. I know.'

The ancient Norwegian's eyes narrowed into slits Hather, who was comforting Astrid, missed the monk's words altogether. Gerard, his heart pounding and his temples throbbing with confusion and fear at his unwitting betrayal, felt the Christ-cross hilt of his sword grow loose in his tremorous fingers. The moment passed.

'Of course,' Starkadder smiled. 'You were calling my name when you came to help us. Am I really so famous in this country?'

'Everybody . . . knows Starkadder,' Gerard mumbled, struggling to return the smile.

It was too late now. He had failed, and the best he could hope for was another chance at another time. Now that he stood in front of this old man who embodied all the strength of paganism, now that he had seen the skill and ease with which his adversary dispatched those foolish enough to come against him, he knew that he could only hope to slay him by stealth. All he could do was pray to Christ that the familiarity he would now be forced to assume and maintain wouldn't blind his eyes to the godless evil of this man. He had to stay close and feign friendship. He had to gain the ancient killer's trust. He had to wait and woo, all the time looking for the chance which would enable him to complete his great and godly design.

'And so you came to help me, Gerard? That was kind. Now, forgive the habitual suspicion of an old and weary man, but will you tell me why?'

He scrabbled in his thoughts for a lie which might serve for an answer. Then, even as it came, even as it passed his lips, he knew that the lie itself was divinely inspired, that the White Christ had wrought a miracle and shown him the way through falsehood into truth.

'I . . . need your help,' he said.

Starkadder nodded. 'What is it you want us to do, English Gerard?' the old Norwegian asked. 'Tell us.'

'I want you to help me free Omund Olisson.'

'To what end?' Hather asked, peering down from the platform to see what manner of man their new companion might be.

The question pleased Starkadder. True, it looked as if Gerard's intentions were the same as their own, but Hather had learned, despite his years, that the same means might be employed by different people to very different ends. It was

201

a good lesson, one that might keep him alive in years and battles ahead of him.

'I've come this far,' Gerard replied, his face, calm and almost serene, belying his inner turmoil. 'So I'll tell you the truth.'

Was it still a lie or was it, through the power of Christ, now the true purpose of his life? Had any read his thoughts and asked him, not even Gerard could have answered with total honesty. 'I want to free Omund and put him on his father's throne. You know me to be a Christian, so you can guess my purpose. He will be grateful to those who save his life. He will incline towards the new, greater faith I am bringing to the north. He will be a powerful convert for me, Hather Lambisson.'

'Why not convert his father instead?' Starkadder questioned.

'Because Oli is old and stubborn. Besides, the common people have no love for him. Not while there's Omund to replace him.'

The priest was right. Foreigner he might be, but he understood how the land lay, and how to destroy all opposition to his cause. Starkadder grinned with satisfaction. Then he said: 'The fortress here at Dalalven is one of the best-built and most secure in the whole of Sweden. Our first, our greatest, difficulty is to get inside it.'

'I can get you in. There are converts amongst the guards. The commander doesn't care what gods they worship so long as they do their jobs. He allows me in to bring Christ to them. All you have to do is hide your weapons. Then you can come in with me. Will you help me?'

Starkadder grinned broadly. 'I owe you already for your help here tonight. To turn down an offer of further help would be churlish, English Gerard. What say you, Hather?'

Since he had left Lambi Nef's estate and his mother, Hather had found freedom and worth in the company of the old Norwegian, he had learned the true nature of loyalty. It went beyond simple service and obedience into uncharted realms of subtlety and decision. He had learned the nature of dwarfs and curses and the horror of dark shapes and hidden castles. He had travelled and fought

202

and now, as he comforted Astrid in the gloom of the strife-ridden smithy, he was upon the threshold of finding something which might grow into love.

Yet his choice was easily and quickly made. Whether it led to glorious life or ignominious and painful death he must follow the doomed old warrior to whatever fate the Norns had written.

'When do we make our way into the fortress?' he asked.

CHAPTER SIX

Omund

IN THE early light of dawn, whilst Omund slept and Oli's men, driven by Thorvald Brotamad to press on and reach their destination before noon, broke camp, whilst the watch began to change within the mounded palisades of Dalalven, Hather, Gerard and Starkadder carried the bodies of the slain down to the river and threw them in. There were no rites, no observance of the ceremonies for the disposal of those slain in the fight. It was too late for all that. Either Odin wanted them for Valhalla or he didn't. If they were amongst the chosen they had already joined the one-eyed father of the gods. If not, then all the funerary rites in the world wouldn't ease their lot in Hel's dark empire. It was as simple as that. So their remains were tossed into the river like the butcher's offal they had become.

Hather had slept with Astrid that night, though sleep, after their experience in the smithy, was all that either had wanted. Towards dawn, smelling the warmth of the girl's sleeping body, Hather had tried to sustain an erection which might permit him sexual entry, making the shared experience a *fait accompli* when Astrid woke, as she surely would. But the image of his mother, Hervara, writhing beneath him upon his father's high seat had clouded his emotions and desires, leaving him unsure and hesitant, depriving him even of the strength he might expect to achieve and sustain as a result of his own dextrous manipulations. The girl remained asleep, unaware of his unspoken

204

failure. Besides, he reasoned to himself, it was unfair to inflict the possibility of a child upon one who had suffered so much, and who might suffer more if he was to die upon the uncertain morrow.

It was dirty, nasty work, staining hands and clothing with the blood and excrement of dead men. But they closed their minds and mouths to the slime and stink, grimly aware that fate alone had kept them from the same end.

Then, with the dead consigned to the currents which would bear them down towards the Baltic shore, Hather, Starkadder and Gerard prepared to leave. They ate what food was left in the smithy, washing it down with water drawn after the corpses had gone seaward. Starkadder, knowing what lay ahead of them, gave Astrid all the money they had left in case they failed to return.

'For food,' he said, pressing the purse into her bony hand, 'and for something better than rags to wear.'

'And to remember you by?' she smiled wistfully at Hather.

Starkadder shook his head. 'Remember us by our deeds, not by our gifts,' he said.

'If we can come back for you, we will,' Hather assured her.

She nodded and turned away, unwilling to let him see the unexpected tears which were threatening to streak her face.

'We must go,' Gerard said, his voice firm with resolution. 'The guard is changing. The men I know will be manning the wicket gate on the river-side of the fortress. They are our way to Omund, Starkadder. I don't expect them to do anything more for us, but at least they'll let us in. Are you ready?'

Starkadder followed Gerard out of the door, pausing only to look back at Astrid and Hather, who stood together, she with her back to him.

'A moment only, my young friends,' he said gently. 'I regret you can have no more.'

He left them there and went out, closing his ears against whatever sweet folly their youth might be promising. He knew that Hather had lain all night awake because Astrid slept close by, not daring so much as to stretch out his hand to touch her. He loved the boy as if he were his own son, not Lambi Nef's, but could not shield him from all that his fate might bring.

For once in his long curse-laden life, Starkadder wanted to go on living, to watch Hather growing into a manhood which would make him one of the greatest vikings of the age. Perhaps it was true that the Yngling dynasty was growing old, ready to crumble and pass from the minds of men. But whilst there were other, younger men such as Hather Lambisson, there was a chance that the future would not be so bad, that from the fall of the Ynglings a better world might grow, a world where men would not walk in fear of their rulers, where peace and order would triumph over disruption and uncertainty.

'Come on,' Gerard hissed, breaking the old mercenary out of his dreaming. 'Get Hather out here. We've no time for this.'

Starkadder sighed and knocked on the side door of the smithy. It opened almost at once and Hather stumbled out into the dawn, while Astrid's saddened face hovered pale in the dark behind him.

They made their way through the town, early shadows trailing behind them, to the wicket gate on the river side of the fortress of which Gerard had told them. As they approached, stealing silently into the darkness of the towering palisade, they drew their cloaks close, making sure that their weapons were hidden by the folds. When they reached the little wooden doorway they stopped, and the priest tapped lightly.

The door opened a couple of inches. Mistrustful eyes peered out at them from under a leather helmet. 'Who's there?' a voice hissed.

'Come on, Halli, open up,' Gerard laughed. 'Surely you know me by now.'

For a moment the eyes narrowed suspiciously, then the door swung open and they stepped inside the fortress.

'The Lord be with thee,' Gerard said, waving his fingers in the air.

'And with thy spirit,' the guard replied. Hather could make nothing of these strange words, which were clearly part of the English priest's new faith.

'These two,' the sentry gestured towards Starkadder and Hather, muffled in their close-drawn cloaks. 'Who are they? What are they doing here?'

'They are brothers, Halli,' came the reply. 'Brothers like myself, who have come to Sweden to bring Christ's words from a distant land. Now, quickly, close the gate before someone sees us.'

Halli closed the wicket-gate, bolting them inside the fortress, and Starkadder chuckled to himself under his hood. The White Christ might be a pain in the arse, but he'd done superb work that morning.

Halli led them past the stables to an empty guard-hut. As he bent to pour milk from a jug into horn beakers, Gerard drew his sword and dealt a hefty blow with the pommel to the back of the sentry's skull. With hardly a sound the Christian collapsed across the trestle table and slid onto the floor.

'God forgive me,' Gerard muttered.

'Freya's tits, man!' Starkadder hissed. 'Find Omund for us and even Odin will forgive you.'

'We have to make our way around the perimeter until we can begin to slip between the longhouses,' the priest whispered, his green eyes bright in a shaft of early sunlight. 'Omund's quarters are almost in the middle of the fortress.'

'Why don't we just go straight there?' Hather asked.

'Because it's too risky. By using that gate we managed to get inside with only one man seeing us. This fortress is round, though, built in such a way that a man on the palisade can see every inch of open ground between the longhouses. We must stay in the shadow of the walls until we find somewhere to cross towards the middle without being seen.'

They left the hut cautiously and began to edge around the outer stables, following the line of the defences until the shadowed gable-end of a longhouse covered their approach to the central buildings. There they paused, listening to the footfalls on the wooden walls, waiting for the moment when the patrolling guards could no longer see them strike out for Omund's quarters. For an eternity they crouched hidden, each listening to the beating of his heart, knowing that discovery would lead to capture and certain death.

The waiting became unbearable as the pounding of their hearts threatened to drown out the footfalls of the sentries above them, sentries who watched for a threat from without which had already come in. At last the moment came when they could make the crossing unseen. Keeping low, their dull cloaks blending with the shadows on the ground, they ran for the cover of the nearest longhouse, moving from shadow to shadow, from wall to wall.

'This one?' Hather demanded in an urgent whisper as they reached one of the four central longhouses.

Gerard shook his head and pointed to a building set across the one they were pressed against. 'In there,' he muttered. 'But be careful. There are guards.'

'Work for me, I think,' Starkadder smiled. He detached himself from the timber wall and walked boldly into the vestibule which stood out from the side of the longhouse.

The sun was behind him as he opened the door and strode inside. The two guards in the vestibule straightened at his approach, noting the glint of armour beneath his long, back-flung cloak.

'Orders,' he began firmly. 'Fetch Omund Olisson.'

The guards hesitated, peering to make out his sun-ringed features in the sudden brightness. Without so much as breaking his stride the old Norwegian stepped between them and slammed a solid fist into each face at the same time. The guard to his left crumpled and went down. His companion needed another blow to the stomach and a knee in the jaw to lay him out.

Smiling at the ease of his victory Starkadder signalled to his companions. As they half-ran into the cover of the vestibule he closed the door behind them.

Up on the wooden walls of the fortress the sentries continued their patrolling, unaware of what was happening in their midst.

'Through there!' Gerard snapped, pointing to the inner door. 'There will be guards in the main hall.'

'Many?' Hather asked.

'Enough,' Starkadder replied, slipping the thong from

Tyrfing's hilt and easing the blade in its sheath. Without waiting to see if his two companions were ready to follow he stretched out his fingers towards the latch.

Then, as the sun rose, bathing the wooden walls of the fortress beside the Dalalven with light, as the guards patrolled and Omund Olisson slept within his bed-closet, as the common people began to rise to the daily struggle of winning a livelihood from the little town, time itself began to alter for Starkadder. He watched a hand, his own hand, yet also the hand of another person at another time in another place, reach out to the brazen fastenings of the inner door. There was nothing strange in the action, nothing that he had not done a thousand times before, yet he felt the tugging at his temples and the hammering in his chest. It was beginning.

He had felt that same sense of being someone, somewhere else, only twice before. It was not the feeling he had when he spoke with Mother Skuld at the waterfall. It was a different, more urgent, more powerful thing, and he knew its meaning all too well.

He had felt it before Vikar died. He had felt it before Frothi died. Now he felt it a third time.

The last betrayal was at hand.

It might take a moment. It might take hours. Yet it was coming. As surely as the sun was lighting up the sky the third betrayal was coming. Before the day was over, before the sun set, the third betrayal would be done.

Hather saw his hesitation and reached out to touch the back of his hand. The old mercenary forced a smile. Hather and Gerard watched his lips draw back to show his age-yellowed teeth. Both of them read his face in different ways; the priest saw blood-lust, Hather saw unbearable pain.

And Hather too knew that Starkadder's weird was all but done.

Starkadder hesitated before the inner door. Then he drew Tyrfing and, with more strength than the feat required, forced the door open.

Four guards were sitting at the trestle table between the inner door and the farther wall, behind which lay Omund's bed-closet. At the kicking of the door they sprang to their feet and reached for the weapons they had carelessly laid aside. In deathly silence Starkadder leapt across the hall with Hather and Gerard close behind him, Tyrfing scything in a glittering arc of dwarf-forged steel.

The first, his sword only half-drawn, fell to the straw-strewn floor almost in two halves. The second, his feet tangled in the bench, pitched over with blood spewing in a furious jet from his torn throat. The third fell to Hather's blade, his own spinning uselessly away from death-weak fingers, and the fourth, the last, took Gerard's rush before his buttocks had even left the seat. The priest's booted foot crushed down on his breastbone, forcing a death rattle out of him, as the sword pulled free.

It was over in moments and the hall was grave-quiet.

And still Starkadder was someone else, obeying a will that was not his own, in a place he had not chosen.

'This way,' came Gerard's urgent whisper. 'Omund is through here.' He led the way to a doorway in the farther wall. Hather and Starkadder followed him, eager to be done with the danger, eager to be free of their fear, free of the fortress of Dalalven.

In the guard-hut near the wicket-gate Halli was beginning to feel a throbbing at the back of his neck. A moment, perhaps a minute more, and he would remember how he came by it.

Gerard, the sweat of fear and fighting matting his greasy brown hair, reached out for the latch. Before he could lift it Starkadder's gaunt hand clamped itself about his wrist.

'Stand away!' the old mercenary hissed. 'There may be more guards inside.'

The monk stepped back towards the centre of the hall to stand among the dead men. His ears were straining for the alarm which must surely come soon.

He had done it. He had led them into the very centre of the fortress, to the place where Omund was kept. For him there was still a chance of success. For Hather and

Starkadder, though, there could only be betrayal and defeat. Did the fools really believe they could get out with Omund alive? Halli hadn't seen who struck the blow. It would be easy enough for Gerard to deny it, to blame it on the man they had all feared for so long.

All that remained was to choose the right moment. He would have to make Oli's men believe that he'd been forced into leading Hather and Starkadder into the fortress, that he'd been their prisoner, obeying under threat of death, waiting only for a chance to warn Omund's gaolers of the treachery in their midst.

And Oli would be grateful. Oli would listen to the Word that Brother Gerard had brought to Sweden, the way of the White Christ from the south. Even Brother Hugo, dragged and tortured by the pagan king until his death-struggle was ended by Starkadder's Odin-offering, would be avenged with the king's baptism by Gerard.

Gerard the monk. Gerard, slayer of Starkadder. Gerard, first Bishop of Sweden.

Starkadder loosed the latch and pulled open the door. A youth, not much older than Hather, was sitting up on the dragon-carved, straw-mattressed frame. His limbs were spindly and his large, grey eyes blinked in the light from the hall.

Halli's shouting rang through the morning stillness. Sleep was shattered, hands flew to weapons and grabbed for clothing.

Gerard was trembling with fear and excitement as he threw his sword away. He turned and ran shrieking from the longhouse, his voice joining in the general alarum.

Hather spun round in amazement as the monk rushed out. Starkadder growled, his eyes narrowed. Something deep inside him, neither instinct nor premonition, had let him down. He should have known. He should have guarded against this. Yet perhaps he *had* known all along that Gerard was playing a game of his own devising, a game not unlike

211

that older, deadlier game which the gods played on their *tafl*-boards.

His heart hammered. His eyes burned. Tyrfing hummed, hungry for the fighting.

End it now, said a voice. Finish it. The third betrayal, Starkadder. Betray the one you came to save. Kill Omund.

Dvalin, high on his gargoyle-crusted tower, was gloating, Tyrfing's evil singing sweetly in his ears. Perhaps at last the White Christ had come to destroy the Yngling dynasty for ever. And perhaps, the dwarf mused, the burning cressets glittering in his eyes, he had hidden from the sunrise for the last time in his night-wrapped life.

The running feet came closer. Gerard stumbled. Rough hands seized him and held him fast.

'Not me, you fools!' he howled, his green eyes wild with terror and exultation. 'In there. Starkadder! He's come to free young Omund!'

Askel Horsetail and Vermund Bjarnisson, dragged by the tumult from drink-bought slumber, confronted the struggling monk.

'Starkadder?' the marshal demanded. 'With Omund?'

Gerard nodded furiously. 'They made me bring them in,' he lied. 'I warned you the first chance I had.'

Horsetail grunted. Then he turned to his captain. 'Secure the vestibule and throw a cordon around the longhouse,' he ordered. 'No one goes in or comes out without permission.'

'And use your best men,' Vermund added. 'The king will have our guts spread out in a thousand blood-eagles if Starkadder or Omund gets away.'

Hather's eyes darted about the hall. One way in or out. One way only. They were caught like flies in a flask. His heart was pounding with mingled excitement and fear. If they were taken, if they lived, there was only death by the blood-eagle to look forward to. Better to die here, the youth thought, and sell their lives for a higher price.

212

His one regret was that he would never see Astrid again. She would be alone in an unkind world. But the skalds would sing of the man who died beside the mighty Starkadder. Hather's legend might be short, but it would be a mighty one.

'We can . . .' He swallowed hard, trying to wet his fear-dried throat so that the words would come out. 'We can take them as they come through the vestibule,' he said. 'They can only come in one at a time.'

Starkadder looked down at the cowering, frightened Omund. Yngling he may be, and Oli's son, but his spirit was gone, broken by the long years of his imprisonment. He could never be the king the people needed.

The third betrayal, Starkadder. Kill him. Then you can die.

A sudden strength flooded into the hand that was almost not his own. He knew that this was what Dvalin wanted, that Omund's death would bring about the fall of the Ynglings as surely and more swiftly than Omund's reign. That was why he had Tyrfing. The sword was dwarf-crafted and could, in the right hands, be dwarf-wielded.

'This is a cruel world,' Dvalin had said, 'and the cruelty is not all of your making, or of mine.'

If the god-forged empire of the north were destroyed the gods would lose their power. Only then would the dwarfs be safe. Only then could they hold their own realms in the face of the invading Christ.

So kill Omund.

Hather's ice-blue eyes were wide with unspoken questions. The ancient warrior's arm was shaking with the effort as he returned the reluctant Tyrfing to its scabbard and slipped the loop over the guard.

'The Norns have written your fate as surely as they have written mine,' he began, speaking gently to the youth who might have been his son. 'Our fates may differ, young Hather. Perhaps yours is to die here, but mine is not. Dvalin wants Omund killed to bring the Ynglings' rule to a rapid end. I'll not give him that satisfaction.'

He closed the door upon the forlorn figure in the bed-closet, and walked slowly, purposefully, into the centre of the hall.

213

'Vermund Bjarnisson,' he called. 'Are you there, Vermund?'

The soldiers gave way before the king's marshal. 'I'm here, Starkadder,' Vermund said quietly.

'I will surrender to you, Vermund,' the old mercenary began, 'if you'll let the boy go. He has no part in this. I'm the one Oli wants.'

Hather dashed forward to stand by him. 'No,' he shouted. 'I won't let you. We stand together, Starkadder, you and I. I came with you of my own choice. I'll not let you sell yourself for me.'

His sword ready, he stepped swiftly between Vermund and the ancient Norwegian.

Vermund sadly shook his head. 'I can't accept your offer, Starkadder,' he muttered, his voice regretful. 'I must take you both or kill you both. King Oli wouldn't have it any other way.'

He stepped forward, his sword drawn. Askel Horsetail and his men began to file into the hall.

Hather, his blade levelled, backed towards Starkadder. Then a sharp blow from the mercenary's mail-gloved hand fell across the back of his neck and he fell senseless to the straw-scattered floor.

CHAPTER SEVEN

The third betrayal

WHEN HATHER recovered his senses it was to find himself bound hand and foot with Starkadder beside him. They lay in the darkness of a dungeon dug out of the rock and shored with timber planking. What little light there was filtered through between the boards of the trapdoor overhead.

The old Norwegian was calling his name, very softly. His grey eyes were sad, still fired by a little of the old weary determination. Hather shook his head, and sat up.

'Why?' he demanded accusingly. 'I could have killed him. An ageing soldier with one eye. I could have killed him easily.'

'Could you?' Starkadder asked. 'And if you had, what then? Kill Horsetail? Perhaps. You've learned well and quickly. You might have taken Askel Horsetail, Hather. But then what? How many more could you have killed? Two? Three? Five, before they cut you down? At least you're still alive.'

The youth snorted. 'For what?' he snapped, derision ringing in his voice. 'For mad Oli to carve me into a blood-eagle? He'll kill us slowly, Starkadder. Make no mistake about that.'

'Listen to me,' the old man began. 'I can't remember what a normal life with its hopes and fears is like, but I can try. Whilst you're alive and in one piece you can hope. There's always hope until the sword plunges in or the executioner severs the last rib. Keep hoping, Hather. Whilst I'm alive you may still be able to live through all this. The third betrayal hasn't happened yet.'

The words had hardly left his lips before he regretted them. His temples still felt that tugging which signalled the nearness of the deed. His heart still hammered away within the gauntness of his ribs and the sense of being unable to control his actions, of not being himself, persisted still. Perhaps the third betrayal had been to strike Hather down. Perhaps his own fate was to die painfully in front of Oli after all . . .

Above them dust from the dry courtyard sifted down through the cracks in the trap–door. The sounds of rumbling wagons and moving horses came to their ears.

King Oli the Great had arrived at the fortress at Dalalven.

Vermund was called to report to the king as he lolled in his wooden bath. The blackness in his eyes penetrated the depths of Vermund Bjarnisson's soul, and the glittering was madder and more crazed than the marshal had ever seen it. The king, sure of his triumph, was giving instructions for Starkadder to be put to the blood–eagle, '. . . and Omund as well,' he cackled.

At that the marshal knew that King Oli the Great was stark gibbering mad. But he had to ask. He had to question that last monstrous order.

'Omund? Your son?'

Oli sighed and lazily splashed water over his shoulders with a flabby hand, the fingertips wrinkled by long soaking. 'Do you really fail to understand me, Vermund?' he asked quietly. 'It's simple enough. Omund is a threat to me for as long as he lives. If he no longer lives there will be no more threat. You see? Simplicity itself. Kill Omund together with Starkadder and Hather Lambisson and you will not only set an example, you remove all reason for treachery.'

Thorvald Brotamad, standing beside the king's bath, suppressed a shudder at the barbarity of the king's reasoning. Yet for all that it filled him with revulsion, he could not deny its logic.

Vermund was only too aware of the choice which faced him. It was all too simple. Obedience, or the blood-eagle.

He saluted and left the royal presence. He remembered his journey north from Uppsala, the people of Oli's kingdom cowering in the flimsy shelter of their homes rather than come out to watch the soldiers march by. The words sprang unbidden to his mind, the words which could turn into gory reality with the death of Omund.

Fear. Courage born of fear. Rebellion.

Could he lead Oli's soldiers against Oli's fear-bold people? More importantly, with his loyalty sworn to one man out of thousands, did he want to? He shook his head as he walked, unsure as to which of the choices frightened him most: obedience, or the consequence of betrayal.

Oli beckoned Thorvald Brotamad to bend his ear. Oli had no illusions about the Norwegian mercenary with the scarred face and the blue-black hair and beard. He knew that this soldier of fortune was little more than a swaggering bully, yet sensed in him a ruthlessness which Vermund Bjarnisson lacked and which made Thorvald the obvious choice for Vermund's successor. Thorvald would obey without questioning his orders. Vermund, on the other hand, appeared to be developing a dangerously womanish softness which might one day damn them all. For Oli, decisions were simply a matter of choices to be weighed, and orders to be given.

Starkadder, Omund and that useless brat of Lambi Nef's. Doubtless, with the son dead, the father would be intriguing against him. So, Lambi Nef would follow his son. After all, even the most ignorant and fumbling of leeches knew that if you find a growth you cut it out before it spreads, and Lambi Nef was a growth to be cut out.

Then, with Starkadder, Omund, Hather and Lambi Nef dead, that choice little whore Hervara wouldn't mind saving her life by a little bed-warming, even with a decaying old man. Oli had his concubines, of course, but they were nothing special. In all his long life there had only been Hervara who was special . . . Give her something to fight for and she'd do anything. Lambi Nef's rewards had made

217

her cold and complacent. She'd need his death to remind her what royal power really was . . .

And, after Lambi Nef, it would have to be Vermund Bjarnisson who died. The one-eyed marshal was still a good man, perhaps the best general in the kingdom, but he questioned too many orders, and that would never do. Trusted men had to give instant obedience. It was the only way to maintain efficient rule. Thorvald might not be as clever, and he was, after all, a foreigner, but at least he knew how to obey.

'Watch Vermund,' Oli hissed. 'At the first hint of treachery his position is yours. Do you understand me, Thorvald Brotamad? Am I making myself clear, Thorvald the Disrupter?'

The mercenary nodded. 'As the waters of a summer sea, King,' he replied.

Halfway across the yard the king's marshal was stopped by Lambi Nef. Hather's father's dark hair was wind-tangled from the journey and his eyes were red with dust and tears. His mind was full of the offer he had made to Starkadder, that same Starkadder who now languished in a dungeon beside his son, Starkadder whose stubborn refusal to kill Oli now threatened to destroy them all.

'Is there any hope, Vermund?' Lambi Nef asked, his voice rough with desperation.

Vermund shook his head and continued to walk in silence towards his quarters. Lambi Nef followed at his heels.

'The blood-eagle? Is that it?'

Vermund made no reply. The question held its own answer.

'When is it to be?'

Four more paces and Vermund stopped. 'Tomorrow,' he muttered, gently. 'I'm sorry, Lambi. I'm really sorry.'

The courtier felt the tears start into his eyes again. Tomorrow. So soon. So little time.

Hervara had entered Uppsala to find it bereft of both her husband and the king. Neither did she find her son or that accursed Starkadder. There was only one thing to do.

218

Despite the protestations of old Tisti and Thorkel Tongue she must continue north, following Oli's soldiers towards Dalalven. Moving with less baggage and with only the two members of her household who had chosen to follow her, she was journeying more swiftly than the king.

In the underground prison Starkadder's sense of displacement was growing stronger. Somewhere Mother Skuld was drawing the threads of their lives together, and the gentle music of the waterfall was beginning to steal into Starkadder's death-hungry ears.

Hather waited, defeated, for the day to darken and the night to come. Then it would be morning and, with his last dawn there would be an hour, perhaps two, of pain so terrible . . . Then there would be nothing but the peace and silence of an early death.

In his bath, Oli was giggling to himself. No one had seen him step across the line into madness. Not even Oli could have known when he crossed it, for the line was a fine one, all but invisible. Only the inane giggling told of his crossing. He could never step back again.

'Free him, Vermund. For the sake of our old friendship I'm begging this of you. I don't care what happens to Starkadder, but free Hather for me.'

The marshal shook his head. Then he laid a gloved hand upon Lambi Nef's shoulder.

'You must understand,' he whispered, his throat choked with held-down tears. 'Not for anything can I betray the man I serve. Oli has ordered your son's death. I may not, I cannot, disobey his command. His word is our law.'

'Even if he's mad? Listen to me, Vermund. I'm going to make you an offer. I made it once to Starkadder and he refused me. One hundred pounds' weight in gold for my son's life. No, don't answer me. Hear me out first.'

219

Vermund already knew what his answer must be, but he had to listen to the offer for the sake of his long friendship with Hather's desperate father. And through the words of Lambi Nef, the voice of King Oli's unspoken and treacherous thoughts stole upon his ears:

'Lambi Nef after his son. Then Vermund Bjarnisson. He's finally questioned one order too many.'

'Oli's mad,' Lambi Nef continued. 'You've stood, as I have, through all those executions. You know the so-called crimes which caused them. They might have served as examples once, but we've seen too many of them – they don't mean anything any more. The only person who still watches without wanting to vomit is that mind-rotted creature in there! If you free Hather I'll give you a hundred pounds' weight in gold. You can be out of here before Oli knows anything about it. Go to Norway. You'll be a rich man. Leave me to take my chances with my son. I'm not asking too much of you, Vermund. You know Oli's mad. I only have to tell you to remind you. That's all. Just to make sure you know the truth about the man you insist on serving. He'll not only kill my son if he's given the chance, he'll kill his own as well. Now, what sort of a creature does that? A sane man? A sane man would rather drown in goat's piss than kill his own son. You know he's mad. And you know that I'll follow Hather to a useless death because he's my son and Oli knows I'll never forgive him. And if you hesitate for a moment you'll follow me, and we'll all be dead. Take up my offer. Be rich and free whilst you can. Believe me, Omund will follow Hather. Oli will destroy his own son because he thinks the poor, useless little worm is a threat to him.'

Vermund dropped his hand from his friend's shoulder. There was no way in which Lambi Nef could have known of his orders, yet he had guessed. Lambi Nef was not a fool.

The king's marshal, too, was beginning to understand that the Oli he was sworn to serve no longer truly existed. In his place, seething with immeasurable corruption, racked by foul jealousy and hatred, sat a decrepit, despicable monster, a monster with no shred of honour left.

He could no longer refuse to see it. Oli was mad, unfit to

rule. Yet even the king's marshal couldn't face the terrifying depths of those black eyes. He couldn't kill Oli. Another would have to do that.

Thorvald Brotamad's ears strained through the shadows to hear. He'd caught Lambi Nef's words: 'Oli's mad', but little more. Still, it was enough. He knew it for the truth, yet truth could be set aside when the prospect of advancement was so close at hand. Truth was, after all, only so weighty a matter as the gold which might fill his saddlebags.

The question which faced Thorvald was simple, like Oli's logic, but it was also unanswerable. Should he report back to the mad king or continue to watch, hidden in the shadows, waiting to see what treachery would be hatched by those death-doomed fools.

But Vermund's reply, which he could scarcely hear, told him nothing. He simply said to his old comrade: 'Come with me.'

To follow them was to leave the shelter of the shadows and risk exposing himself and his motives. Thorvald hesitated, unsure of his purpose, and in that hesitation planted the seeds of his own destruction.

Oli, in his bath, wasn't to know what was happening. It would be an easy matter to return to him, to tell him that he'd overheard Vermund Bjarnisson and Lambi Nef plotting together to free Starkadder and Hather. The king's orders, upon receipt of such intelligence, would be harsh. Kill them both, he'd say. Don't wait. Don't take them prisoner. Just get rid of the threat before it grows any greater. No need to leave the shadows. No need to expose yourself or your ambitions. Just do it. That's all.

'Lift the trap,' Vermund commanded his men. 'Free the prisoners.'

Hather and Starkadder blinked in the sudden daylight. Their bonds were cut, and they climbed the lowered ladder up onto the dusty earth of the courtyard.

Hather had not seen his father since his defilement of his mother, and almost shrank from Lambi Nef's clasping arms.

The moment passed, and his father released him to address Starkadder.

'You refused me before, Starkadder. But there'll be no bargaining for your life now. Kill Oli.'

Vermund nodded at the words. Around him his men waited, their weapons, on his order, still sheathed.

'Oli's ordered your deaths,' the marshal muttered. 'In the morning. Young Omund is to die with you.'

Will it be such a betrayal to kill the man who's sentenced you to the blood-eagle, Starkadder? Doesn't it make the third betrayal that much easier?

Omund's still alive. So's Hather. That means it has to be King Oli I'm to betray. There's no one else it can be.

'Kill him, Starkadder,' Lambi Nef began to beg. 'There's no one else who can face his black eyes or his black heart. Only you. Kill him, Starkadder. Kill Oli. Before he kills us all.'

Starkadder studied the anxious features of those around him. It made sense as much as anything else did. Besides, Lambi Nef had saved him twice now, and a debt twice owed was a debt crying out to be repaid.

Beside the waterfall Mother Skuld was smiling. In the sky above her, denied until the last, Odin's ravens were circling.

King Dvalin waited in his grotesque castle lapped by the acid lake for the coming of the final night. He would see, no matter what the distance. He would know when the third betrayal had been committed. And then his curse would lift from Tyrfing. Then at last he himself would face the coming of the dawn.

And Hervara, ruined Hervara, re-made by ancient Tisti and sustained by the care of Thorkel Tongue, but hovering upon the edge of the same madness as chained King Oli,

222

rode on through the night towards Dalalven, towards the consummation of her dreams.

The death of Starkadder.

Tyrfing hummed in his hand as he wrenched open the door. Thorvald Brotamad, his eyes glittering, his pride stiffened by mad Oli's promises, stood dark and bristling between Starkadder and the cackling creature in the bath. Behind the old mercenary Vermund and Horsetail stood with Hather and Lambi Nef. They were afraid, as Thorvald was afraid, but if Starkadder should fall they were ready to take his place.

Sooner or later one of them would kill Thorvald Brotamad. And, after that, sooner or later one of them would kill King Oli.

The third betrayal was at hand.

Starkadder looked at the fingers locked about Tyrfing's humming hilt. He felt once more that sense of otherness, of being little more than an observer. All that was needed was a little simple butchery, and the berserk rage which was even now sinking its talons into the depths of his soul, would take care of that. No need to think. No need even to be. In such moments he was a killer, not a man. They all knew that. That was why they hung back, why they left him to face Thorvald Brotamad and Oli's black eyes alone. He did not need them, did not even know they were there.

Mother Skuld began to laugh.

Hervara sighted Dalalven. Thorkel Tongue glanced at old Tisti, shuddering at the vicious smile which creased the aged crone's features. It was a smile that held too much of vengeance for the steward's liking.

The ravens wheeled closer. Beyond the palisaded walls Odin's wolves howled grimly, eager for the deed of blood.

★

Hather shivered. He began to fear for Starkadder, for his father, for Astrid, and for the future which they might not share. He sensed what was to come.

Hervara was laughing, whipping her flagging mount ever closer to the fortress.

'No! He's mine! He's mine! Mine! Mine! No! No! No!'

His brown hair whipping wildly about his head, Brother Gerard raised the makeshift crucifix of ash-wood and thrust it in Starkadder's face.

Dvalin, chuckling softly, began to climb the massive spiral staircase for the last time. As he climbed the tower, dwarfish servitors dowsed the cressets and torches about its base. They had their orders. To disobey was to risk exposure upon the outer wall, and the slow, terrible death which the day would bring.

'Can you thwart me this time, Starkadder?' he asked himself. 'Can you deny me in the evening as you denied me at the dawn?'

The ancient mercenary seemed to hesitate for a moment, to acknowledge the power of the English monk's home-made cross. Tyrfing flashed.

Hather felt the god-given power which held Starkadder in its death-grip. He felt it sear him and rob him of all strength. He crouched low on the floor and covered his face.

The tip of the blade hooked under the cross-piece of the crucifix, dragging it out of Gerard's clutching fingers. As the cross flew from his grasp, the monk followed it with his eyes, suddenly uncertain of its power. Felled by panic he dropped to his knees and began to pray.

The prayer saved his life. Had he still been on his feet when Tyrfing slashed above his head he would have lost his throat to that murderous sweep.

Struggling to control his blade, putting his own will against its fearful treachery, Starkadder booted the whimpering Gerard out of his way. The priest didn't matter. Whether he lived or died, whether he had kept faith or betrayed them, whether he believed his own *hoc-est-corpus* or not, none of it mattered. All that concerned Starkadder was the rotting creature in the bath, the once-great king whose dead black eyes, even then, were fixed on the ash-wood cross smashed on the floor.

'Stay there, Englishman,' the old mercenary ordered. 'Move again before I'm done and not even your Christ will save you.'

On his buttocks, pushing himself by his feet and hands, the gibbering monk who had seen himself as the first Bishop of Sweden, scrambled for the sanctuary of the nearest corner.

Thorvald Brotamad felt the power of Starkadder's icy gaze boring into his skull. His knuckles whitened as they struggled to keep a grip on his sword, the hilt dangerously sweaty in his frightened hand.

'You told me you'd kill me one day, Thorvald,' Starkadder grinned. 'Is it to be today, my friend?'

Behind the mercenary captain Oli's lightless eyes were cold with the dark fire of his madness. 'Go on, Thorvald,' the king urged. 'Go on. Kill him. Kill him!'

'That . . . was a . . . long time ago,' Thorvald Brotamad replied.

Thorvald Brotamad's fingers went limp, the sinews slackened, and his sword clanged to the floor. He stepped aside.

'Do what you have to, Starkadder,' the mercenary said. 'It's all the same to me now. I might fight you, but I can't fight the gods and the Norns who stand beside you.'

King Oli began to laugh. It wasn't over yet. There was a great deal of blood to be shed before his reign was done. Old and sick he might be, but he could still defy Starkadder, and he could still defy the curse which drove Starkadder on.

'I've spent my life serving great kings, Starkadder,' Thorvald continued. 'I've been proud to do it. But I'm not proud any more. Oli's greatness has fled him with his wits.

He's so mad he doesn't even see that death is the only thing left to him.'

Starkadder stepped forward.

King Oli's laughter ceased. He was still smiling, still amused, but now his scabrous chest was beginning to heave with its panting as his fingers groped for the hilt of the sword hidden beneath the water.

Dvalin stepped out on to his balcony, his wolf-yellow eyes sweeping across the deepening darkness. He locked the door which led back to the staircase and threw the key out in a graceful swing across the acid lake. It took a long time to fall, glittering as it caught the moonbeams which escaped from behind the rushing clouds. As it vanished for ever, boiling and hissing into nothing, Dvalin ascended his ornate throne with a wry smile.

The king of Trollheim was beginning to scent blood.

Starkadder watched himself, the yet-unblooded Tyrfing in his hand, moving towards the pitiful, drooling figure in the bath. The berserker rage was humming in his blood, strengthening its grip upon his old heart. Gerard and Thorvald watched him, their hearts hammering. They truly didn't matter to the ancient mercenary. They had simply been obstacles to be overcome before the third betrayal was committed, hurdles to be leaped or swept aside.

Askel Horsetail hid his face. Vermund Bjarnisson covered his single eye against the maddening gleam in the monarch's crazed black gaze. Lambi Nef stepped nearer, closer to the mad king who had ordered his son's death mere hours before.

'Now, Starkadder,' he hissed. 'Go on. Do it now!'

Raven Munin's ebony eyes, seeing through rooftops and rafters and walls all her one-eyed master required her to, hovered upon midnight pinions overhead. Beside the banks

of the Dalalven, with Hugin upon his shoulder and Geri and
Freki prowling the hem of his light-blue cloak, Odin's gaze
darted between the hovering darkness of the raven and the
approaching riders, riders destined to witness the last terrible
moves in the game played out between the gods and the
Norns.

Seconds, mere seconds. Death, mere death.

All about Allfather were another time and another place.
Above the thatched roofs and wooden walls a waterfall
cascaded like a cloud. Beside it stood a stone hut, and a
runestone stabbing towards the blackened sky like the
phallus of an anguished god.

'Are you here, Skuld?' Odin called aloud. 'Have you
come to see the ending of a hero's curse, Mother of Destiny?'

For the briefest moment he glimpsed a young, lovely girl
clad in the finest Byzantine silks. Then the image wavered
and faded, leaving the tattered figure of a bent old hag, her
wrinkled features covered by a heavy wadmal veil.

Oli slashed upwards, shrieking wildly, the hidden sword
trailing beaded strings of water as its point darted towards
Starkadder's throat. Tyrfing, swishing through the air in
unholy glee, rang against the bear-greased blade, shivering
it into a multitude of glittering shards. Jagged splinters of
metal rained back into the water, showering the mad king
like thorns, until the water in the bath was red and the
demented laughter died.

His sword was gone. Now only his awesome black eyes
could save him. His awesome black eyes, and his cunning.

'Can . . . you . . . kill . . . me . . . Starkadder, my . . . friend?'
he panted. 'Those . . . weak fools . . . can't.'

He raised his right arm and swept the ruined hilt towards
the men clustered in the doorway. 'Is . . . this the . . . third
betrayal?' he asked, glaring. 'Even . . . if you . . . kill . . . me,
is it over for you?'

Doubt. Work on Starkadder's doubt. He's stayed his
hand thus far. He might stay it yet further.

Starkadder towered over the king, his gnarled hands
clenched round Tyrfing's hilt, the blade high above his

head, slanting downwards for an impaling thrust. The old mercenary's face was livid with berserk rage, the lips drawn away from his age-yellowed teeth in a ghastly grin.

Oli dropped the broken sword hilt, a flick of his wrist tossing it lightly from him. His hand flopped back into the water, and he shrugged his bleeding shoulders, as if he were surrendering to his fate and accepting it.

But beneath the surface of the water his hand closed upon the haft of the beard-axe which had lain hidden with the sword. With speed surprising in so sick and ageing a man, the king sprang up, scything the edge of the axe towards Starkadder's unprotected neck.

'Now!' screamed Lambi Nef. 'Do it now.'

'Yesss!'

All uncertainty left Starkadder's blazing grey eyes. For a moment he had wavered beneath Oli's words and the hypnotic power of his terrifying eyes, but that moment had passed. As Starkadder himself had sprung from the shrouding snow upon Angantyr and his berserks, as the crystals of ice had flared in the sunlight around him, so King Oli had risen in a spray of flashing water, a spray which broke the hold of his malignant black gaze. Tyrfing flashed down before the axe could bite Starkadder's neck. Its point struck the naked king's breastbone and tore down, glancing off the ribs, penetrating the unprotected belly just above the navel and skewering his body through.

Blood began to bubble from both points of the wound. Falling rivulets stained Oli's belly and legs, rolling down into the reddening, dirty water. The axe, its swing checked, tumbled from his hand and his body stiffened with shock. His arms, the elbows slightly hooked, were held out from his body like the wings of the raven overhead.

Tyrfing withdrew.

King Oli stood there, his back bent away from the transfixing blow. His mouth worked without speaking and his black eyes flickered from side to side, seeking the mercy he had denied his own victims.

In a moment of stark sanity his right hand reached out and clutched at Starkadder's shoulder. The panic fled from his eyes, leaving them calm, almost forgiving.

'S . . . Starkadder?' King Oli asked, his chewed lips dribbling blood.

When he crashed down in a great flood of bloodied water, Tyrfing began to work again.

'Stark . . . adder?'

The berserk couldn't hear the whisper. His sleeves were swishing past his ears as he plunged the dwarf-forged weapon again and again into Oli's body.

Up. Down. Up. Down. Up down. Murderous. Up down. Mindless. Up again. Down again. Up down, up down . . .

By the seventh blow Oli's life had fled for ever, but the rage refused to yield, refused to let go. Starkadder worked on and on, his knees straightening, bending and straightening again with every thrust. Tyrfing chopped again and again into the dead king's shredded corpse, and only on the nineteenth blow, when the ruined flesh was butchered enough for the point to catch and stick in the bottom of the bath, did the unholy flashing and plunging cease.

Yet still the rage burned on.

Still there came the tugging and hammering.

Still he stood apart, seeing himself drenched with sweat and bloody water, panting hoarsely, while Tyrfing dripped blood.

Hather felt the pit of his stomach churn as if a giant were winding it about some enormous distaff. It wasn't over, not yet.

Brother Gerard began to pray again. Thorvald, Askel Horsetail and the marshal turned away from the ghastly sight. The king's open, sightless eyes, floating in blood, were even more terrible in death than in life.

Lambi Nef stepped forward warily.

'You've done it, Starkadder,' he said quietly. 'You've killed King Oli.'

But it wasn't enough. Odin required something more of the old warrior before he would grant him his death.

It wasn't over yet.

Lambi Nef took the old man's arm. 'Long life to King Omund,' he cried, smiling broadly.

Slowly, as if fighting off the doubts which still beset him,

Starkadder shook his head. No. Not Omund. Not that broken weakling. Omund would damn the Yngling dynasty with his feeble blood-line as surely as mad Oli would have done.

No, not Omund. Anyone but Omund.

Yet there's no one else, is there, Starkadder?

'Not Omund. It can't be Omund.'

Lambi Nef turned in amazement. 'Your work is done, Starkadder,' he said in a firm, gentle voice such as he might use to an angry child. 'You'll be well rewarded for it. Now it's up to those who know the court and its business to decide what happens next.'

Starkadder shook his head again, still dazed with the hammering, the tugging, the berserk rage which refused to let him go now that its work was done.

'Not Omund,' he snarled. 'Not that weakling Omund.'

Lambi Nef forced a laugh. 'Then who would you have us choose, old killer? Who else is there? You? The king is dead, long live the king-killer king? Haven't you lived long enough already, Starkadder?'

Lambi Nef had not meant his words to be dismissive, but they struck at the raw heart of the berserk's rage. Starkadder felt himself stiffen, stood outside himself, suddenly sure of the dreadful act he was to do, which none might turn aside.

Not Omund. 'Not Omund!'

'It's not for you to choose!' Lambi Nef snapped.

'*Anyone but Omund!*'

His arm was shaking. Tyrfing's laughter was ringing in his ears as the echoes of his shout were ringing about the darkened rafters, a laughter as brittle and keen-edged as Oli the Great's. His grey eyes burned within their hollowed sockets with a terrible fire, a fire not even Oli at his death had seen.

'Oh God,' Gerard moaned, rocking on the floor in the corner. 'Sweet Jesus.'

Vermund gasped. Horsetail's eyes widened in sudden knowledge. Thorvald felt the thrill, the tingle in the air, the warning of horror to come.

Hather crouched on the floor, beyond thought or fear, watching the two men he loved best in the world.

230

Dear god dear Odin. Dear Odin, not this. Anything but this.

Lambi Nef's right hand flashed to the hilt of his sword. Two, perhaps three, inches of metal had been drawn from the scabbard before Tyrfing's curse-born shriek filled the blood-heavy air.

The third betrayal.

Tyrfing hissed as it clove through the air. Hervara called for the gates of Dalalven to be opened for her. Dvalin clapped his talon-nailed hands in grim glee. Odin nodded sadly, and turned to Mother Skuld. She was nodding too.

The third betrayal.

Munin called into the night, and Hugin answered her. Geri and Freki threw back their shaggy heads and howled.

The third betrayal.

Starkadder's arms corded and shook with the effort of trying to check Tyrfing's scything arc, but he could not halt it. After the blow the sword flew from his hand, trailing a spray of blood, and dug deep into the wooden wall eight feet away.

Lambi Nef's headless body hesitated. Then it pitched over, and his blood pumped out to run with Oli's on the floor.

Only then, with Tyrfing gone from his hand and the act done, did Starkadder feel the rage in his blood begin to die. Suddenly it didn't matter any more that Omund was the only Yngling left to rule his father's lands. Nothing mattered any more. All that remained was the grim, wrenching sickness which went with each of the betrayals.

Now at last Starkadder knew why he and Hather had been brought together at the meeting of the streams south of Uppsala. He understood the aweful design of the Norns and the gods in their playing with men's souls. There had to be a blood-feud between Hather and himself.

Angantyr's death on the plain at Roliung had not been the cause of any blood-feud and Hather knew that now. But this, the betrayal and needless slaughter of a good man and true friend, was the last step in the measured tread of events which had brought them here. All their journeyings, the dangers and horrors they had lived through, had brought the time-wearied warrior and the battle-hardened boy to this. The old man had slain Lambi Nef and the Norns had written that his son must avenge his killing. Not all the love that the two felt for each other could wipe out that terrible decree.

Hather stood up, his father's head hanging by its hair in his grasp. Starkadder tugged Tyrfing from the wall and forced the reluctant blade back into its sheath.

'The blood-feud is between us now,' he muttered, his eyes cast down so as not to meet Hather's. 'I'll meet you at dawn to settle it, Hather. I'll be waiting for you on the plain in front of the fortress.'

Hather clutched at his arm with trembling fingers, his eyes bright with tears.

'Starkadder,' he asked, 'why did it have to be?'

The old man gently pried the fingers away. Still without looking Hather in the face he shook his head.

'How should I know?' he growled. 'Isn't it enough that it's happened? Do I have to be able to tell you why? I can't do it, Hather. Not this side of the grave. Only the Norns can do that.'

CHAPTER EIGHT

Starkadder dying

HERVARA WEPT that night for Lambi Nef as she had never thought she could. His death left her alone with a stranger for a son, not even to be consoled by the thought that in the morning Hather would be fighting Starkadder to the death. At last all her planning, her lusting and scheming, had come to a sort of fruition, yet it was a fruition which held nothing of triumph for her and little even of revenge.

Starkadder walked from the fortress. No one moved to stop him. With the news of Oli's death spreading through Dalalven like fire none would even think to challenge the terrible old warrior. Those who saw him shrank away, for death walked at his back.

And Dvalin, trapped on his high throne to wait for the numbing death of dawn, watched, and muttered: 'I haven't forgotten, Starkadder. You've played the game and shall reap the rewards I promised. You will be the last owner of Tyrfing to be killed by my dwarf-forged blade.'

Voices cut into Astrid's sleep like wolves' teeth, chasing her dreams and setting her heart a-hammer, voices shouting of a murdered king, of a duel to be fought between the two men who had saved her from Magnus Gydasson. She didn't understand but she knew that the death of King Oli heralded some change through all the north, a change which hung upon the death of either Hather or Starkadder.

Odin and Skuld said nothing. Munin returned to Odin's

233

shoulder and told Allfather of the things which had come to pass, things which Mother Skuld already knew too well.

The waterfall flowed on; the runestone jabbed at the heaving sky. Ragged, rushing clouds masked the moon. For the age of gods and heroes was ending, and even the sky seemed to know it.

The wolves keened on and the sentries shuddered. When Odin was abroad there was little sleep to be had. When Odin was abroad in the world of men it was for one purpose alone. He was seeking heroes for Valhalla.

Someone was going to die. Starkadder walked out of the gates of the fortress and saw the waterfall cascading white as a veil among the rolling clouds, and knew that it was to be himself.

The end was coming. All he had to do was to wait for the sun.

Hather stood before his mother. Haggard from weeping for Lambi Nef she showed little of the beauty which had lured her son to defile his dead father's high seat. This night had set a seal on the door of Hervara's life. She could never step back, never be young again.

'I still love you, Mother,' Hather said, 'but I can't live with you any more.'

Old Tisti nodded sagely at his words. Whatever secrets she still held were hers alone. She had read the runes for Hather for the last time. They had fallen onto her white cloth and they would never fall there for Hather again. They told her that Astrid wouldn't be his only love, but she would at least be his first. They said that his mother's grief for the man she had never loved quite well enough would free her son to be a man again, to be the one to return Astrid to the life she had known before her father's death.

And Tisti had seen that Omund, weakling Omund, last of the Ynglings until his thin blood was bred into a son, would do what he was told. Strong men would rule in his name, men who had earned his gratitude, men like Vermund Bjarnisson and Askel Horsetail and even Thorvald Brotamad, to preserve the kingdom for a little longer. The fall of the Ynglings would be slow through the years. Tisti had already seen the slaughter of the six chieftains of Ingjald Firestarter, heard Uppsala aflame and crackling like a funeral pyre. The slow steps of time were turned towards that day, the day of the fall of the great house of Yngling. But even Odin and Mother Skuld would have to bide their time a little longer for that.

Starkadder led no horse this time as he went to meet the Norn beside the waterfall. He went on foot, asking no questions, seeking no mercy. He was content, knowing that the cruelty which had ruled his life was slackening its hold at last.

And Skuld waited, a sad smile hidden beneath the veil for the age-worn hero.

Towards dawn, when that long night was over, the townsfolk of Dalalven gathered in a broad swathe before the gates. They could see Starkadder kneeling in the centre of the enclosure they had formed, his helmet thrown off and his head bare, muttering to himself or to someone none of them could see with mere human eyes.

Astrid came with a cloth soaked in the river and bathed the old man's brow. He looked up, but whatever he saw it wasn't the girl from the smithy.

'Thank you, Mother Skuld,' he said softly. 'At last I thank you for your kindness.'

She was dressed in rags. In days to come Astrid would again wear silk from Byzantium.

Does it have to be like this? Hather thought. My father's dead and gone. Must I really kill the man who was my other father, my teacher, my friend, to pay for the shedding of my father's blood? Is there nothing left, nothing more than killing, killing, killing?

Be patient, came a voice from a one-eyed face. There is more, little Hather, but the killing must come first. You know that this is more than a simple blood-feud. You know that you have to kill Starkadder for the sake of your honour in the eyes of men. Yet he must also die for another reason, a greater purpose. It is for that greater purpose that the killing must be done, not just for honour or for blood-feud.

He felt no fear. He was going against the greatest, most deadly slayer that the north had ever known, but he felt no

235

taint of fear, only the knowledge that the deed must be done, and that it must be his alone.

Starkadder was going to die.

The palisade walls were already crowded with soldiers, and more marched out through the great gates behind Vermund Bjarnisson and Askel Horsetail. Not one understood why they were there, save that they were to witness the dying of a legend. Not one knew that Starkadder's death meant not only the ending of a curse, but the dying of an age.

Astrid dropped the cloth and ran forward to Hather who walked beside his mother, her steward, and old Tisti. Their lips met in a fire of sudden passion. Hervara, wild-eyed and tangle-haired, saw, but felt no anger, no jealousy. She was heart-numbed and felt nothing.

Starkadder waited alone and Hather walked to meet him at the waterfall. Those who waited with him, the ravens, the wolves, Odin One-Eye and the old Norn, were hidden from the sight of all but he.

'Does it have to be?' Astrid asked. 'Must you really fight him?'

Hather nodded then thrust her gently to the side as he stepped forward.

'Do you know why?' Starkadder called, his grey eyes looking over Hather's head to the horizon where dawn was creeping into the eastern sky. 'Do you know why we have to fight?'

'I've come to love you as a father,' Hather replied. 'There's no reason, no purpose that I can see. Only a silly, stupid blood-feud. I have to fight you, Starkadder. I have to kill you because it's expected of me. I don't want to, but I have to. For the sake of my life amongst the living I have to kill you or die myself.'

The distance between them narrowed to a few yards. Dawn grew stronger, more rosy, in the east.

'You say it's expected of you,' Starkadder smiled. 'Yet do you know who it is who expects it, Hather? Shall I tell him, Mother Skuld?'

'He won't believe you, Starkadder,' came the reply. 'He can't see me, and he will only believe what he can see.'

Hather was struggling to hold back the tears which might blight his skill and bring about his own destruction. The distance between Starkadder and himself narrowed to mere feet. The dawn grew brighter.

On his throne King Dvalin felt the numbness begin to steal upon him, yet still he watched. He had to see it through right to the end, though it meant the certainty of death to him.

Starkadder drew the dwarf-forged sword, Tyrfing, from its scabbard. Hather drew his own weapon, the one which Starkadder had given to him in exchange.

Astrid wanted to rush forward, to separate them, to place herself between them. But old Tisti knew more of the truth than any there, and her gnarled hands held the girl back.

Geri and Freki patrolled with glittering eyes. Hugin and Muni wheeled silently overhead. Mother Skuld and Odin, even though they had no substance, stood aside.

Dawn flooded the plain. Dvalin stiffened. Hather struck.

Astrid gasped and turned to bury her face in Tisti's shoulder.

Tyrfing, strangely silent, parried efficiently and aimed a cut at Hather's legs. Almost as if they were playing the youth jumped up, allowing the blade to pass beneath his feet. Then he chopped down and sideways, swinging at Starkadder's neck.

Thorvald Brotamad felt the breath catch in his throat. Gerard's makeshift cross slipped from his fingers and fell unnoticed into the dust.

The mercenary's knees buckled, allowing the blow to fly harmlessly above his head. Tyrfing turned in his hand and swept back, ringing triumphantly against Hather's parry. Both weapons vibrated with the force of their meeting. The combatants straightened and stood upright a little way apart.

'Try harder, lad,' Starkadder muttered. 'You'll have to do better than that to bring me death.'

'I . . . don't want to kill you,' the youth replied. 'Can't we end it? Now?'

Starkadder shook his head. 'Your honour demands my death,' he growled. 'And so do I.'

237

Hather cut to the chest. Tyrfing flashed up to meet the blow then slashed towards the youth's throat. Hather's blade blocked, twisted, then lunged for Starkadder's heart.

Tyrfing parried down to the side. Hather stepped back panting, his forehead beaded with the cold sweat of fear.

'Tyrfing,' Dvalin muttered through his stiffening lips. 'Only the dwarf-blade can kill old Starkadder. You can't do it, boy. It has to be Tyrfing.'

'Don't trust him,' the shape of Svafrlami hissed. 'Whatever you do, don't trust King Dvalin.'

Vermund gritted his teeth, his single eye following the intricacies of the deadly battle on the plain.

The swords met and clashed. Again they met, parry deflecting blow, blow being blocked by parry.

Astrid turned back to watch the conflict, her heart racing. Hervara, revenge no longer important, prayed silently for her son.

The sword in Hather's hand cut sideways towards Starkadder's body. Tyrfing blocked the blow and forced it upwards.

Then Hather twisted his weapon down, its speed wrapping the glittering blade around Tyrfing like a whip, catching the dwarf-weapon, tearing it from Starkadder's fingers. Tyrfing flew into the air, and sang.

'Don't trust him!' Svafrlami hissed. 'Don't trust King Dvalin!'

Up flew Tyrfing, as it had flown when Starkadder tore it from Angantyr's grasp. Thousands of eyes watched it go, saw it hang blood-red in the dawn light. And their ears hummed with Tyrfing's death-song.

Starkadder watched its flight. So Tyrfing was about to kill him. He would die as Angantyr had died.

Dvalin grinned with unholy mirth as Tyrfing turned in the air. There was time for one last jest before he turned to stone. With Oli dead and Omund on the throne the Ynglings were finished anyway, sooner or later. What need was there for him to keep his word to Starkadder and Hather? Why should the fated one die as he had intended? Tyrfing turned in the air and began its fall, flashing down, not to Starkadder, but to Hather.

Astrid screamed. Starkadder sprang forward. He felt Hather's unseeking blade pierce him through. It didn't matter. The thrust wouldn't kill him. Only Tyrfing could kill him, so it didn't matter.

Just so he should die, and not the boy.

Thorkel Tongue couldn't bear to watch the young master's death and covered his eyes. Old Tisti stared up at the evil, gleaming blade, and willed it not to fall.

Angantyr might have laughed in his grave on Samsey Isle, but his body had fallen to the teeth of the grave-worm, his flesh and bones long gone.

The corpse-fires gleamed in Hervara's eyes. She knew at last how her father had met his death. 'Not like this,' she whispered. 'It mustn't end like this.'

Dvalin fought to clutch his failing senses to himself a little longer. He never knew the moment when he finally froze in the sun and turned to stone.

And still Tyrfing continued to fall, for as long as a mortal man might live three lifetimes.

Hather stood, clasped to Starkadder by his grip on the sword.

In a last grim, determined gesture, Starkadder hurled him clear.

Tyrfing struck.

The point entered Starkadder's open, upturned mouth, passed through his jaw and behind the collar-bone and plunged down to find his heart. He stood there, kept erect by the length of the fateful blade which had sunk to the hilt, crossing the sword which Hather had thrust through him seconds before.

He wanted to shout his triumph, to give thanks to Odin for his death, but Tyrfing wouldn't let him.

'The cross,' Gerard gasped. 'The sign of the cross. The swords have shown him the Christ.'

Starkadder didn't hear him. Nobody heard him.

It was over.

Starkadder had tasted the blade of his death and was free.

Another watcher near the plain beyond Dalalven

HE STOOD beside Odin, the wolves nuzzling at his legs, the welcoming ravens flapping about his shoulders.

Beyond him a body, Starkadder's body, transfixed by two swords, bearing within it the shape of the White Christ's cross, rocked backwards on its heels and struck the hard earth of the plain.

'Is it over, Allfather?' he asked. He saw Astrid rush forward, sobbing, to embrace the trembling, tear-racked Hather.

'You're dead at last, Starkadder,' came the reply.

'And the living, Allfather. What of the living?'

Odin shrugged. 'Life goes on,' he smiled. 'But it's nothing to concern yourself with. There's a place, a special place, I've been keeping for you in Valhalla, Starkadder.

'Of all who've worshipped me, of all who've served me and earned such a place, you're the one who's worked hardest for it. The curses have seen to that.'

Starkadder saw it all at last. The Norns, older and more wise than the gods, had grown weary of the knowledge they held, tired of their existence and their duties. Their rest, however, could come only with the Ragnarok, the doom of the gods, and that doom would be hastened when the Yngling dynasty no longer sustained the deities of the Norse pantheon. That was why they so desired and encouraged the coming of the White Christ from the south. That was why the curses which had plagued Starkadder, himself the embodiment of the power and aspirations of those older gods, had to end.

'Will you tell me about their futures, Allfather?'

Odin smiled, then he nodded. 'I think we can do that much for you. Who would you like to start with, Starkadder?'

'Hervara?'

The god sighed. 'She'll continue to love her son,' he said, 'but she's about to realise that it was Lambi Nef she truly loved. His death has blighted her, Starkadder. She'll linger for a year or so, but then she'll die.'

'And Omund? Horsetail? Thorvald? Vermund Bjarnisson? What of the princes and warriors who are left? What about the House of Yngling itself?'

'Good men in their way,' came Odin's reply. 'Omund will marry and father sons. His great-grandson will be Onund Roadmaker, the father of Ingjald Firestarter. Ingjald will be the last of the Yngling kings. His son will never live long enough to take the throne, and then the Yngling line will be gone from the north for ever.'

'And the rest, Allfather? What of the rest?'

Odin allowed himself a wry smile before he continued. 'Dvalin's already turned to stone,' he replied. 'Hather will bury Tyrfing with your body. It will go to the grave with you in the same way that it went to the grave with Angantyr, and there it will lie, with your bones. As for the rest, old Tisti will see her mistress in the grave and live long enough herself to impart much of her wisdom to Hather. Thorkel Tongue will give the boy the same fidelity and service that he showed his father. Askel Horsetail and Thorvald will fall together fighting a threat to the kingdom's unity, but not for some years yet. Vermund Bjarnisson will cut the spear-rune into his flesh before he dies of old age. And that's all, Starkadder. There's little more to tell.'

Astrid wiped away Hather's tears with her fingers. He held her tightly to him, crushing her against his chest, aching in his victory for the comfort which only she was left to bring. The curses and the doubts were all behind him, he was free, but he knew in his heart that the memory of an old warrior called Starkadder would always be there to haunt his future happiness.

'We'll take his body away from here,' Hather muttered, fighting the sobs which threatened to fill his throat. 'We'll raise a grave-mound for him, and for Tyrfing, in the place where my grandfather died, at Roliung.'

'And what of Hather?' Starkadder demanded. 'What about the one who might have been my son? Will he and Astrid be happy?'

Odin simply smiled.

'You've looked out across the future,' Starkadder pressed. 'You know what is to be, Allfather. Won't you grant me this last glimpse of human life before I go with you to Valhalla?'

A hand slipped into his own. It was a girl's hand, young and soft. It shouldn't have belonged to Mother Skuld at all, but it was hers.

'They will be happy for a little while,' she told him. 'Everyone is fated to be happy for a little while, as you in your own way were happy these last few days with Hather. It won't last, though. They'll both find other loves in other times and other places. That's the way of humans, old Starkadder. It's a way you're well out of.'

He knew that he no longer had a body, but the knowledge wasn't enough to keep him from weeping. Tears fell down his cheeks, tears for the dead and for the living. They fell for the knowledge that nothing, not youthful love, nor life itself, was destined to last. They fell for Oli and Hervara, for Tisti and Lambi Nef, for Horsetail and Dvalin, for Thorvald and Thorkel Tongue, for Vermund and for Astrid and for Hather. They fell for Odin and Mother Skuld, and for all the gods, doomed by greater forces than themselves.

Yet there was one person Starkadder didn't cry for. He didn't cry for himself. For he was free, and in his freedom was a life in death. His three lives had lasted no more than a moment, after all, scarcely as long as it took Tyrfing to turn singing in the air, and fall.

'I love you, Hather,' he whispered. 'Live your life well. For me.'

Mother Skuld was smiling at him gently. He looked at Odin and saw that the Allfather was smiling as well.

They both took his hands.

'Shall we be going now?' Allfather asked.

Not wishing to let such a magnificent champion lie without a tomb, Hather gave orders for Starkadder's corpse to be buried in the plain which people call Roliung.

Saxo Grammaticus – *Gesta Danorum* Book 8, 274.